*W*hat the critics are saying...

ఈ

PURSUIT

Gold Star Award! "I believe that Cariboo Lunewulf: Pursuit is an extraordinary book that deserves a Gold Star Award. This is romance writing at it's finest level. ~ *Just Erotic Romance Reviews*

Five Stars "This is another home run for Ms. O'Clare." ~ *Fallen Angel Reviews*

Four and a Half Blue Ribbons "PURSUIT is a wonderful story of paranormal activity that will intrigue readers and keep them turning the pages." ~ *Romance Junkies*

Five Stars "With exciting characters and a fascinating plot, Ms. O'Claire weaves a tale that will leave you panting and longing for a werewolf of your very own." ~ *EuroReviews*

Five Unicorns "I just loved this book! The story line is intriguing and I just couldn't put this novel down." ~ *Enchanted In Romance*

Four Hearts "I am impressed by the alternate reality Ms. O'Clare continues to develop. The author's unusual vision of werewolves living in our world differs from so many in this growing subgenre." ~ *Romance Readers' Connection*

Five Cupids "Pursuit is another page turner by Ms. O'Clare." ~ *Cupid's Library Reviews*

Five Coffee Cups "Ms. O'Clare's world of werewolves is ingeniously created. The story is artfully blended with a plot and scintillating dialogue that keeps you turning the pages." ~ *Coffee Time Romance*

Four Roses "Pursuit is an amazing story that brings readers deeper into the world of the Cariboo and shows that its females are just as aggressive and demanding as its males." ~ *A Romance Review*

CHALLENGED

Five Cups "Ms. O'Clare is a gifted author who has penned yet another terrific werewolf tale that has me totally entranced." ~ *Coffee Time Romance*

Five Stars "Ms. O'Clare once again enchants her reader with the ability to feel and relate to her very realistic characters." ~ *eCataRomance*

Four Blue Ribbons "The love scenes are steamy with an animalistic flare that will leave readers panting for more." ~ *Romance Junkies*

Four Stars "Lorie O'Clare has written another winner. She is at the top of her game with Challenged." ~ *EuroReviews*

Five Stars "As always, Ms. O'Clare makes her characters appear believable. This story fascinated me from the first chapter until the last." ~ *Just Erotic Romance Reviews*

Five Stars "Challenged is the third in the Cariboo Lunewulf series and it continues to deliver the wonderful storyline and sizzling sex that I've come to expect from Ms. O'Clare." ~ *Fallen Angel Reviews*

"As a conissuer of WOLFIES, Lorie O'Clare is my goddess." ~ *A Romance Review*

LORIE O'CLARE

Challenged Pursuit

ELLORA'S CAVE
ROMANTICA PUBLISHING

An Ellora's Cave Romantica Publication

www.ellorascave.com

Challenged Pursuit

ISBN 1419954091
ALL RIGHTS RESERVED.
Pursuit Copyright © 2005 Lorie O'Clare
Challenged Copyright © 2005 Lorie O'Clare
Edited by Sue-Ellen Gower
Cover art by Syneca.

Electronic book Publication June 2005
Trade paperback Publication November 2006

Excerpt from *Nuworld: The Saga Begins* Copyright © Lorie O'Clare 2005

Content Advisory:

S – ENUOUS
E – ROTIC
X - TREME

Ellora's Cave Publishing offers three levels of Romantica™ reading entertainment: S (S-ensuous), E (E-rotic), and X (X-treme).

The following material contains graphic sexual content meant for mature readers. This story has been rated E–rotic.

S-*ensuous* love scenes are explicit and leave nothing to the imagination.

E-*rotic* love scenes are explicit, leave nothing to the imagination, and are high in volume per the overall word count. E-rated titles might contain material that some readers find objectionable — in other words, almost anything goes, sexually. E-rated titles are the most graphic titles we carry in terms of both sexual language and descriptiveness in these works of literature.

X-*treme* titles differ from E-rated titles only in plot premise and storyline execution. Stories designated with the letter X tend to contain difficult or controversial subject matter not for the faint of heart.

Also by Lorie O'Clare

෨

Also available from Cerridwen Press

ഈ

Nuworld: The Saga Begins
Nuworld: Tara the Great
Nuworld: All for One
Nuworld: Do or Die
Nuworld: The Illegitimate Claim
Nuworld: Thicker than Water

About the Author

ഈ

All my life, I've wondered at how people fall into the routines of life. The paths we travel seemed to be well-trodden by society. We go to school, fall in love, find a line of work (and hope and pray it is one we like), have children and do our best to mold them into good people who will travel the same path. This is the path so commonly referred to as the "real world".

The characters in my books are destined to stray down a different path other than the one society suggests. Each story leads the reader into a world altered slightly from the one they know. For me, this is what good fiction is about, an opportunity to escape from the daily grind and wander down someone else's path.

Lorie O'Clare lives in Kansas with her three sons.

Lorie welcomes comments from readers. You can find her website and email address on her author bio page at www.ellorascave.com.

Contents

Pursuit

Dedication

&

*So many of you have helped build the strength of the
Cariboo Lunewulf.
With your love for the lunewulfs,
the wild Cariboo grew stronger.
I really want to thank Sue Ellen Gower,
who never grew tired of editing my books,
and working with me late into the night when neither of us
could clearly see the computer screen any longer.
And to Renee and Jaynie
for their endless persuasion that I create a series just for
this more wild and primitive werewolf.
And of course to my dear friend Lora Leigh who has always
believed in me and my talents to create worlds so similar to
ours, yet different.
You are all such wonderful friends and I wouldn't be here
without your love for my books.*

Chapter One

෨

Gabriel McAllister pulled the straps over the logs stacked on the rollback truck and then hollered at the driver. He stood back as the driver took off.

"Gabe? You want to head down to Howley's?" Stone, Gabe's twin brother, wiped his brow.

Gabe squinted at his twin. Stone's blond bangs stuck to his forehead. In spite of the chill in the air, they were both sweaty and dirty.

"Well, if I look half as bad as you do, the only place I'm headed is home for a shower."

Stone curled his lip. "The bitches like a werewolf who's a bit sweaty. Turns them on."

"It amazes me that you ever get past hello with any of them. You're a fucking prick."

"Yet I do. Again and again."

Gabe shook his head. His twin, although continually coming across as a crude asshole, was actually his best friend.

There were three of them in the McAllister den here in Prince George, Gabe and Stone being the youngest of the littermates. Their older brother, Marc, had always been the protector, the good guy. Gabe figured his twin got away with his mouthy attitude because of Marc. No matter what trouble he caused, their older littermate was always there to get him out of trouble. Gabe always figured Stone caused enough trouble for the both of them, so had grown up keeping his own nose out of trouble.

"After we head to the den, find food, then maybe Howley's."

Gabe's cell phone started ringing. He pulled it off his belt while following his brother down the uneven dirt road toward the sawmill.

"Yup," he said, answering his phone while at the same time getting a whiff of something different in the air.

Stone smelled it at the same time, his pace slowing as he squinted and stared through the trees that surrounded them.

"Are you two still out by Wright Creek Road? I just got word there's an abandoned car out that way. Before we get human cops combing my land, I want you two to find out who's out there." Rock Toubec, the owner of the ranch they worked at, never cared too much for humans. He wanted his land exclusively for werewolves.

"We'll check it out." Gabe clicked his phone off.

"What's up?" Stone had stopped.

The two of them stood in the middle of the road, the surrounding trees shading the area around them. A cool breeze brought the smells of the forest to them. The clearing where they'd worked today was filled with the smell of sawdust and diesel from the trucks. Those scents mixed with something new, something fresh that hadn't been there minutes before. Gabe would have noticed it.

He didn't have to tell his twin to be quiet, to put some muscle on and to follow him. They didn't need to communicate to know someone—another werewolf—was out there, buried in the forest, and they were moving quickly.

Small branches and underbrush didn't stop Gabe. Leaping over a fallen tree, his muscles stretched, the blood pumping through his veins. His heart pulsed with new life, beating harder than a human heart should pump. New life surged through him. The beast within, his carnal side, ached to come forth and take over, offering him stronger instincts, more power and more aggression.

Stone ran alongside him, moving with similar agility through the woods. Tracking in his flesh didn't offer the acute senses he would have in his fur, but neither of them knew what or who they were dealing with. They wouldn't jeopardize the pack before they knew exactly who was out there.

Tall fir trees surrounded them, while a bed of needles crushed under their boots. The thickness of the forest would be enough for most people to get lost. Trees reaching for the sky, growing several feet from each other, made everything around them look the same.

It wasn't the visual surroundings that led Gabe. Allowing the change to consume him just a bit, enough to make his senses more acute, he relied on smell and his hearing.

And it took his werewolf senses to draw him toward the intruder.

Moving slowly, sensing they were being watched, Gabe spotted her first.

He slowed and then stopped, staring at the tall, willowy blonde not fifteen meters in front of them. Her breathing was wild, something close to panic surging through her.

Stone moved next to him, his attention locked on the mysterious female who stood frozen, her body pressed against one of the trees not too far from them. His brother allowed a twig to snap under his foot. Even if the woman had been in her fur, she was too close to escape them in a full chase. It was just like Stone to ensure that the prey realized they were officially being hunted.

Fear and distrust were carried by the breeze. She looked around her with large blue eyes, her breasts moving up and down as she breathed heavily and searched the dense trees around her.

When her gaze locked with his, Gabe wasn't sure he'd ever laid eyes on a prettier bitch. Tall enough that he would guess her *Cariboo*, she wasn't from around here. He would have remembered such stunning good looks. Well-tanned skin made her pale blonde hair appear even lighter. It fell straight around her face, fanning over her shoulders and past her breasts. Wearing jeans and a tight-fitting sweater, her thin figure appeared to be close to perfection.

She didn't take her gaze from his as she stepped backwards, and then within the next second disappeared behind the tree.

"Let's get her," Stone whispered, already stripping out of his shirt.

"I'll get her." He wasn't sure why he said that, but Gabe didn't bother to dwell on why he suddenly had the urge to overpower her, discover the reason for her panic and why she was hiding out here on Toubec's land.

There was a slight movement and it took Gabe a second to realize she'd stripped out of her clothes. He caught the briefest glance of flesh before the woman dropped to the ground, allowing the change to consume her.

Fire already burned through his veins. Muscles contorted, growing heavier while his bones stretched, adjusting to allow the heavier weight. Blood pumped in a heated rush, his heart pounding as the change surged through him.

Quickly he yanked off his clothes, feeling fur creep over his human flesh, the prickling of hair puncturing through his skin. Instincts too raw, too pure for any human to experience, overtook him.

When she took off running, he realized she was *Cariboo lunewulf*. A larger, more muscular creature than the pure *lunewulf*, this female came from the same line that he and his brother were from. But Gabe knew he'd never seen her before, or at least he was pretty damned sure. The woman bolted, disappearing before the change consumed him.

Stone pounded the earth alongside him, the two of them taking up the chase, instinct ruling their thoughts. All Gabe focused on was that he would catch her, learn what made her run into the woods and then flee from them the moment she caught wind of them. Nothing mattered other than catching her.

And Gabe and his brother had the advantage. They knew the land.

The female's scent guided them, her fear and determination so rich in the air she was easy to follow. Yet she put up quite a chase. Within minutes they had left the thick growth of tall firs and headed toward open meadows. His boss, Rock Toubec, another *Cariboo lunewulf*, used the rich ground for cattle. The large ranch helped support and feed most of the pack.

After a couple of miles it was obvious she ran blindly, panic taking over so that she gave no thought to her direction. When she crossed over Wright Creek Road and bolted onto land no longer owned by werewolves, it was time to end the chase. Only one problem—none of them had their clothes with them, and it wasn't yet dark. In their fur, or naked, it would be hard to explain to humans.

Their own den was just a few miles down the road. There was only one thing to do.

We're taking her down, he barked at his twin, Stone more than likely already thinking the same thing.

Separating, they moved so that they were on either side of her, making it impossible for her to do anything but run forward. If she diverted off on either side, she would run into one of them.

The small cabin, which the twins had made their den ever since moving here from the Canadian Rockies, was less than a quarter mile away. Perfect. Gabe moved in on the female.

Their panicked little bitch was going home with them whether she liked it or not.

Coming up alongside her, he saw her blue eyes turn silver with outrage. Obviously she didn't like the idea of losing her self-inflicted chase. Well, today she would overcome her pride.

Their claws tore at the ground, speed being an asset to their breed as they raced across the countryside. Gabe moved closer until he had her alongside him. The silly bitch snarled at him, as if she could actually take him on.

Bumping into her, she stumbled and then rolled over the ground. When she would have come up snarling, Gabe moved over her. The heat from her body, a mixture of fear and anger, rushed through him. And it was the strong odor of fear that kept his more carnal instincts at bay.

In spite of that fact, the urge to dominate, to claim victory and make her submit, warred in his mind. Even in his fur, a werewolf was still more than animal. The focused intelligence of his human half was enough to keep him from claiming her.

Stone danced around him, growling and yelping. Gabe knew his twin battled the same carnal desire to fuck the beautiful creature lying beneath him.

Neither one of them were rapists though. The adorable bitch had gone limp, not belly up, but almost cowering underneath him. Nothing they had done should have her so terrified.

You're fine. Get up, Gabe barked at her, sidestepping while Stone continued to prance around the two of them. His pent-up energy matched Gabe's.

Her growl mixed with a whimper. She backed up away from them, her belly close to the ground, and her nose almost touching it. Silver eyes shaped like almonds glowed brightly at them. Then she turned, almost leaping into the air, as she bolted away from them.

Well, hell. Gabe broke into a run. There was no reason to take her down a second time. Within minutes they were at their cabin, appearing just as quickly as the woods around them ended. On their own land, and using the female's surprise that she'd just run into a home against her, Gabe took that moment to grab her, gripping the loose fur at the back of her neck.

Stone changed first, his body altering while hair disappeared and his muscular body appeared. He straightened, his head being the last to resume human form.

"Let's get her inside." He leapt up the stairs of their back deck, his human scent filling the air with the smell of body sweat.

Wonderful. The first impression this terrified bitch would have of them was that they were two stinky men.

Stone had the back door open, and Gabe almost carried the female by the nape of her neck into their home. As soon as the door was closed, he allowed the change to take over him.

"It's all right. We aren't going to hurt you," was the first thing he said when his mouth could form words again.

For the life of him, Gabe couldn't utter a word after that. The female changed, slowly standing naked before them. Never had he laid eyes on a more beautiful woman.

Chapter Two

✆

Pamela sucked in her breath, doing her best to not shake noticeably. She'd either gotten herself into a worse nightmare than what she'd run from, or she'd found the perfect sanctuary. If she could get herself to calm down for just a moment, she was sure she could figure out if she was safe or not.

"Mind telling us why you gave us all such a good workout?" The man who'd had his mouth on the back of her neck crossed his arms over his chest.

It was hard not to stare at both of them. Obviously twins, she wasn't sure she'd ever laid eyes on two better-looking men. Not that her own pack had a good selection of werewolves to choose from.

Although she was well into the years of finding a mate, most bitches were mated at her age. She was only twenty-three, and regardless of what her sire had thought, she had no problem holding out for the best she could find.

"Do you have a shirt or something that I could put on?" No matter where she put her hands, there was no way she could hide her nudity from them. Although with the eye candy both of them were offering her at the moment, it was probably only fair.

"I kind of like you like that," the one who'd opened the door and entered first said.

"Stone," the other one reprimanded, and then turned his attention to her, pulling a folded afghan from the back of a chair and handing it to her. "I'm Gabe McAllister, and this is my brother Stone. And you are?"

There couldn't be any harm in offering her name. It wasn't like her pack would send out an all-points bulletin or anything.

"I'm Pamela, from the Bordeaux den."

"Why did you abandon your car and take off running?"

There was no way she could answer that question. Telling them she ran from a werewolf she despised, who abused her and forced her to do things, wouldn't help matters. No one in her own pack believed her. Why should she expect anything better from strangers?

And with this werewolf, Gabe, standing in front of her showing off his perfect body, getting her brain to conceive a believable lie was impossible. He was nothing like Jordan.

Her stomach twisted in knots. "I ran out of gas."

The way his eyes darkened at her lie caught her off guard for only a moment. She was a pro at dodging the first punch. When Gabe lunged at her, she leapt on to the couch, ready to jump over it and bolt out the back door.

That damn afghan he'd handed her was too bulky. He grabbed her arms, the still folded, knitted blanket the only barrier between their naked bodies.

"That will be the last time you lie to me," he hissed, pulling her to him.

Her heart pounded with enough ferocity to trigger the change. Her muscles ached to grow. This was exactly why she'd run. No werewolf would ever bully her again.

"Get your hands off of me." Her fear dissipated.

Possibly a fool's mission, but her temper had pushed her through more than one predicament in the past.

The phone rang, making her jump. Instead of digging his claws into her flesh, bruising her, Gabe simply held her in place, looking over his shoulder when his brother reached for a cordless resting on their kitchen counter.

The open family room area spread over into a large kitchen, divided only by carpet ending when plain vinyl spread over the kitchen floor.

Once upon a time in her past, she remembered her mother telling Pamela and her littermate that you could judge a person by their den. But it was hard to focus on the type of home these two lived in when hard, corded muscle filled her vision.

His biceps bulged, while tanned skin was covered by a sprinkling of dark blond hair over his broad chest. She worked to swallow, barely hearing the twin answer the phone while she took in Gabe's strong jawline, his broad shoulders and then blond locks that were damp enough that they curled around his face.

This man was fucking hot as hell.

"Yeah, we got her here," Stone was saying to whomever he spoke to on the phone. "Yeah...her. Have your bitch send over some clothes. Or we could just keep her naked until she tells us why she was running without an escort."

Gabe turned to look at her, his amused expression at his twin's words showing when his blue eyes sparkled. Pamela's heart skipped a beat, making her breath catch in her throat.

"Sounds like you better tell us what we want to know," he whispered. "The torture could get intense."

Strong fingers stroked her arms ever so slightly, sending chills rushing through her. She gripped the afghan to her chest, knowing her nipples hardened from his gentle touch.

It was more than his touch that sent a rush of interest through her. The amusement she'd caught in his gaze filled the air around him as well. This werewolf was different from the assholes in her pack. This was the kind of werewolf who would never give her the time of day. More than likely he had a bitch in town he brought his kill to. Some refined lady who was dignified and classy. Not a mountain bitch like herself.

"He's calling Rousseau." Stone had hung up the phone and moved to stand beside his brother, his gaze traveling from one of them to the other. "We're gonna have a houseful here before long."

This was the last thing she needed, an entire fucking pack coming down on her. Jordan would contact the pack leader, whine like the puny ass he was, and they would be turning her over to him before she had a chance to speak. And that would be the end of it.

"Go put some clothes on." Gabe glanced at his twin. "I'll watch her and then you can stay with her while I dress."

Stone nodded and then turned and headed down a dark hallway. Pamela caught herself staring at buns of steel as he disappeared into the other end of the house.

"I'm not going back." She wasn't sure what to tell this werewolf, but if she was going to convince him to take her side, it sounded like she needed to do it fast.

"The smell of your fear is filling my living room." Gabe let go of her arms and then ran one of his large hands down the side of her head.

Such a gentle touch, yet with hands at least as large as Jordan's. She let the afghan fall open, struggling to wrap it around herself. Somehow she needed a convincing story. Her mind raced with options.

Gabe took the blanket from her, unfolding it and then wrapping it around her shoulders. She looked down, and then her mouth went dry at the sight of his thick, long shaft. His cock was twice the size of Jordan's and it wasn't hard. Dear God. This werewolf was beyond perfect, gentle-natured, yet powerful-looking and confident.

She licked her lips, unable to quit staring at how perfect his cock was.

She spoke quickly before she lost her nerve. "Jordan Ricky will be coming to fetch me. You can't let him take me back. I won't mate with a werewolf who keeps beating me. I won't do it."

His cock straightened, and her brain seemed to shut down. It took a moment to realize every muscle in his body had hardened, while he grew before her eyes.

"That's all I needed to hear. You aren't going anywhere." He spoke with such conviction, enough finality, that it was hard to believe that this werewolf wasn't pack leader.

Surely any man who radiated the power she sensed coming off him had to be a leader among werewolves.

Pamela looked up at him, as his expression hardened. His lips formed a narrow line. Small silver streaks that hadn't been there a moment before raced like lightning across his blue orbs. He suddenly looked incredibly dangerous. Yet for some reason, he didn't scare her.

"Thank you," she mumbled.

Stone came back out into the living room, and Gabe simply nodded at her before retreating into the back end of the house.

Thirty minutes later, Pamela followed a *lunewulf* bitch to the other end of the house. The woman was quite the knockout, dressed in gothic style with a black mini dress and black boots. However, the woman was several inches shorter than Pamela, and the clothes she'd brought were somewhat tight.

"I brought a few outfits. You can borrow them while you're here." The woman leaned against the closed bedroom door, surveying the black jeans Pamela had managed to slide into. "I'm Simone, by the way."

"I have some clothes in my car." Pamela pulled a sweatshirt over her head and then frowned when she realized there was no mirror in the bedroom.

"My mate is having it towed over here." Simone crossed her arms, pursing her lips as she nodded in approval. "Those will do for now. Hold on to them as long as you need."

"That's kind of you." Pamela wouldn't be rude, although she didn't sense friendliness coming from this woman.

Simone was being kind, but her reservations about Pamela were obvious. She smelled the hesitation in the air, something akin to a lack of trust. Simone's reaction didn't surprise her. Pamela wasn't a mated bitch, and she'd just raced into their pack. There was no way she'd trust a bitch in her position either. Trust was earned, and so easily broken.

More than anything she wanted to go back to Gabe. His claim to protect her and his powerful good looks called out to her. His twin, Stone, had identical features. It might be dangerous staying in the den with the two of them. That thought suddenly made the small bedroom seem a bit too warm.

"You know, I know your kind." Simone had a no-nonsense tone about her.

The hairs prickled down Pamela's spine. She straightened, searching the bitch's expression, which had turned hard.

"My kind? And what kind do you think I am?"

"You're running from a werewolf. Been there and done that. And now you've found a den with some damn good men. Don't use them." Simone's pale blue eyes pinned her where she stood.

Even though the bitch was several inches shorter than Pamela, she had no doubt the woman would defend her pack members. After the day from hell she'd had, the last thing she wanted to do was spar with a stranger over the right to have a roof over her head.

"They offered to let me stay."

Simone shrugged. "I'm sure the two of them would love to fuck you."

"Sounds like they would be using me then." Just thinking about Gabe's large cock made her heart race.

She wouldn't give this bitch the satisfaction of smelling her lust though.

"You've got a werewolf out there coming after you. You don't need to tell me shit for me to be able to figure that out. And that will bring trouble to the McAllister den." Simone took a step forward, waving a perfectly manicured fingernail at her. "Gabe has a heart of gold. And although Stone can come across as an ass, he's a werewolf who will always have your back. Don't bring trouble to this den."

As much as she wanted to jump in this bitch's face, tell her to quit pointing fingers at her, Simone was right. She didn't know the werewolves out there, but obviously Simone cared about all of them. And Pamela's problems would bring trouble to anyone she stayed with. She let out an exasperated breath.

"I didn't ask to be brought here." She looked around the bedroom, simple and clean with little decoration. She guessed it to be a guestroom. "But you're right. I've got trouble following me, and it's just a matter of time before he finds me. I don't want to bring trouble to your pack."

Simone nodded, looking down and cocking her head. Pamela heard the men in the other room too and knew they would be missed if they stayed hidden back here too long. Once again, she needed to make a quick decision.

"I could climb out one of these windows. But you said they are towing my car…"

Apparently Simone must have been testing her, checking out what level of trouble she might be. Pamela had no rank in this pack. Simone wasn't queen bitch, or she would have introduced herself as such. But her expression relaxed, and the softer smell of compassion filled the room.

"I'm not heartless. You run out of here and you'll have more than one werewolf chasing your ass."

The door opened behind Simone at that moment, and she almost jumped out of the way to avoid being hit. Gabe gave her a quick glance before taking in Pamela. The way his gaze soaked through her made her tummy twist into knots.

What was it about this werewolf?

"You're not going anywhere." Gabe's voiced boomed off the walls in the small room.

A wave of panic rushed through Pamela. Gabe sounded so serious, almost dangerous. The last thing she needed was to run into another werewolf who would dominate and control her, imprison her and not allow her to think for herself. Life like that was simply unacceptable.

Gabe stood to the side of the doorway, silently making it clear that the two women had been alone in the bedroom long enough and he expected them to return with the others.

"You're going to scare her to death," Simone muttered, punching him playfully in the chest. "It's obvious she's already terrified. I'm sure she doesn't need to think all werewolves are brutes."

Pamela immediately envied the way Simone so easily talked to this werewolf. Sauntering past him, this bitch who had just tested her made her way back to the living room and into the arms of a *Cariboo lunewulf* that Pamela guessed was her mate. The werewolf showed no jealousy over his mate being so playful with another werewolf, but instead rolled his eyes as he stared at Gabe.

"She giving you grief?" he asked, his size so much larger than the *lunewulf* male who stood alongside him.

"When isn't Simone giving someone grief?" the *lunewulf* male said. "And you must be our visitor. I'm Johann Rousseau, pack leader."

"I'm Pamela Bordeaux." She straightened, extending her hand to the pack leader, who took it in a firm and warm handshake.

His smile was brief though as he quickly turned all business. "We've had your car towed over here. We realized you'd run out of gas and will accept for now that you abandoned it for that reason."

All eyes were on her and she smelled their curiosity. It didn't take a rocket scientist to guess that they all were speculating why she was there and what her past was. She licked her lips, fighting to clear her mind the way she'd mastered doing at such an early age so that her own emotions wouldn't be smelled.

Johann must have guessed she had no comment. The less they knew about her the safer she would be.

"You've already met Gabe and Stone McAllister," Johann went on. "This is Rock and Simone Toubec."

She nodded to the large *Cariboo lunewulf* who had pulled Simone into his arms. Maybe it was a good thing that there were *Cariboo* in this pack—that is, as long as none of them knew Jordan.

"Are you mated?"

She bit her lip at Johann's question. He knew her name, and it wouldn't take too much effort on his part to put word out to the few *Cariboo* packs in the mountains to confirm anything she told him.

"No." She looked down, praying her pack wouldn't betray her. "I refused the mating," she added quietly.

"The werewolf who wants you as his mate is following you?" Gabe asked.

Pamela didn't need to look up to feel the tension that suddenly filled the air. She was bringing trouble to this pack.

"I don't know if he's in Prince George or not." And that was the truth.

It wouldn't help matters if she told them that she'd managed to escape Jordan twice already since leaving the Canadian Rockies. One thing she was almost sure of, he wouldn't find her in this den.

"What's his name?" Gabe asked.

Pamela looked up at him. She didn't know a thing about this *Cariboo*. The McAllister den didn't ring a bell with her, but there were *Cariboo* scattered throughout the mountains. Some of them so rural that just a few dens created a pack. Jordan Ricky had come from such a pack. *Cariboo* like that made their own laws.

"What's his name?" Johann repeated.

Pamela let out a sigh, glancing around at the werewolves who all stared at her intently.

"His name is Jordan Ricky." She made eye contact with each of them quickly, searching for an immediate reaction.

Her gaze settled on Gabe. Pamela was a tall woman, a common trait of her breed, but he was still at least several inches taller and so damned muscular. Hard blue eyes captivated her, stealing her breath away. With the quick realization that she wanted his approval for some bizarre reason, her tummy twisted into knots.

Gabe looked away from her first. "She'll be safe here," he told Johann.

Johann shook his head. "She isn't mated. She can't stay in a den with two single males."

"Oh, good grief," Simone muttered. She looked at Pamela. "You're welcome to stay with us if you'd like."

"Trust me. If she's got a *Cariboo* after her, he'll track her down." Stone's comment made Pamela's heart swell painfully.

She glanced at Stone. He looked so physically identical to Gabe, although something about his mannerism, and a very different scent, made him seem so unlike Gabe.

"I don't mean to bring trouble to your pack." She focused on Johann and thought she saw something soften in his gaze.

He wasn't *Cariboo*. She'd never really associated with *lunewulf*, but stories told of the smaller breed fit his behavior. They were more refined, gentler than *Cariboo*.

"I need to contact your pack leader. But for the time being, we offer you protection. If the Toubecs will take you in, I approve."

She should be grateful. This was more than she'd hoped for. But contacting her pack…her stomach twisted in knots.

"Thank you. But…"

"But what?"

She didn't know enough about *lunewulf* to know how this werewolf's mind worked. His scent was relaxed though, sincerely curious about her. She sensed no hostility, no indication that he would force her to do anything. Another strong difference in their breed.

"If you contact my pack leader, he will simply tell you to send me back. It's the way of the *Cariboo*." She glanced at the other men in the living room, all watching her intently.

"What is the way of the *Cariboo*?" Johann focused on her, like she was the only *Cariboo* in the room.

She shook her head. "Our pack leader has final say over who mates with whom."

Johann's brow wrinkled. "All packs have been that way for centuries."

Pamela sucked in a breath, licking her lips, which were suddenly way too dry. "I will not be Jordan's mate. No one will force me."

Chapter Three

🔉

"What's your deal with this Pamela bitch?" Stone asked as they parked outside the hardware store in town the next day.

"I don't have a deal with her." Gabe walked toward the front of the truck, meeting Stone on the sidewalk.

Glancing quickly up and down the street, he wondered if he would pick up the scent of a new *Cariboo lunewulf* if he entered town. The thick smell of humans made it hard to detect anything else. But he told himself he would be able to. If Jordan Ricky dared enter into his pack, he would know it.

"Aside from the aggravation I've smelled on you all day, you're jumpier than a pup who's about to get into trouble." Stone followed his gaze up and down the street.

"Say what you want. You're out to protect her as much as I am."

Anyone else, and Stone would have denied it. He didn't fool Gabe though. Ever since Pamela had left with Toubec and his mate the night before, there had been a sullen silence in their den.

Stone shrugged. "She's got too much baggage."

After a quick visit into the hardware store, they strolled back to the street at the same time a patrol car slowed behind their truck.

"What's this I hear?" Marc McAllister, their older brother, the oldest of their den, stared at them through silver sunglasses.

Gabe walked between the parked cars and leaned his hand on the hood of the police car. "What have you heard?"

Marc looked past Gabe to Stone, then stared down the street. Gabe smelled how tense Marc was.

"You sniffed out some bitch, a *Cariboo lunewulf*," Marc spoke quietly.

Humans might know they existed, but none of them understood their ways. Gabe kept his voice low as well.

"She's got a werewolf from her pack coming after her."

Marc nodded. "That's what I heard. Get a description for me."

Gabe nodded, slapping the hood of the car and then stepping back. Marc looked up at him. "You going to go after this bitch?" he asked.

Gabe didn't answer. Was he going after her? He didn't know Pamela Bordeaux. And he'd only met her the night before. In less than twenty-four hours though, all he'd focused on was when he'd see her again.

Marc nodded once at Gabe's silence, obviously drawing his own conclusion. Glancing around him toward the street, he pulled slowly into the street.

"Let's get these supplies back to Toubec." Gabe turned and climbed into the truck.

By the end of the day, Gabe wasn't sure exactly what work he'd done. He ached and knew he needed a shower, so there had to have been something accomplished. He'd headed toward the ranch house before giving it any thought.

Damn good excuse he had. His older littermate wanted information.

Toubec's cubs ran across the large yard from one of the outbuildings toward the sprawling ranch. Gabe smelled their happiness, their perfect contentment as they ran across land where they were free to live as werewolves without censorship. Toubec had found paradise for his den, and he was one hell of a werewolf to share it with other *Cariboo* who came to him. Gabe and his brothers had bought a small part of this beautiful land.

The moment the scent in the air changed, everything inside him hardened. Turning toward the large barn at the other end of the yard, he saw her.

Pamela stood in the large entrance, the heavy door held open by a rock propped against it on the ground. Wearing blue jeans that hugged her legs as if they were painted on, and a flannel shirt, buttoned down so the material parted in a V, showing just a glimpse of her cream-colored skin. Her long blonde hair fell behind her shoulders, and a breeze made the ends of it blow from behind her. Staring at him, her blue eyes almost perfectly round, and her red lips puckered, her scent drifted through the air, calling him to her.

He stuffed his thumbs in his front pockets and strolled toward her, watching as she shifted her stance, her sudden awkwardness doing nothing to damage her alluring smell.

Pamela stood a good several inches shorter than he did. She looked up at him, her expression wary as she ran her tongue over her upper lip.

"You need a shower." Her gaze never left his.

A bold female sure as hell turned him on.

"You smell wonderful." He wasn't daunted by her implying that he stank.

She nibbled at her lip, and he had an overwhelming urge to do the same.

"Where did you sleep last night?" he asked instead, letting his gaze drop to where the top button of her shirt kept the material from showing off any cleavage.

Nibbling off that button sounded pretty damned good too.

"In the house." She nodded in that direction, looking away from him for the first time. "There are cabins. Simone told me about them. They have extra housing for *Cariboo* dens and a few are occupied. I offered to stay in one of those."

Gabe knew without asking that Toubec wouldn't approve of that. "You need the protection."

Pamela let out a sigh, once again nibbling on her lip. The action was driving him nuts.

"I just want it to end." She shook her head, looking down, and the overwhelming smell of sadness and frustration filled the air between them.

Unable to keep his hands off her any longer, Gabe ran his hand through her hair, tangling it between his fingers. Pushing enough to make her look up at him, he leaned into her.

Pamela took a step backwards, her scent growing stronger. Desire filled the air around them.

"We'll see to it that it ends then." His tone had deepened, a more carnal, rough side of him pressing forward.

He didn't know why he needed to kiss her so badly. Already he'd determined that she wasn't just another piece of tail. Something about the fact that she would run, take on her own pack and any other pack that stood in her way, really appealed to him. The whys though wouldn't distract him. At the moment, all he knew, and accepted, was that he had to taste her.

They'd stepped into the shadows of the barn, blocked from view just inside the doorway. The large structure was used primarily to store equipment used to work the large ranch. Werewolves didn't get along well with horses. At one time, probably, this large barn had been home to a fair amount of livestock. But for Toubec, it served as a workshop to repair and store equipment that he and the ranch hands used to work the land.

The smell of engines and sawdust didn't hide her lust when he leaned forward, capturing her mouth. Nibbling on the lip he'd been craving ever since he'd seen her, he captured it with his teeth.

"No. You shouldn't..." she whispered at the same time that her hands pressed against his chest.

Her scent deepened though, growing richer, sultrier. And her hands glided over his chest, reaching his shoulders and then holding on.

Gabe never forced himself on a lady. And he never would. Glancing down at her, his vision blurring with need, he watched her long lashes flutter over her blue orbs. She realized he watched her, their mouths releasing, and simply stared up at him momentarily.

Her lips parted, still moist from his mouth, her breaths quick and short. Putting his hands on her hips, he pulled her closer, still watching her, and let her feel his hard cock pressing against his jeans. Her fingers tightened over his shoulders but she didn't pull away. Nor did she speak.

Her scent grew so intoxicating it reached out and grabbed the more carnal side of him. It made his heart pound, while blood pumped with a fierceness through his veins. It drained through him, leaving him lightheaded with need while his cock throbbed. The heat of her body surged through him.

He had to have her. His hands snaked around her, crushing her to him, while he stole the gasp that escaped her lips when he devoured her mouth.

For the briefest of moments, she hesitated, remaining stiff against him.

When her fingers stretched over his shoulders, and then her palms pressed into his flesh, stroking him, moving until her hands wrapped around his neck, he knew she wanted this. Her body stretched against his. Long and slender, she moved along him.

No one woman had ever turned him on the way Pamela did. It made no sense but he didn't give a rat's ass. Regardless of the fact that they didn't know each other, that he had no knowledge of her den, her pack, Gabe knew he needed Pamela.

He ran his hands up her back, feeling her spine, her ribs, the beat of her heart. Her long blonde hair draped over his hands, tickling his flesh, adding to the fever that already burned through him. For the briefest of moments he could see why a werewolf would chase her across Canada.

That thought brought clarity to his brain. He would fight for this bitch. Damn it to hell, he didn't even know her and he wanted her bad enough to take another werewolf down. No female had ever made him feel that way.

"Pamela," he growled, taking a hold of her hair.

Twisting it in his fingers, its silky texture torturing his senses, Gabe pulled her head back. His mouth left hers and he tasted the flesh of her cheek, her jaw, her neck.

A growl escaped her and her fingers quivered, stroking his neck. She then gripped his shoulders again, digging her fingernails into his flesh.

Something carnal ripped through him. Raw and untamed, she had managed to call his beast forward without his consent.

He returned the growl, nipping at her neck and then stroking her flesh with his tongue. Tasting her simply added to his craving for her. The urge to take her right there, in broad daylight, just inside his boss's barn, suddenly sounded like a damn good idea.

Lifting her, he moved away from the doorway of the barn.

"What?" She looked and sounded disoriented for a moment.

When he put her down, she stumbled backwards a step or two until she backed into the wall next to a long wooden worktable. She brushed long strands of hair away from her face and stared up at him. Silver streaks glowed in the blue of her eyes and her teeth had lengthened, pressing against her lips.

"Wolf man. Don't take what isn't yours." Her voice was gargled, the change lingering in her, threatening to take over.

"Then who do you belong to?"

She straightened, her round breasts pressing against her shirt, stretching the material. "I belong to me!"

The distance between them was too great. Moving in on her, the way she pressed against the barn wall, watching him warily, made his blood boil even further. It had been a number of years since he'd enjoyed a *Cariboo lunewulf* female. Her arousal filled the entire barn with its rich scent. The way her muscles bulged against her clothing, and her breath came in pants, told him he could let go, be himself without holding back.

Damn. If he didn't fuck her right now he would go insane with need.

That pussy of hers had to be soaking wet. The flush in her cheeks, along with her rich smell, had him aching to find out.

She raised her arms, holding her hands in the air as if that would stop him. He grabbed her wrists, pinning them on either side of her head against the wooden barn wall.

"I need to fuck you," he said into the nape of her neck and then bit at the tender flesh there.

"God. Gabe." Her breath quickened, making her breasts press into his chest.

He let go of one of her wrists and cupped her breast through her shirt, kneading the full, soft flesh. Her nipple was so hard it thrust into his palm. Moving fast, the urge to rip her shirt leading his thoughts, he pulled at her shirt, yanking it free from the inside of her jeans.

"I can't…"

It took a moment for her words to register.

Gabe lifted his head, the taste of her flesh still on his lips when he straightened and looked down at her flushed expression.

Pamela straightened, not looking up at him. Straight blonde hair drifted over her face.

His hand snuck under the fabric and he rubbed his fingers over her breast, the swollen roundness so damned appealing.

"You can't what?" He didn't want to ask. But no matter the pain he would endure, he wouldn't fuck an unwilling partner.

Footsteps outside told him some of the ranch hands were nearby. He hadn't noticed them before and wondered if possibly Pamela had.

She shook her head, pushing him back until his hand slipped out from under her shirt.

"I just can't." She shook her head and turned to leave.

Gabe grabbed her arm, and she turned to look at him. The turmoil in her expression and scent matched the feelings twisting through him.

"Describe this werewolf to me," he told her. "What does the one who is coming after you look like?"

"You don't know me well enough to fight for me." The sadness in her tone about ripped his heart out. "But thank you."

She pulled her arm free and ran out of the barn.

Chapter Four

🕭

Over the next couple of days, Pamela kicked herself in the rear repeatedly for running from Gabe. Every inch of her ached for him to touch her again, stroke her skin with those rough, capable hands, nip at her and kiss her the way he had when they were in the barn.

He distracted her during the day, haunted her dreams at night. It just wasn't fair. The longer she stayed there, the more miserable she was. And that wasn't right either. Rock and Simone had opened their den to her, offered her sanctuary. The last thing they deserved was a moping houseguest.

To make matters worse, the night before, someone from Rock and Simone's pack had called suggesting there were new *Cariboo lunewulf* in town.

Pamela hadn't slept a bit last night. And while a run in her fur would have helped soothe her nerves more than anything right now, that was the absolute last thing she could do.

Every muscle ached when she padded down the hallway toward the stairs. Dark shadows lingered at the end of the hallway. Cubs still slept. Their heavy breathing and the gentle smell of clean laundry crept from their bedrooms. She moved quietly past the two doorways, not wanting to disturb them. The next bedroom was Rock and Simone's. She didn't need to pause at their doorway to know that neither one of them were in there.

Reaching the top of the stairs, she heard soft voices downstairs. Several werewolves, their concern drifting up toward her, spoke with an energy that warned her something wasn't right.

She chewed at her lower lip while gripping the banister at the top of the stairs. Barely sunrise, a time when many werewolves headed home after enjoying a night under the stars, a group of this pack remained inside, discussing something that bothered them.

Their energy, their emotions grew stronger the longer she stood there.

Her breath came harder as blood rushed through her veins, her body hardening as the change challenged her human half. No matter that she was *Cariboo*, a breed considered wilder, more unruly, than most werewolves. Even she knew better than allowing the change to take over while inside. She did have some decent breeding in her, even if her pack thought her little better than chattel.

But there was no way in her human form she could tell who was downstairs and what they were saying. Interrupting a private conversation would be rude.

Of course it wasn't right to eavesdrop either. But the level of concern she smelled alerted her that the only way she'd truly know what was going on down there was to keep her presence quiet and allow enough of the change to go through her so that she could fine-tune her hearing.

Ignoring the sweet pain that ached to consume her, Pamela held on to the banister, feeling the sweat soak her palm. The baggy sweatshirt and sweatpants clung to her skin, tightening around her as her muscles grew slightly.

Control it. You are the master.

Maintaining her human form while her werewolf blood coursed through her veins made the pain more acute. But it also heightened her senses. The dark shadows surrounding her faded. Individual scents — Simone, Rock, one of the ranch hands and another werewolf she didn't know — drifted up the stairs to her. Their quiet voices, the deep baritones and Simone's sultry tone, sharpened, making it easier to hear what they said.

"Where is he right now?" Rock Toubec asked.

"We've put him up in Power's Bed and Breakfast. And I will say he's not too happy to be there." The werewolf whose scent she didn't recognize spoke. "He's already contacted his pack, stating his rights are being challenged."

"What does he expect? For us to just turn her over to him?" Simone asked.

"If Ricky brings his pack into it, we'll have controversy hit the ranch." Martin Hanson, Rock's ranch manager, growled as he spoke. "We sure she's tellin' us the truth?"

Fire rushed through Pamela. Outrage and humiliation warred through her, clogging the air around her. Her emotions would be detected if she remained standing there. And she wouldn't be caught standing at the top of the stairs, eavesdropping.

It was hard to move. Her muscles had thickened, aching to change, allowing her emotions to be free to roar through her. But she had to keep her wits about her and get out of there. What she'd heard downstairs, the hushed whispers spoken before dawn had even arrived, were enough to let her know that Jordan had found her.

Damn her pack. Damn everyone of those *Cariboo* who'd decided what was best for her. None of them cared what she thought, least of all Jordan Ricky. He probably cared about her the least. It was what she had, what her den had left her. And that land was a curse. Jordan would kill her, destroy anything in his path just to own her so that he could have what she had. And she wouldn't be mated to a werewolf who didn't love her. Worse yet, who hated her and reminded her of that fact every chance he had.

Everyone downstairs would know she was awake if she paced her bedroom, which was what she felt like doing. Crawling onto her bed, she hugged her knees to her chest, fighting the burning tears that threatened to fall. Forcing herself to be patient, she stayed put when the cubs woke up, racing downstairs toward the smells of bacon frying.

Her stomach growled and her head pounded as the morning started in the Toubec home. The strong smell of coffee, bacon, eggs frying, and toast and butter made her stomach turn.

Thoughts of the night her sire had gone to that blasted pack meeting, informing her that he would announce her dowry, find her a mate, made her stomach turn.

"I don't need help finding a mate," she'd argued with him.

"You'll do as you're told. I won't have a werewolf shacking up alongside me that I don't approve of."

"But I'll have to live with him."

Her sire had thrown his arms up in the air, turning to glare at her mother, and then had stormed out. It had been later that night that Jordan Ricky, drunk as a skunk from celebrating his mating to her, had found her. The *Cariboo* in her pack had confirmed and celebrated her mating without even talking to her about it. How fucking archaic could a pack be?

Pamela rested her head on her knees, refusing to feel sorry for herself. That would get her nowhere. *Take action. Don't wallow in pity.* Her mother's soft-spoken words still encouraged her forward.

It was time once again to take action. Jordan Ricky was here. This was a larger pack, with what she hoped was more forward thinking than her own pack. There was no doubt in her head though that the pack leader here would honor the words of her own pack leader. They all seemed to think they had to control their bitches. Like she didn't have a mind of her own.

The ache to lunge through the window, spring to the ground below and race across the bountiful land outside sounded so damn good.

She stayed put though, sitting on her bed in the small bedroom she'd considered sanctuary. Waiting quietly until the house grew quiet, as the day began, she didn't move until she knew she could escape without being noticed.

Simone left the house with the cubs, taking them to school, and that was the moment Pamela waited for. Once the bitch of the den was gone, she had a better chance of escape. The werewolves wouldn't pay as much attention to her. Werewolf culture was the same no matter the pack or breeding. The bitches answered to the bitches. It was the way it was in this den, and the way it had always been.

Running in her fur during the day was a dangerous and more than likely foolish feat. Accepting the fact that she would have to hoof it across the meadows toward the miles of rambling trees that surrounded the lumberyard where Gabe worked, she put speed to her gait, running faster than a human could run.

Maybe running to Gabe wasn't the answer. She knew little about this *Cariboo*. For all she knew, he might be as bad as Jordan.

No fucking way! Quit being paranoid. No Cariboo could be as bad as Jordan.

The chilly air didn't stop her from breaking out in a sweat. By the time the rich smell of freshly cut wood filled her senses, her heart pounded in her chest, partially from running so fast, and more so from the excitement of seeing Gabe again.

And what if he wants nothing to do with you?

Remembering when they were last together, his hands on her, his mouth nipping at her neck, made her heart race all the faster. She could barely keep her breath when she heard pounding footsteps racing behind her. Turning quickly, ready to take on her pursuer, she didn't have time to react when a large body slammed into her, taking her to the ground.

"Where the hell do you think you're going?" Gabe's growl ripped through her.

Panic had consumed her. Too many memories of Jordan tracking her down, capturing her every time she'd tried to escape his mountain cabin, rushed through her before she realized who was on top of her.

Kicking furiously, she bit and scratched while Gabe lifted her to her feet.

"Calm down, my sweet bitch." His tone was relaxed, not the nasty criticism she'd heard so many times from Jordan.

It took a moment to catch her breath. Gabe put her on her feet, running his hands down her arms before releasing her. He put his hands on his hips, staring down at her, looking at her as if he waited for an explanation.

"Jordan. Jordan Ricky." She inhaled deeply, ordering her heart to quit pounding in her chest. "He's here. He's in Prince George."

"And so you run from your protection? Are you trying to seek him out?" Gabe didn't look pleased.

His aggravation filled the air around them. Anger filled her nose with its spicy aroma. Pamela nibbled her lower lip, forcing herself to remain calm at his preposterous implication. Were all werewolves so damned bull-headed?

"Hell no, I don't want to seek him out." She matched his stance, fisting her hands against her hips. "I overheard them this morning. They are worried about Jordan bringing his pack to the ranch. I'm going to bring trouble to them and I won't have that."

"And so where are you going?"

"I was looking for you."

Something changed in his expression. Gabe grew before her, his muscles bulging while his mouth formed a thin, determined line.

There was no way she could move when he reached for her, grabbing her tangled hair and pulling it to the side, forcing her to arch backwards as he tugged.

"You won't turn me away twice," he grumbled, and then captured her mouth with fiery need.

So many emotions had tumbled through her since she'd awoken that morning. The exhilaration of her run, even if while in her skin, had unleashed adrenaline that now needed a direction. Without thinking, she reached for Gabe, gripping his hair as he did hers, and holding on, deepening the kiss.

When he growled into her mouth, she about exploded inside, moisture soaking her inner thighs against her jeans.

It hadn't crossed her mind what she would do once she found Gabe. But his aggression put all of her energy into focus. More than anything right now she needed to fuck him. Damn the possibility that more of the crewmen could be out here working. She needed him inside her, and she needed him now.

Grabbing his shirt, she ripped at it with her fingernails, hardly giving thought to the partial change rushing through her.

"Woman." His growl fed her fire, the one word giving her chills.

"I'm not turning you away." She could barely talk, barely think.

Ever since overhearing the conversation that morning, knowing Jordan was so close, she'd been in a state of panic. Somehow being in Gabe's arms, feeling his hard body pressed against hers, gave her a sense of grounding.

This *Cariboo* would protect her. She didn't know why she knew that. But instinct told her that he wouldn't hurt her, wouldn't use her like Jordan did. His strong scent, dominating and predatory, wrapped around her. Her pussy throbbed with a demanding need. And more than anything she needed him inside her, realizing that it would bond them but at the moment not caring.

Gabe's hand moved between them, grabbing onto the waist of her jeans. With a quick tug he ripped the button free, tearing the zipper so that it broke free of the material. His aggression fed her fire, having her almost panting when she stumbled as the material tangled around her legs.

Her jeans gathered at her knees, the cool air attacking her feverish cunt as he exposed her. There was no time to regain her footing before he turned her around, pushing until she collapsed to her knees.

And then he was over her, mounting her as if they were in their fur. His hard cock pressed against her ass and then slid down toward her cunt while she braced herself on all fours.

There was no foreplay, no intimacy. Gabe thrust inside her with a need matching her own.

"Holy fuck," she cried out, feeling his stiff cock penetrate her.

The hard ground dug into her palms but she didn't care. Birds chattered noisily above them while the small wildlife clamored around them, crying out while shaped as humans they fucked like animals.

Gabe filled her, reaching her most sensitive area. Her vision blurred, a massive tidal wave of lust breaking inside her as he pounded her cunt. Never had she been taken so quickly, with so much energy, and craved it so badly. Sex had never been so damned good.

With each thrust the pressure grew inside her. Her sensitive muscles quivered, moisture soaking both of them while he built the momentum. The friction between them created a heat that smelled so damn good she could get drunk on it.

Gabe fucked her, grunting behind her while his hands dug into her hips, pinning her so that she couldn't move. Shaking her head from side to side, her long hair fanning around her face, she didn't want him to ever stop.

"Sweet bitch. You are one hot fucking woman." His words came to her as if they were whispered through a tunnel.

Everything around her seemed to fade. Nothing mattered but his cock gliding in and out of her. The world consisted of the two of them, everything else fading into nothingness.

And when his fingers dug deep into her flesh, while his cock inside her swelled and stretched her further, she couldn't hold back.

Pamela arched her back, throwing her head back when she felt him explode inside her. Howling loud enough that her throat stung, she didn't care who heard. Never had she felt more free, more alive.

"Pamela," he growled, his baritone vibrating through her as he collapsed on top of her, swollen and stuck inside her.

She collapsed as well, unable to hold up both of their weight. Gabe remained inside her, locked deep within her cunt while he rolled to the side, wrapping his arms around her. For a moment, all seemed right with the world. Staring up at the tall trees, with the endless blue sky beyond that, she almost believed that she could find happiness. Possibly a *Cariboo* did exist who would treat her right. Taking a long deep breath, she slowly relaxed against the warmth of his embrace.

Chapter Five

ஐ

Gabe paced in his living room, glaring at his twin, who stood facing him with his arms crossed against his chest.

"This is crazy. I'm causing headaches no matter what den I go to." Pamela sat cross-legged on his couch wearing his bathrobe, which she about drowned in.

After bringing her to his den, she'd informed him she needed the rest of her clothes. Apparently the zipper in her jeans no longer worked. It didn't bother him in the least that he'd ruined her jeans. And he had no problem keeping her naked. But the woman had to have clothes.

The way she scowled at him when he'd called Toubec, letting him know that he had Pamela and now needed her clothes, made the phone call all the more enjoyable.

Unfortunately, that was when his pleasure for the day had ended.

"Your pack has sent an administrator." Stone's expression was hard. "He's accompanied Ricky and they're demanding their rights to have you back."

"Jordan doesn't want me. All he wants is that damned land."

"What land?" It was time to get all of the facts out of Pamela.

Pamela sighed, twisting the tie to his bathrobe in her hand nervously. She didn't look up at either of them.

"My sire offered up a piece of land on the side of our mountain as a dowry. They bid on it at a special pack meeting. I wasn't even aware that it happened until Jordan, drunk from celebrating his mating to me, showed up at my den to take me. When I told him I wouldn't be his mate..." She paused for a moment, looking like she wanted to rip the tie in two. "Well, he dragged me out of my den, took me to his own den and then beat me for humiliating him."

She looked up at both of them. "I ran during the night."

"So you're mated?" Gabe could feel his blood start to boil.

Pamela stood quickly, the bathrobe parting to show off the beautiful swell of her breasts. She either didn't realize how she'd exposed herself for the two of them or she didn't care. Her anger flared though, its spicy smell filling the living room.

"I am not mated!" She tossed her hair over her shoulder, glaring at him as her breaths came almost in pants. "The only time Jordan touched me was to beat me."

Gabe glanced over at Stone, who had his gaze fixed on her exposed cleavage.

"Sounds like your pack seems to think otherwise." Stone didn't move when Pamela took a step toward him, her hand raised as she made a fist.

At the last moment, she pointed at him, poking him in the chest. "My pack can go to hell, along with any other werewolf who is going to have such an ass backwards point of view."

Stone took her hand, holding it when she tried to pull away. Gabe watched the action, knowing his littermate would respect whatever bitch Gabe claimed. And right now, he wasn't sure if he had a right to claim her. There was investigating to do. For the moment, hearing everything Pamela could offer them would have to do. Then he would take that information and see how free Pamela actually was.

Dear Lord. Was he actually thinking about mating with her?

He knew the answer to that one, regardless of what he wanted to think. Pamela ran circles around any other bitch in his own pack. Her fire and her spunk turned him on almost as much as that sexy body of hers. She'd gotten under his skin the first day he'd met her. And in less than a week, she'd consumed his thoughts. Their sire had always told them that they would know the bitch that was for them the second they laid eyes on her. Gabe knew he would fight for Pamela. And it was starting to sound like that might be exactly what he would have to do.

"No one in this room is challenging anything you're saying," Stone told her quietly.

She looked down at her hand that Stone continued to hold, and then looked over her shoulder at Gabe.

"I don't want to go back with them." Her words were a plea, a roundabout way of asking for his protection.

"No one will make you do anything you don't want to do." Gabe reached for her, stroking her soft hair. "You have my word on that."

"And mine," Stone added.

A firm knock disturbed the brief moment of silence between the three of them. Gabe watched Stone let go of her hand and walk past them. But in that moment, Gabe knew that Pamela had bonded with the two of them. His brother, his littermate, was part of him. Gabe and Stone had shared everything almost since birth.

In that brief moment, he'd sensed the acceptance in Pamela. They'd both had their hands on her, and she'd relaxed, her anger fading, while a glimpse of peace settled through her. She would take his protection and Stone's too.

That acceptance on her part let Gabe know that Pamela was the bitch for him. She took him as he was, a twin. And with him, she would accept Stone. Whatever it took, he would make this woman his mate. She would have all of him, and he would share her with Stone, making their den even stronger. It was how he'd known it would be all his life.

Stone opened the front door and the smell of Simone's perfume filled Gabe's nose before he saw the female stroll into the living room, carrying a bundle of clothing.

"How come every time I come over here, you don't have any clothes on?" There was a glint of amusement in the saucy bitch's eyes.

"We like to keep our women naked," Stone said easily.

"You are such a brute." Simone rolled her eyes. She then focused on Pamela and her expression turned serious. "I'd like to speak with you alone."

Pamela nodded and then glanced up at him. Gabe gestured toward the hallway. "Take her back to the bedroom."

He watched the two bitches disappear into the small guest bedroom that once had been their oldest littermate's bedroom when he'd still lived there. He knew that it didn't bother him that Pamela came with so much baggage, so many issues that they would have to work out. His older littermate, Marc, had taken a human for a mate. Gabe had it easy when he thought about all the issues Marc had to deal with in order to do that.

He turned his attention to Stone, who met his gaze with a piercing stare. "You're going to have to fight for her."

Without even telling him, Stone knew he planned to make Pamela his mate.

"Yup." And he would do it too.

"You have my approval. And I'm sure Marc will give you his blessing as well."

Gabe nodded, knowing both of his littermates would back him without even having to ask. Not that he'd planned on asking, but neither of them would have expected that anyway.

"Once Simone leaves, we'll contact Rousseau and find out what he's learned about her pack. You know as well as I do that the *Cariboo* ways won't impress him." Gabe had no problem with Johann Rousseau, their pack leader. But he was *lunewulf* and the *Cariboo* had their own way. "He'll view the laws of her pack as antiquated and overrule them."

"And if he doesn't?" Stone asked.

"Then we'll overrule them."

Stone nodded. "Then we make her part of our den."

Gabe didn't miss the underlying meaning Stone meant. "Yes. We make her part of our den."

The two of them stared at each other. Gabe had just agreed to allowing Stone to fuck her too. It didn't need to be voiced. Making her part of their den meant that what belonged to one of them belonged to both of them. And when the time came, Stone would share his mate as well. The bitches that they brought into their den would understand that, if they were to understand them. And Gabe knew that Stone had sensed it too. Pamela would agree to it.

The two females came out of the bedroom, Pamela now dressed in a pair of leggings and close-fitting sweater. Her long, willowy body was nicely displayed in her clothes. His cock stirred to life, anxious to be inside her again. Never had he seen a more sexy woman.

Simone headed toward the door. "Rock told me to tell you that he's got you covered," she said.

"Tell him thank you." Gabe had never doubted that Toubec, another *Cariboo*, would support him in fighting for Pamela.

Simone left the den and Gabe turned his attention to Pamela.

"What did she say to you?"

She shrugged. "She just wanted to make sure that I really wanted to stay here, that I wasn't here against my will."

Gabe could have guessed that was what Simone had planned on doing. Bitches in a pack looked out for each other.

"And what did you tell her?"

"That I was here of my own free will." She straightened, her expression solemn as she met his gaze.

An instinct rose in him with such strong vengeance that he couldn't stop it from filling the room with its ripe scent. A protector's instinct, a powerful ownership, something more raw and untamed than he'd ever experienced in his life. Bones popped inside him without his consent. Blood rushed through him with a vengeance that he could barely control.

Mine!

He pulled Pamela to him, almost yanking her off her feet with his need to have her in his arms, to hold her, to feel that ripe body of hers against his. Grabbing her chin, he lifted her face to his.

"And that was all that was discussed?" He needed to know everything she did, that she said, such powerful ownership rushed through him that he couldn't focus on anything else.

"No." She shook her head slightly, her pretty blue eyes clouding as she hesitated in enlightening him as to the rest of their conversation.

"There will be no secrets," he growled, aching to be able to simply crawl inside her, know her thoughts.

He wanted to know everything she felt, every emotion that sprang from her the moment it blossomed.

Pamela licked her lips, glancing down for just a moment before stiffening, straightening in his arms, although she didn't pull away.

"She warned me about you two," she whispered.

"Oh?" He already knew what Simone had told her but needed to hear Pamela voice it.

He sensed Stone standing behind him, watching, waiting to hear what he also needed to hear.

When Pamela pushed away, he let her go. Damn it if he didn't want to keep her in his arms, but he would give her this space, not force any part of him on her. She would have to accept all of him, every bit of how he was. But she would do it of her own accord. He waited for her to speak.

Pamela walked into the adjoining kitchen, her ass swaying deliciously in her leggings that hugged her as if they were painted on her.

When she turned, hesitation seeped from her. She gazed from one of them to the other.

"She warned me that you would share me with Stone." The way she spoke, with such conviction, holding her head high, showing that she would stand up to the unknown, embrace it instead of run from it, made his heart pound with excitement.

"Nothing will happen until you are ready." Until you are mine, he wanted to add, but held his tongue.

She nodded and then turned her back on both of them, searching the kitchen as if she ached for something to do, anything to remove the awkwardness that he smelled swarming around her.

Glancing at Stone, his twin took the silent hint and headed out the back door. Gabe walked over to Pamela, aching to hold her, deciding her knowledge of his need to share what meant the most to him with his brother was enough for right now.

"As soon as the sun sets, we'll run. It will do all of us some good to be in our fur for a while."

He pulled her to him, feeling the sweet curve of her ass nestle into him.

"That sounds real good," she murmured.

There were other matters to tend to as well. But they would be best dealt with once they all had time to run off the emotions that cluttered his den at the moment.

Chapter Six

§ō

The smell of fish frying turned Pamela's stomach. There was plenty going on to make her lose her appetite. She knew she should eat, and helping make supper was something to do to stay busy. But every time she turned around in the kitchen, she brushed against one of the oversized *Cariboo* helping to prepare their meal.

"You're going to spoil us working in the kitchen like this," Stone teased, reaching into a bag to help peel potatoes. "Now all Gabe has to do is train you to cook naked."

Gabe reached around her to swat Stone on the side of the head with a dishtowel. Stone ducked, letting out a hoot while grabbing her to use her as a shield against his twin.

"Ignore him," Gabe retorted, managing to smack Stone with the towel against his thigh. "He was our mother's least favorite and so was ignored as a cub."

Stone jumped around her, grabbing Gabe in a headlock. "You're just jealous 'cuz she gave me the best of the kill and you got the scraps."

Gabe wrapped his arms around Stone and the two of them fell into the wall, making the house shake as they laughed and wrestled.

It was hard to stay out of their way, but part of her didn't want to. They had succeeded in lightening the mood, giving her a glimpse of Gabe in his own environment, at ease in his den.

Happiness warmed through her for the first time in ages, it seemed. She could smell the relaxed state of the two men, their laughter and roughhousing making her ache for a den like this, with relaxed emotions and no hostility or tension.

Muscles bulged through their shirts, adrenaline mixing with the smell of their amusement. She let her gaze stroll down the two of them, noting the similarity in their bodies. As far as physical appearance went, their bodies appeared the same. Tall and well-built, broad shoulders with thick muscles corded under well-tanned skin. Gabe had light red streaks highlighting his blond locks and Stone had lighter, blonder hair. But that was the only difference she could see between the two of them.

"Just because you're a few minutes older," Stone growled, speaking through laughter and heavy breathing when Gabe tackled him and the two sprawled to the floor. "Don't think you're going to take me down in front of any bitch."

Pamela laughed, getting into the moment. "You're both acting like a couple of pups. And the fish is going to be tough if we don't eat it soon."

She managed to get around them and flip the filets that fried in butter and onions.

The phone rang then, and Pamela turned quickly, staring at it, while Gabe and Stone parted, both of them still laughing.

Her heart suddenly started pounding in her chest as she watched Gabe grab the cordless. His smile slowly faded as he listened to the man's voice that tickled Pamela's ears, although she couldn't fine-tune her hearing enough to hear what was said.

"You can ask her yourself, but she wants to stay here."

Silence fell around the room as the spicy smell of anger drowned out the smell of butter, onions and fish frying.

"I'm aware of that." Gabe's tone had hardened, matching the anger that radiated through him. "Don't you think I already know that? Whatever it takes. Yes. I've made up my mind."

Pamela turned quickly, not daring to think about what Gabe had made up his mind about. Her hand shook when she reached for the fork on the counter and stabbed at potatoes boiling in water on the fire at the back of the stove. Water splashed and she stepped backwards, feeling the quick sting of burning water against her flesh.

Stone silently took the fork from her. "Go sit down," he said quietly.

She looked up at him, into eyes so similar to Gabe's. At that moment, she saw something in him that she hadn't seen before.

Gone was the crass expression, the sarcastic look that he wore as a mask. Stone could be as compassionate as Gabe. He would make a good mate for some bitch.

Pamela licked her lip, looking back toward the cooking food.

"Go," he repeated, and nudged her backwards.

Pamela crossed her arms over her chest and walked out toward the adjoining living area.

Gabe paced from the length of the room back to the kitchen. When she met his gaze, he looked away, making everything inside her twist with nervous energy. There was nowhere to go, no other room to escape to. Hell, she couldn't even leave. Neither of them would allow it, and she wasn't stupid enough to think she could escape the filthy paws of Jordan twice. The ugly sensation of being trapped crept through her, and her heart started racing too quickly.

"Listen to me." Gabe's baritone had such a hard, serious edge to it that chills rushed over her skin. "She claims that she isn't mated. And I believe her."

"I'm not. I swear it. No one ever asked me if I wanted Jordan for a mate."

She would have gone on, ridiculed her pack for their antiquated ways. Gabe raised his hand, silencing her. Tension grew in the room. Gabe was fighting her battle for her, and in the end it would mean him fighting Jordan for her. Werewolves had come a long way over the centuries. Very few packs treated their bitches the way she was being treated, sold over for the price of a dowry. But there were still many traditions that remained hard, fast and intact. And challenging a mating, demanding the right to claim a bitch as his own, would mean a fight to the death.

A female could do the same, and it would always be this way. Werewolves didn't divorce, and by human standards they didn't marry either. The law was simple. When two werewolves wished to unite as one, they approached the pack leader. If the mating was approved, then it was done. But if another werewolf laid claim on either the werewolf or the bitch, then it was resolved in their fur.

A simple law with little recourse. Two werewolves who both wanted the same female would fight—until one of them died.

Jordan Ricky wouldn't stand a chance against Gabe McAllister.

"Very well. Show me the papers, and we'll take it from there. In the meantime, unless she wishes otherwise, she stays here."

The voice on the other end of the phone once again tickled Pamela's ears. Allowing any part of the change to go through her would be too easily detected though. There was no way she could understand what the man on the other end of the line said.

Pamela couldn't handle this any longer. She would go nuts just standing there. The urge to run out the door into the night, run once again from all of her problems, almost overwhelmed her.

Gabe hung up the phone with a bit too much aggression. Without looking at her he returned to the kitchen. He and Stone made plates, no one speaking. She was going to go nuts and explode if someone didn't say something soon.

"What was that all about?" She had a right to know the details. The conversation was obviously about her.

"Jordan Ricky claims you two are mated. He's approached our pack leader to have you returned to him. Obviously somehow he's learned you are in our territory."

Gabe carried two plates into the living room and handed one of them to her. His eyes were an icy shade of blue that captivated her and twisted her stomach in knots at the same time.

"What papers are you going to look at tomorrow?"

Realizing he held a plate of food at her, she took it, doubtful she'd be able to eat a bite. The relaxed mood in the den was gone.

"Apparently he has proof that you own land together, have joint checking accounts and several credit cards in both of your names. The signatures show that you've signed them with Jordan's last name." Gabe's lips barely moved as he spoke. Although for all appearances, his body appeared relaxed, the thick smell of aggravation couldn't be missed. "Even by human standards that would make you pretty damned mated."

Pamela didn't know what to say. "It's all lies." She shook her head, suddenly needing to sit down.

There was no way he could have all that information. It had been one night—one terrible night—that she'd spent in Jordan's den. And she'd run before sunrise.

"Eat your supper. We'll make sure there are clean sheets in the guest bedroom before you sleep."

The hardness in his tone bothered her. She had no clue what Jordan had up his sleeve, what he was trying to prove. *Cariboo* pride ran deep. And saving face with the pack would be imperative for Jordan. She didn't doubt that. Obviously, Gabe's pride was just as strong. *Cariboo* were *Cariboo* no matter what part of the world they lived in.

"I want to see those papers too." She sat down on the couch, resting her plate on her knees. Staring at her food, she wondered what efforts had been gone to for Jordan to have such proof. "They're forged. I've never once signed my name using any other last name than my sire's."

After a long moment, Gabe finally spoke. "I believe you," he said quietly.

"Then why do I smell your doubt?" One thing she would never do would be to cower in front of any werewolf. "The room is frigid from the emotions that are running through it at the moment."

Gabe didn't say anything and Pamela shoved at her food with her fork. Stone still stood in the kitchen, jabbing at his food, which was on the counter. He didn't look her way when she glanced over at him.

Pamela had had enough. Standing, she walked over and dumped her food in the trash then put her plate in the sink. Turning to face both of them, she crossed her arms over her chest. Nervous energy rushed through her. She didn't know either of them that well. Granted, she had the best sex she'd ever had earlier today with Gabe, and pursuing a relationship with him sounded mighty damned appealing. She wouldn't be doubted though.

"I'm going for a run," she announced.

"No," Stone piped up quickly.

"Not alone you aren't," Gabe said at the same time.

"Then we come to a truce right now." She glared at both of them. "You believe me or you don't. But say now what is on your mind. I won't stay in a den where I'm not welcomed as a friend."

"Friend?" Gabe stood, suddenly looking very dangerous.

Walking toward her, he dumped what was left of his supper in the trash and then moved in on her. When he was mere inches away, he reached behind her, placing his plate on top of hers in the sink. The rattling of the two plates made her jump, and she cursed her frazzled nerves.

"Is that what you want? Friendship?" he whispered, pressing against her so that the counter pinched against her back. "I think we've moved way past friendship, my dear."

There was no way she could see past his broad shoulders toward Stone. But the smells in the kitchen changed quicker than she could blink. Lust drowned out even the smell of the fish and onions.

"I smelled your anger." Even with him this close, his body hard against hers, scorching her senses, she wouldn't let her desire for him fog her senses. "You doubted me."

"What you smelled was my outrage that someone would challenge what I might consider calling my own."

Pamela's breath caught in her throat. Suddenly there was no air to breathe that didn't swarm with his strong emotions. She gasped for air, pushing hard against his chest until he took a step backwards, allowing her to jump around him, gather space she could call her own.

"You…you barely know me." Her heart raced too quickly in her chest to make her breathing slow. She almost panted as she looked from him to Stone. "I've just run from a werewolf who decided to call me mate without my consent."

"And will you run from me too?" Gabe didn't move but leaned against the counter.

His expression was suddenly so relaxed she could almost convince herself that she'd imagined the harsh emotions she'd smelled moments before.

"No," she said, uttering the word before she'd even given it thought.

But she didn't need to think about it. Gabe was the kind of werewolf that a bitch would fight for, not run from. The ache in her heart that pulsed through every inch of her body told her she wouldn't run. Gabe was the werewolf she'd dreamed about in her den every night. Every time she'd looked at another *Cariboo* and found him lacking, she'd been imagining Gabe. Strong and powerful, willing to fight for her. She sensed his honesty as well from the way his pack members respected him. Gabe was a werewolf others looked up to. He wasn't a louse, stooping low enough to lie, cheat, forge documents instead of working with the truth. Gabe was the *Cariboo* she'd dreamed of all of her life. He would lay his kill at her feet. She would see to it.

"I think a run would do us all some good." Stone scraped his fork across his plate, gathering the remnants of his food and then swallowing it. "Pamela can do the dishes when we get home."

He offered her a roguish smile, one she guessed probably got him into the pants of many bitches. He needed a lot of work though. The werewolf had a chip on his shoulders a mile wide. She pitied the bitch who fell for this guy. He was almost as sexy as his brother. But with that attitude that he used to cover his more sensitive side, the good bitches would send him packing.

Out of nowhere, the thought of fucking both of them sprang into her mind. Her insides fluttered to life. Damn it. She'd dealt with all of the intense emotions she could handle for one night.

"You can do your own damn dishes," she growled, fighting the thought that had invaded her senses. Hostility would be a better emotion for them to smell. "Damn. You need a leash."

Stone shook his head, walking past both of them as he pulled off his shirt. "I can see already you're going to need help training her."

"We'll all do our own dishes when we get home, just like we always do." Gabe's muscles swelled in his arms and chest as he pulled his shirt over his head.

Pamela swallowed, closing her eyes and slowly pulling her shirt over her head. There shouldn't be anything different about undressing in front of these two. She'd stripped in front of her pack members all of her life. Somehow telling herself that didn't stop the warmth from spreading from her cheeks, deep inside her straight down her middle. Heat rushed through her, lodging between her legs, making her pussy throb.

"You'll stay right by us. Do you understand?" Gabe opened the back door.

Stepping to the side, he allowed her out into the cold night air. Stone was just ahead of her, his muscles rippling against his flesh. Teeth pressed against his lips, which caused his words to garble.

"You know what they say about single bitches who run with a couple of werewolves." He grinned, and she didn't miss the fact that he'd acknowledged her single.

And she did know what werewolves thought of single bitches willing to run without an escort or before they were mated.

"They say the same thing that they say about bitches who run from a mating," she said, sighing.

Gabe pulled his shirt off, then reached for the buttons on his jeans. Stone bent over in front of her, pushing his jeans down muscular legs. There was no way she'd be able to slip out of the rest of her clothes. She would make a complete ass out of herself. Allowing the change to rip through her without even undressing was a childish act, certainly something a grown bitch would never do.

Her fingers trembled while a fire burned deep inside her, screaming for release. Blood pumped through her veins, her heart pounding harder with new energy as the beast inside her, the other half of her whole, slowly woke, fighting to consume her.

Too much man, too much werewolf — *Cariboo* — filled the space around her. Their scent smothered her and her insides reached out, burning her alive, making her crave to have more.

Yet this was madness. She closed her eyes, blocking out the incredible view. Sensing the change take over, her muscles grew as her bones began to stretch. Quickly stripping out of the rest of her clothes, she embraced the sweet pain, craving the fullness of emotions, the pureness of her soul, the completeness of who she was.

"The smell of your lust is addictive." Gabe's breath tickled her flesh.

Pamela turned, her legs already aching to bend. Barely able to stand on two feet, she stared into his silver eyes. Blond hair streaked with red stood almost on end. His look was wild, animalistic, carnal and possessive. Her breath caught in her throat, and she gasped at the wild sight of him.

"All in due time," he told her, his voice garbling as his teeth grew. "You shall have both of us when I say the time is right."

Falling forward, landing on four paws, her skin prickled as fur spread over her body. Growling her answer, letting him know she wouldn't be mastered, not even by a powerful *Cariboo* male, she lunged forward.

I'm not in search of a keeper, wolf man.

Gabe dropped to all fours as well, letting out a howl while his body rippled, powerful muscles bulging under flesh that quickly covered with fur.

She laughed, her vocal cords making it sound like a high-pitched growl. Leaping off the back deck, she took flight, tearing at the ground as she embraced the night.

Gabe and Stone matched her pace, running on either side of her. They had the strength to outrun her, outmaneuver her best actions. Between them she was safe though, free, her problems momentarily left behind.

What happened tomorrow, later this week, in the near future, was not a problem for this evening.

For tonight she would enjoy the moment, knowing her freedom ran deeper than the speed her legs could carry her. Somehow running between the twins, tearing at the earth while the three of them ruled the night, Pamela knew she left behind her fears, her uncertainty of where her life would lead her. As the power of her beast bled through her, she realized she ran toward a new life. From this point forward, she ruled her own destiny.

No one would make her decisions for her. And that included Gabe McAllister. She would say what she wanted and when she wanted it. That included when she would take the two of them to bed.

Chapter Seven

ରେ

Sweat clung to Gabe's flesh as he allowed the change to grab a hold of him. Confining the beast, quenching the power while his body once again took the form of a man, he watched Pamela as she straightened, her woman's body as sultry and beautiful as her werewolf form.

They had run long and hard. All of them had pent-up energy needing release. Fighting for Pamela would challenge and drain all three of them.

Pamela's small hand reached for the back door, pulling it open and then disappearing into his den with her clothes balled in her hands.

"There's only a few hours until dawn," he told Stone, grabbing his own clothes and heading for the door. "And it's going to be a hell of a day tomorrow."

"Are you going to fight for her?" Stone asked, putting his hand on the door. He needed to know where they stood.

And Gabe understood that. If Gabe wanted Pamela, Stone would put his life on the line for her too. Gabe didn't have to discuss that with Stone to know it was true.

"I doubt Ricky came all this way to just turn and head home with his tail between his legs."

Stone stared off toward the yard, not saying anything for a minute. The dampness in the air clung to Gabe's flesh, mixing with the sweat. He needed a shower. His brother needed answers. Gabe just hoped he could give them to him.

"Fighting for her will make her your mate." Stone met his gaze, his own expression hard. "She'd be yours for life."

"Don't you think I know that?" Gabe pushed past Stone, pulling the door open.

The bitch was in a situation. And he could solve her problems by challenging Jordan Ricky. Gabe didn't doubt he would defeat the *Cariboo* too. He'd never lost a challenge. But to fight for a bitch, an act that would make the bitch his mate, twisted his insides into hard knots.

The primal side of him, the beast that would conquer and claim, said to mate with her—fight for the bitch and make her his own. The human side of him knew he couldn't make that decision on his own. He needed time to get to know Pamela, know in his heart that she was the woman for him. Prior to meeting Pamela, no bitch had put those thoughts in his head. That realization brought him pause too.

The warmth of his den surrounded him, along with feminine smells that were new to it. He could hear the shower running, knew Pamela soaked under the flow of hot water while she used perfumed soaps and shampoo that she'd obviously brought with her. Never had his den smelled so nice. The image of soapy water flowing over her curves brought his cock to raging life.

Walking down the hallway took more effort than he'd imagined. When he stopped at the bathroom door, he glanced toward the living room. Stone stood at the other end of the hallway, watching him, his cock as hard and ready as Gabe's. He stared into his twin's eyes for a moment, knowing Stone wanted to fuck Pamela as bad as he did. But Gabe had his mark on her, and Stone would respect that. Every time in the past when they'd shared a bitch, it had been because the woman meant something to them. Well, Pamela sure as hell was getting under his skin. But he needed to know those feelings were mutual, that Pamela would accept Gabe for all that he was. Once he had that assurance, he would offer Pamela the best gift he could offer. He would have both of them fuck her. Without a word, he turned the knob on the door, closing it quietly behind him.

Steam wrapped around him, carrying her scent. It soaked through his flesh, his arousal throbbing while he grew drunk on her smell.

He could rip the shower curtain from the bar. When he grabbed the damp fabric, the thought entered his mind. His beast still lingered in his system, more carnal and untamed. The human side of him stopped him, and he pulled it back instead.

Pamela jumped, wiping water from her eyes while beads of water clung to her naked body. Her eyelashes stuck together and she blinked, staring at him with large blue eyes. Her breath came quickly, her large, full breasts moving up and down with each inhale.

"A girl doesn't get any privacy around here?" There was a teasing note in her tone although her expression turned pouty.

"You don't want to be left alone." He stepped into the shower with her, the warm water quickly rinsing the sweat from his body.

"So now you know what I'm thinking?" She turned, blocking the water, while her fingers spread over his chest.

"I smell your lust. Do you see what it does to me?" He watched her lashes flutter over her eyes when she glanced down at his cock.

"You're just horny after a good run." She pressed against his chest although they both knew she didn't have the strength to keep him from her.

Her blonde hair was darker when wet, and clung to her head and down her back. Gripping her narrow shoulders, his hands slid down her arms until he touched the swell of her breasts. The way she sucked in her breath when he fondled them, cupping them gently at first, made his insides boil with need.

"I don't deny my needs. But will you take what I don't offer?"

He tugged on her breasts, watching the water stream over her hardened nipples while her mouth moved but no sound came out. Her lips formed an adorable circle while she gasped, yet still formed no words. Lust hung so thick in the moist steamy air surrounding them that it filled his lungs.

"Are you telling me no?" he asked, running his hands over her breasts and then pinching her nipples.

"Oh God," she cried out, her fingernails digging into his flesh.

A thick rush of her cum filled the shower, a rich, ripe smell that drove him forward.

"Do you want me to do this?" He let one hand slide down her slender abdomen, and then brushed his fingers over the source of her heat.

"Yes. You know I do. This isn't fair," she rambled quickly, holding onto his shoulders while her forehead collapsed into him.

"What's not fair? You didn't want me to come to you?" If she told him no, he wasn't sure he'd be able to walk away.

"Whether I did or not isn't the point." She chewed her lower lip when she looked up at him.

Gabe pressed her breasts together, loving how the water pooled at the top and then streamed down over her full ripe flesh.

"Then you do want me," he suggested, tiring of conversation, needing to be inside her more than he needed to breathe.

He wouldn't take her if she didn't want him. But damn it, he knew that she did.

The water splashed against her, spraying both of them as he lifted her into his arms.

"You fool. You'll slip." She wrapped her legs around his waist while pressing her arm against the damp shower wall.

"You need to learn to trust me," he growled, her body pressing against him sending a fever surging through him.

If he did slip, he doubted he would notice or feel any discomfort. Her pussy opened when she spread her legs, strengthening her scent. All blood flooded through him, his heart pounding almost too hard as his cock swelled.

Pamela adjusted her body, her breath torturing his skin. "What do you want, wolf man?" she whispered, moving her cunt against his cock.

"You know what I need," he growled, thrusting his hips forward and burying his cock deep inside her heat.

"Oh, fuck yeah." Her arms moved quickly over his shoulders, her fingers clasping behind his neck.

Arching her back, she let her head fall back, sliding deeper over his cock.

Adjusting his grip, he cupped her ass, lifting her and feeling her cunt muscles tighten as they glided over his cock.

Hot water sprayed over them, splashing against feverish skin. Slightly blinded by the shower, Gabe closed his eyes, letting his senses take over. Gripping her ass, he raised and lowered her body, feeling her muscles constrict throughout her body as she moved with him.

Heat swelled through him, the fire inside Pamela's hot pussy making it impossible to focus on anything else. Her fingers tightened behind his neck when he gripped her ass harder, drilling into her with a need more intense than he'd ever experienced before.

His cock grew, pulsating with a need he could no longer control. A growl escaped him as he moved faster, harder, his carnal side taking over.

"Gabe," she cried out, her head falling forward.

Her wet cheek pressed against his while she wrapped her arms and legs around him with more strength than he would have guessed she possessed. She moved with him, gliding her cunt over his cock until he could take it no more.

"I'm going to come," he hissed, barely able to talk as all blood surged to his cock.

"Fill me, wolf man. I want it all." Her brazen words were like molten lava, tearing through him, raking over his senses until he lost all ability to focus on anything but his release.

She cried out again when he thrust into her one last time, holding her over him with a fierceness fed by his primal need.

Her body tightened, her hands digging into his shoulder muscles, the sweet pain causing him to explode.

"Oh, shit. Yes. Oh, hell yes." Her quivering muscles vibrated against his shaft as her own explosion soaked him with creamy heat.

When she collapsed in his arms, he took a careful step backwards, leaning against the shower wall.

"Sex with you is mighty damned good," she said with a sigh.

When she shivered, he realized for the first time that the water had turned cold. Still nestled deep inside her heat, the cold water dropping against his arms and chest barely affected him.

Turning, he blocked her from the shower. "Did you ever fuck Jordan Ricky?"

She raised her head quickly, her blue eyes hardening instantly. "I can't believe you'd mention another werewolf while buried so deep inside me."

"Did you?"

She shook her head slowly, her expression turning wary. "No."

"How many werewolves have you been with?"

"How many bitches have you been with?" she countered, her body straightening.

He couldn't pull out of her yet, his cock still buried too deep inside her. Her pussy muscles constricted around his cock, while the scent around them changed. Straightening one leg, she hit the faucet with her foot, turning off the water. A damp chill suddenly filled the air around their damp bodies.

"I don't know." He narrowed his gaze on her, watching her take in the truthfulness of his statement.

"And do our previous affairs matter at this point?" she asked.

"Only one does." His cock softened slightly, the thought of the *Cariboo* who stalked her settling like a hard rock in his gut.

Slowly he lifted her until his cock slid out of her tight cunt. Regardless of any answer she might give him right now, he doubted seriously that she'd been with that many werewolves.

"I'm twenty-three years old, and up until I left the mountains, I've lived my entire life in my parent's den." Straightening against his body, she stood before him, her anger flooding through the small bathroom. "The affair that you refer to was hardly that. I spent mere hours in his den, as a prisoner, against my will."

She pulled the bathroom door open. Stone stood at the other side of the door, still naked. Pamela grabbed the towel that hung over the rack. Wrapping it around her, she looked at Gabe, then turned her angry stare toward Stone.

"Do you use sex to gather information also?" she asked, and then stormed past Stone toward the guest bedroom, slamming the door behind her.

Stone looked after her briefly then raised an eyebrow as he turned his attention on his brother. "You've got a fucking way with the bitches, don't you?"

Gabe stepped out of the shower, grabbing another towel. "I learned what I needed to know. She's not mated."

Padding past his brother, ignoring his confused expression, he hesitated at Pamela's door. The urge to go in after her, let her know the intention of his questions, distracted him. Her anger still lingered in the hallway. Even her strong emotions smelled good to him. Damn it. What was it about Pamela that made him want to lay his kill at her feet?

Resting his hand on the door, he wondered if she felt his satisfaction. Did his emotions matter to her? Pamela had run from a life she didn't want. Her strength and determination appealed to him as much as her defiance.

For a moment he entertained the thought of witnessing more of her fiery temper. Taking her on, making that anger of hers flare a bit more and then seducing it right back out of her, had a certain appeal.

Stone let out a sigh and Gabe turned to see his twin head toward his bedroom. His own room was behind him, and after standing a moment longer in the empty hallway, he turned and went to his own bed. Her scent continued to filter through his system as he climbed into bed. It would take time to fall asleep. All he wanted to do was go pull her into bed with him.

And when his phone rang, he swore he'd only been asleep a few minutes. Blankets twisted around him and he kicked them to the floor, then headed to the kitchen to grab it on the fourth ring. Apparently Stone and Pamela slept through the intrusion.

"What?" he asked, scratching his head until he was sure his hair stood on end.

"You still have the *Cariboo* bitch at your den?" Rousseau sounded tired, but it could have been just that Gabe was exhausted.

"She's asleep in the guest bedroom."

"The guest bedroom?" Now Rousseau sounded amused.

"Yes. The damn guest bedroom." Gabe knew his pack leader wasn't calling first thing in the morning without good reason. "Is there trouble?"

"I don't think she's in your guest bedroom." Rousseau's tone hardened.

Gabe didn't answer. He stormed down the hallway, forcing the door to Pamela's room open. The wood frame groaned and the door flew open, hitting the wall.

"Where the hell is she?" Gabe barked into the phone as he stared at the empty bedroom.

Lunging toward the bed, he grabbed the covers. Her scent didn't even linger on them. A cold morning breeze swept through the open window. He stared at the curtains as they fluttered around the glass pane.

Stone came out of his bedroom, his ruffled appearance matching how Gabe felt.

"She's here at our den right now." Rousseau's cold tone didn't waver as he added, "I'm not sure why I'm holding her. She's got me seriously pissed off."

Chapter Eight

৪১

Pamela couldn't stay sitting any longer. Jumping up, she paced across the large master bedroom, ignoring the pensive looks the other bitches in the room gave her.

The door opened and Samantha Rousseau pushed herself away from the wall, letting her arms uncross. The smell of annoyance didn't waver when she smiled at the pack doctor.

"Is everyone okay, Bertha?" Samantha asked.

She gave Pamela a side-glance. Pamela knew she blamed her for all injuries that transpired that morning. Hell, she would if she were queen bitch. Samantha had every reason to be upset with her.

Several werewolves from the Rousseau pack sat out in the living area with minor injuries because of Pamela.

No. Not because of her. Because of that bastard Jordan Ricky. Every muscle inside her hardened.

"Just a few minor injuries." Bertha shrugged and then turned watery blue eyes on Pamela. "So you are the bitch of the moment."

"Bertha." Samantha let out a sigh. "Pamela, do you need the doctor to look you over?"

Pamela could still feel Jordan's hands on her. Her throat still burned from screaming when he'd dragged her from Gabe's yard. She hadn't had the chance to change before he'd knocked her over the head. When she'd come to, he'd dragged her almost to his car, parked down the road. Thankfully, Jordan was a stupid ass. He hadn't bothered to consider that the neighbors might also be werewolves.

Pamela shook her head, knowing that if she showed lack of appreciation to the queen bitch, she could be sent packing. She was tired of running, and her anger no longer consumed her.

"A good night's sleep and the bruises will be gone."

"Seems like Jordan is mighty desperate to get you back." Simone Toubec moved to stand next to Samantha, narrowing her gaze on the queen bitch when Samantha shook her head. "Of course, you aren't part of this pack, and your affairs are none of our business."

"She's in our territory, under our protection," Samantha reminded her.

"You don't know Jordan." Pamela guessed that the two bitches worried her presence would continue to bring trouble to her pack.

"And you do know him really well?" Samantha asked.

"Not *that* well." She was under trial here, these three bitches with their gazes locked on her, their scents full of distrust and concern.

"I can smell that you've had sex recently. Did you get raped?" Bertha asked.

Pamela shook her head slowly, looking down. What would Gabe think if she told his pack leader's mate that they'd had sex? Her stomach twisted, knowing that she had to give them an explanation. The ranking in packs didn't sway no matter what pack it was. Pamela would show her respect to these bitches. Right now, she had no rank, no place among the other females.

"I wasn't raped. I had sex before Jordan caught me." Her embarrassment filled the room with its sour smell, like a pile of overripe lemons.

Pamela fought her temper that tried to step forward once again. Getting angry had gotten her into this predicament to start with. Gabe suggesting that she'd been with many werewolves, that her relations with Jordan were more than she'd told him, had pissed her off. When he'd questioned her right after coming inside her, while still locked deep inside her pussy, it had been enough to set her over the edge. Never in her entire life had her integrity been questioned so much.

And it was all Jordan Ricky's fault. Damn him to hell for screwing with her life like this.

"Well, like it's any surprise that you would do Gabe," Simone said, her smile appearing sincere.

"Simone! Would you stop," Samantha threw her hands up in exasperation.

Simone giggled and then walked over to Pamela, squeezing her shoulder. The bruises Jordan had left on her would be gone by tomorrow — werewolves healed quickly. But they were still fresh and she winced when Simone touched her.

"That does it," Bertha said, moving around Pamela. "Strip. You're gonna show me if you got any broken bones. Don't want them mending crooked on you, now do you?"

"I don't." She glanced at Samantha, who sincerely looked concerned. The other women watched her carefully as well. "I mean, if you want me to go through an examination, I will. I don't want to cause even more trouble."

"Well that's what we're here to resolve right now," Samantha said. "When Marc McAllister saw Jordan dragging you, he was more concerned with your protection and didn't chase after Jordan."

"More than likely, the werewolf freaked out when he came across a werewolf being accompanied by a human on a motorcycle." Simone laughed. "Not many werewolves are prepared when they come across a human and werewolf out on a run together."

"What?" Pamela vaguely remembered the scene she'd woken up to early that morning. "I remember humans and werewolves. I hadn't given it any thought at the time. All I could think about was how I was going to escape from Jordan a second time."

"Marc is the oldest in the McAllister den," Simone explained, "and his mate is human."

Pamela nodded. "Thanks for the advance warning."

"Might be nice to know ahead of time in case Gabe decides to take you to meet the rest of the den." Samantha let her gaze travel down Pamela. "Let Bertha examine you. Might as well cover all of our bases."

"All of our bases?" Pamela frowned. "What do you mean?"

"Jordan came to Johann and showed him paperwork making it look like he was simply retrieving his mate. I'm not *Cariboo*, but I respect the ways of your line just as I respect the *lunewulf*. I understand that a mating to the *Cariboo* is more of an ownership. It's not our way, but Johann took the werewolf seriously."

"It's not my way either." Pamela pulled her shirt off for Bertha and watched while Simone walked over and drew the blinds. The room darkened and Pamela's eyes adjusted slightly, her more carnal side instinctively kicking in. "I refuse to be any werewolf's property."

"I saw the papers. You have a joint account, showing you've been mated for quite a while."

"Those papers are fakes." Pamela knew how hard it would be to get out of a mating if the bitch and werewolf had been mated for a while. Werewolves don't divorce. "I haven't seen them, but I was in his den for several hours. That was it. And he didn't fuck me while I was there."

"Several hours and you didn't fuck him?" Simone asked.

"Have you met him?" Pamela made a face while raising her arms so Bertha could feel her ribs.

"None of her bones are broken," Bertha announced, standing back and surveying Pamela's naked body.

The other bitches did the same.

"Will your den confirm when the mating occurred?" Samantha asked.

Pamela sighed. It really sucked having her word doubted.

Samantha raised her hand. "For the record, I believe you. But this *Cariboo* has some strong arguments why we should turn you over to him, allow him to take you from our territory."

"It's just not right." Pamela would lose her temper all over again. "Damn it to hell if the *Cariboo* don't need to get into the twentieth century—just that far. God forbid they actually join the rest of us in the twenty-first century."

The other bitches grinned. Pamela grabbed her clothes, stuffing her legs into her jeans. The air in the room lightened, all of their emotions relaxing. There was a sense of bonding, or at least appreciation. Pamela had never had the chance to get that close to the bitches in her own pack. Living in the Canadian Rockies, there wasn't opportunity to hang out with the other bitches that often. For the most part, it had just been her den.

"We are traditionalists," Samantha said seriously. "Werewolves will always be as they are today. Nothing has changed for centuries."

"You just tell me one of your werewolves has mated a human, but then say we can't change?" Pamela shook her head.

The bitches around her snickered. And Samantha nodded, smiling. "The McAllisters are exceptions to even the wilder *Cariboo.*"

"Possibly it is because they are so wild that they stand ahead of other werewolves."

The room quickly grew silent. Samantha stared at Pamela, the other two bitches quietly watching the two of them. After a moment, Samantha relaxed, smiling.

"You're okay, girl," she said, and laughed easily.

She gave Pamela's shoulder a quick squeeze. "Let's go join the men. I'll have Johann show you the proof that Jordan Ricky gave us, Pamela. Just know that we've got your back. I have only one question for you."

"What's that?"

"Do you wish to join this pack?"

Pamela glanced at all of them. Never had other bitches told her they had her back. Honoring the traditions she'd just complained about—although some traditions deserved to be kept intact—she straightened, lowering her head, acknowledging the queen bitch.

"I would be honored to join your pack."

"Very good."

Had they been in their fur, Pamela would have bellied up in honor of the queen bitch. As humans, the position would look rather ridiculous. Samantha smiled, patting Pamela on the side of the arm.

A variety of emotions filled the room when Pamela and the other bitches joined the werewolves. Johann walked over to Samantha, putting his arm around her, while she leaned into him, whispering something that tickled Pamela's ears. The others in the room perked up as well, curiosity besting them.

"We're honored to have you join our pack, Pamela Ricky," Johann said seriously.

"My name is Pamela Bordeaux. I can give you the phone number to my den, if you like." She glanced at the two men who sat in the living room. One of them, a tall blond *Cariboo*, she guessed to be Gabe's littermate. The family resemblance was there. "And thank you for helping me."

The *Cariboo* stood, looking down at her with a hard expression. She didn't smell anger. Hell. She didn't smell anything on him. Her stomach twisted in knots. He looked positively intimidating.

"We haven't formally met. My name is Marc McAllister. I'm Gabe's and Stone's oldest littermate."

She'd guessed right.

Nodding politely, she straightened. The least she could show this pack was that her den had taught her how to behave socially.

"Please let your mate know I'd be honored to bring by a cake or something."

"I'm not sure she'd understand the tradition." Something close to amusement appeared in his eyes. The others in the room shifted and the smell of emotions definitely lightened. "Which pack are you from? We haven't gathered that information from Ricky yet."

She didn't believe him but wouldn't challenge him either. "Our pack was in the mountains. Banff was the closest town."

Marc nodded and paced over toward the kitchen doorway so that he stood behind Johann and Samantha. Simone plopped down on the couch and picked up the small cub who'd crawled into the living room. Everyone appeared relaxed, yet somehow she felt an interrogation coming on. So be it. They could bring it on. She had nothing to hide.

"Our den actually lived in Banff for a while," she added. "Have you ever been there?"

"A few times while growing up." Marc tapped his lips with his finger, watching her with a piercing gaze. "And how old are you?"

"I'm twenty-three."

"And you come from a large den?"

"No. I had an older brother who died when I was a teenager. I'm the only one other than my parents."

"Your sire must have been anxious to find a good mate for you."

She should have known that question was coming. Her stomach twisted when thoughts of arguments flooded through her. The many times her sire grew exasperated with her turning away dates.

"The survival of our den falls in your hands," he had told her more than once. "If you don't find a decent werewolf, I swear I'll do it for you."

"But they don't want me, Father," she'd yell right back at him.

He didn't understand though. As hard as her sire had worked to make a name for his den, proudly claim ownership of so much land, it made no sense to him that she wouldn't be proud of all they had. But all of the money, all of the land, made her a token, out for the highest bidder. Was it too much to ask for love?

"Yes. He wanted a good mate for me," she said, knowing the room waited for her response. "My parents are good werewolves."

"Of course." Marc sounded sincere, his tone softening. "Understand I'm not like these *lunewulfs*. I know *Cariboo*. A proper mating, and at a proper age matters greatly to our dens."

Pamela let out a loud sigh, fearing once again her temper would get the best of her. "What are you getting at? Maybe I am older than most when they mate. But you didn't know how it was. There was no werewolf that I wanted. And mating just to be mated isn't an option."

Samantha straightened, crossing her arms over her chest, silently letting Pamela know that she shouldn't raise her voice.

"He bid you out, didn't he?" Marc's question made her heart stop in her chest.

Damn. Damn. Damn.

"Bid her out? What's that mean?" Samantha asked, her confusion filling the air around them.

That emotion was quickly replaced with the spicy smell of anger.

"No one bids out their cubs anymore," Johann hissed. "I don't think even Grandmother Rousseau would have stooped that low."

"I do," Simone muttered from the couch.

"What does it mean?" Samantha demanded again.

Pamela couldn't handle it any longer. Never again did she want to experience the humiliation like she had the night she'd found out what her sire had done.

"Yes. Okay? Yes." Pamela couldn't keep her voice down. "He sold me. That's what it means, Samantha. My own sire sold me to the highest bidder in order to keep money in the den. And I won't have it. Don't you see? I'm no one's property."

Pamela's heart almost exploded in her chest when the front door burst open behind her. The chill from the morning air and the smell of hard fury wrapped around her before she could turn around.

"Gabe!" Johann and Marc said firmly at the same time.

She didn't have time to react. Large hands grabbed her, lifting her off the ground. Gabe's outraged expression filled her gaze. For the briefest of seconds she saw Stone's concerned look behind his twin.

Her heart pounded too hard in her chest for Pamela to catch her breath. Gabe's hard muscular body pressed against her when he backed her into the wall. The other werewolves in the room grabbed him, but all she could do was stare into those penetrating blue eyes.

"What the hell were you thinking?" he hissed, shrugging the others off him as if they were no more than cubs.

She knew what she'd been thinking. She'd been outraged at his line of questioning while locked deep inside her. His cock had throbbed inside her pussy while he'd implied that she slept around and that she'd lied to him. This wasn't the time or place to answer his question in detail.

"I won't have you, or anyone else, imply I'm lying," she hissed back, unable to discuss the other matters at the moment.

"And so you risked going back to a werewolf that you've run from?" he asked, his fingers pressing so deep into her arms that the urge to change rushed through her without her beckoning.

"Let go of me." When she tried to struggle, Marc leapt on his younger littermate, pulling him away from Pamela.

Panting, she stared at the werewolves surrounding her. A mixture of emotions, from salty, raging anger, and something akin to the thick smell of sadness, filled the room.

Well, the last thing she wanted from any of these werewolves, no matter how friendly they'd been to her, was for them to feel sorry for her.

Marc and Johann held on to Gabe, and he shrugged their arms off him. His gaze never left her.

"How many werewolves are you going to run from, Pamela?" There was pain in his tone, something she hadn't expected out of the large *Cariboo.*

She shook her head. "I didn't run from you. I just left in anger. Get that through your thick head. You were out of line with your questions."

Defiance rushed through Gabe. She didn't have to smell it. His muscles grew before her while his hands clenched at his side into fists.

"Anytime that I ask you anything, you'll answer it," he said, his teeth clenched.

"Not if you're going to ask me preposterous questions while we're…" She couldn't go on. Her cheeks flushed with embarrassment in spite of the anger that had begun surging through her.

What was it about this werewolf that got her so worked up?

Stone stepped in between them, placing his hand on her shoulder but looking at Gabe.

"You two can fuck and make up later," he said, with his usual callousness that she was getting accustomed to.

Samantha quickly moved to her side, putting her arm around her. Pamela's muscles were still tender, but she sighed against her new queen bitch anyway.

"The bitch was bid out, Gabe." Marc put his hand on Gabe's shoulder hard enough to turn him so that the two faced each other. "I've questioned her and I believe her."

Pamela had almost forgotten about the other werewolves in the room. An older man coughed, clearing his throat, and the others turned to acknowledge him.

Sitting in the overstuffed reclining chair by the couch, the older *Cariboo* scratched at whiskers on his chin. "I know your sire. Remember him from the old days. We enjoyed a few runs together. And I know the ways of the *Cariboo* packs back in the mountains. If he mated you, with or without your consent, your pack is gonna back it. You got a fight on your hands, missy."

Chapter Nine

∞

By the end of the week, Gabe was sure every member of his pack had stopped by. Curiosity ran thick through all of them. Many had met Jordan Ricky, who still remained at the bed and breakfast in town. Gabe hadn't met the werewolf yet. But he figured it was about time to pay the asshole a visit.

After calling Pamela to make sure she was at his den, he made sure Stone would head to the den to keep an eye on her.

"Don't go and do something stupid," Stone said when Gabe dropped him off. "Just remember, you fight him for the right to Pamela, then you mate with her for life."

"That won't happen until Pamela and I agree it's time." He hadn't discussed it with her, but she deserved that much. "I'll let you know right now though...she's already mine."

Stone nodded. "I know."

His littermate actually didn't give him shit for such a deep confession. And that's what it had been too. The more time he spent with the spitfire bitch, the more he needed to be with her. So damned sexy and full of life, he'd never met another female like her.

Pulling out of the gravel drive onto the highway, he knew that no matter what, he would have her as a mate. That much he'd decided. Just picturing her long blonde hair flowing around her, the way her eyes sparkled when she smiled, and that damn defiant attitude of hers, made him want to turn back around and fuck her silly before going to see Ricky.

Would serve the prick right to smell her cum on him when he showed up to talk to him.

Evening traffic wasn't too bad, and he made it through town before too long. Pulling into the parking lot of the bed and breakfast in a quiet part of Prince George, his cell phone rang as he parked.

"Yes?" he answered, recognizing his home number on the phone.

"What are you doing?" Pamela sounded breathless.

For a brief moment the thought that Stone would try to fuck her entered his mind. He shoved it to the side just as quickly. Stone wouldn't touch her without Gabe's consent.

"Don't worry about me. I'm fine."

"I got Stone to tell me," she said, letting her words fade off and a brief silence follow.

Gabe waited, realizing he hadn't formed a formal plan of what he would say to the werewolf.

Get the fuck out of town, or I'll kill you sounded pretty damned appealing to him.

"Gabe?" her voice had grown quieter. "Are you going to challenge him?"

It made sense that she'd worry about something like that. And he wouldn't take her without her consent. Pamela had a right to say who she mated with. Beyond a shadow of a doubt, it would be him. But Gabe would wait until she said she was ready.

"Nope." He worked to make his manner light. "Just thought it was time to greet our visitor."

"I see. Well you just do that." The line went dead and Gabe lowered his cell phone, looking at it as if it would explain to him Pamela's suddenly strange behavior.

Shaking his head—he would never fully understand the female gender—he got out of his truck and strolled toward the office of the bed and breakfast.

Several minutes later he returned to his truck, frustrated that Jordan Ricky wasn't in his room. His cell phone rang again and he frowned when he answered it, recognizing his oldest brother's number.

"We've got more company arriving in town," Marc said when Gabe answered.

"Oh yeah?"

"Looks like Pamela's den has shown up. They contacted Rousseau the minute they were in town, demanding to see their daughter."

"I'm at the bed and breakfast. Ricky isn't here."

"What are you doing there?" There was sudden aggravation in Marc's tone. "You owe it to your pack to make an announcement before you challenge him."

Sometimes it got damn irritating that it was assumed he would announce his every move. Often a quick action proved a lot more effective than announcing and planning everything.

"The only one who needs to know when I challenge Ricky is Pamela," he told Marc.

His brother growled instead of answering.

"Where are the Bordeauxs?" Gabe asked, ignoring his brother's frustration.

"They don't want to stay in town. Apparently they don't care to mingle among humans. Toubec has agreed to let them stay in one of the cabins. But they are demanding to see their daughter."

Gabe jumped into his truck, already fearing the worst with this meeting. "I'm headed home. Pamela doesn't go anywhere without me."

"Gabe." Already Marc had that tone he used when frustrated and determined things play out with his plan of action. "She isn't yours. Rousseau has been very generous in allowing an unmated bitch to stay with you."

"But we've already confirmed that her pack views her as mated. It was on those grounds that Samantha agreed to let her stay with us. And since Pamela is now part of our pack, the queen bitch has that authorization over her."

"And I'm not arguing any of that. What I am saying is simple. She isn't yours."

It would just be a matter of time before she was. He would see to it. Cutting out into the slow flow of cars, Gabe shifted into the faster lane and headed toward his den.

"If they want to see her, that's fine. But I'm accompanying her, and no one will say otherwise."

It seemed to take longer to return to his den than it had taken to get into town. Pulling into his drive, he parked the car and hurried inside.

Stone and Pamela sat watching TV and turned when he stormed into the place.

"Your den is here," he said.

Pamela's hand went to her throat, and she suddenly looked panicked as she stared from Gabe to Stone. She stood slowly, the jeans and sweater she wore showing off her slender features. It wasn't hard to see how quickly her breaths came or smell the sudden fear that filled the room.

"Where are they?" she asked, her voice breaking with thick emotions.

"I'll take you to them." Gabe moved to her, running his fingers through her silky blonde hair.

When she looked up at him, fear in her pretty blue eyes, he knew more than anything that he would defend her at any price.

"They are going to want to take me home." She looked down.

Gabe gripped her chin, forcing her to look back up at him.

"Do you want to stay here?" he asked, needing to hear from her what was in her thoughts.

"You've both been very kind to let me stay here." There was a sudden distance in her tone that Gabe didn't like.

Stone shifted on the couch, making a face that showed his own frustration. Gabe wondered what the two of them had been discussing before he arrived. Stone didn't look too happy.

"Very kind?" Gabe said, his jaw clenching from the frustration that suddenly flowed through him. "I'm not trying to be *kind*."

Pamela pulled away from him, crossing her arms as she stalked to the other side of the couch. Stone watched her move, glancing quickly at his brother as if trying to warn him of something.

"Then what exactly is it that you are doing?" she asked, her tone way too calm, too controlled.

Gabe narrowed his gaze on her, anticipating at any moment that his hot little bitch would fly off the handle. He'd come to know her quick temper.

"I'm trying to help you gain your freedom." He matched her calm tone.

Pamela let out a choked sigh, running her slender fingers through her hair.

"Why, Gabe? Why are you doing that? You haven't laid a hand on me in a week. You act so formal around me. Tell me why you are doing this for me."

Gabe narrowed the distance from her, pulling her into his arms. Her scent alone hardened every muscle in his body. But it was that defiant expression, her willingness to take him on, the way she stubbornly puckered her lips that made him mad with need.

Gabe couldn't answer her, his need for her suddenly too great. Fisting her hair in his hands, he pounced on her mouth, taking advantage of her parted lips and tasting her to the fullest.

The way she sighed into him, offered what he demanded as if she was starved for him too, just about made him explode with need for her.

He didn't hesitate. In fact, he didn't even give it thought. With a quick movement, he pulled on her sweater, freeing it from her jeans and then thrusting his hand underneath so that he could feel her warm flesh. Smooth and silky, touching her burned him alive with a craving he couldn't quench.

Running his hand up her sweater, he gripped her breast, kneading it hard and rough. She cried out in his mouth and the blood that rushed through his veins ignited with fire.

He broke the kiss, tasting her flesh as he ran his mouth down her neck. Nothing had ever tasted so sweet, so incredibly perfect.

"You know why I'm doing this," he growled.

"Tell me," she whispered as her head fell back, inviting him to nibble further along her neck.

"For you," he growled, taking her nipple between his fingers and twisting the puckered flesh. "I'm doing this for you."

Pamela cried out, her hands gripping his shoulders as her head came forward. Her blue eyes sparkled with streaks of silver. "Why? Why are you doing this for me?"

His brain was on fire, burning with need for her. He straightened, looking down at her, both of his hands moving under her sweater to caress her breasts.

He wouldn't speculate on what went through her mind. There was reason behind her questioning though. "You want to be free of Ricky. I'm helping you."

Pamela pushed against his chest and then took a step backwards. She backed into Stone, who put his hands on her hips.

Pamela ignored Stone, her deep blue eyes fixed on him. "And what if there was no Jordan?"

Gabe smiled, narrowing the distance between them and sandwiching her between him and Stone.

"You will find out soon enough what life will be like without Jordan Ricky," he told her.

Her eyes widened when he pressed into her, almost smashing her between them. And then he kissed her again, her mouth smoldering with even more heat than it had a moment before.

Pamela groaned into him, stretching her body like a cat between the two men. Her breasts rubbed against his chest while he tangled his fingers in her hair, deepening the kiss. Everything about her screamed to be fucked. She would do both of them, right here and now—exactly where he wanted her to be, trusting him to the point that he could share her.

One problem. Now wasn't the time.

"Pamela." It was all he could do to quit kissing her.

"Mmm?" She was grinding her ass against Stone's cock, and the sway of her ass made her brush against him.

His cock was harder than stone.

He forced himself to take a step backwards, the smell of her lust, mixed with his own scent and Stone's, just about undoing him. That one step backwards was almost the hardest thing he'd ever done.

"Get ready to go." His cock painfully rebelled with a vicious thrust in his jeans.

His body didn't want to do anything other than grab her and drag her back to his bed. But in his mind, the pack waited for him to deliver her to Toubec's and face the fire of her den.

"Gabe," she whispered, her lips moving as if she'd say more, but the smell of disappointment that suddenly drowned all three of them was words enough.

Stone let his hands fall from her waist, turning and running his hand through his hair. Gabe felt his aggravation. They were going to take Pamela and throw her into the fire, force her to endure the traditions that had existed among them for centuries but now worked against them.

More than he knew he needed to breathe, Gabe knew Pamela belonged here.

"Do as I say," he said, forcing strength to flow through him that would be needed to take on her den.

And he had too many pack laws against him. Turning from the disappointment that rushed through her and lined her pretty face, he walked toward the door. God willing, her den would want what made Pamela happy.

She'd shut down her emotions as she slipped into her shoes and grabbed her purse. "I'll get my things too," she said, holding her head high as she glared at him.

He hated how she looked at him as if somehow this was all his fault.

"No." He took her wrist, guiding her to the door. "Stone. You're going too."

"Damn right." Stone followed them out the door, shutting it behind them.

"I don't understand," Pamela said when they reached the truck. "What kind of bitch do you think I am?"

She slid into the middle of the bench seat in the cab, Stone sliding in on the passenger side next to her.

Gabe let the truck roar to life, glancing at her pursed lips and perky nose. Long blonde strands streamed around her face as she looked straight ahead. The protector inside him swore no matter how angry she might be that he was taking her to her den, no one would take her from him.

He didn't answer until they pulled onto Toubec's property and started slowly down the gravel road that led to the cabins where her mother and sire waited.

"You're my kind of bitch," he said with a hard whisper as he dragged her out of his side of the truck.

God. She looked shocked as she stared up at him, her blue eyes widening. Her lips parted as if she would comment, but then she looked down. The intense pleasurable scent that rushed through her undid him. No matter that he could smell other werewolves in the area. Damn it to hell if they wouldn't smell his scent on her. Pulling her to him again, he kissed her savagely, bending her over until the truck stopped her.

"And don't you forget that," he said on a breath when he let her up.

Running her teeth over her bottom lip, she nodded, taking a deep breath and then glancing at the row of cabins lined by dense trees.

Stone shut the door on his side of the truck, and Pamela jumped, then sucked in a breath. Gabe gripped the back of her neck, giving it a gentle squeeze.

"I'll be right there by your side. Stand up to them and be strong. You're part of this pack now. Say the word and we're here to defend you."

She nodded but didn't look up at him. And her pace dragged as he guided her toward the several cars parked around the small cabins, the smell of burning wood and werewolves mixing with the fir trees that surrounded them.

Rousseau's pale blue Suburban was parked down the gravel road ahead of them. Two other vehicles, both showing tags that indicated they were from the Canadian Rockies, were parked alongside it.

The door to the second cabin opened, a rush of a fresh burning fire and strong, aggressive emotions spilling out to greet them.

A tall, older bitch, her gray-blonde hair wrapped in a bun at the back of her head, hurried out of the door, her blues eyes watery when she spotted them.

"Pamela!" She let out a cry and extended her arms, hurrying to hug Pamela.

It was almost as if she didn't notice either him or Stone.

Another vehicle approached from behind and Gabe glanced quickly to notice Marc parking alongside his truck. His oldest littermate was on full alert as he strutted toward them.

Fear wrapped around happiness. That was the only way he could describe what he smelled off Pamela. He and Stone stopped, allowing the two bitches a moment as they embraced, hugging and kissing while the salty smell of their tears added to the moment.

It didn't surprise Gabe that Pamela would be close to her mother. The only cub in the den, the two females probably had a close relationship growing up. Pamela had good breeding, there was no doubt about that. The older bitch holding Pamela tight with her face buried in her cub's neck probably had a good part in bringing up such a wonderful woman.

The mood changed instantly when three werewolves appeared from the cabin, walking toward the bitches.

Pamela's mother held on to her tightly, glancing toward Gabe and his den briefly before glancing behind her.

"Pamela." A huge barrel-chested *Cariboo lunewulf* boomed her name as if it were a curse.

Everything inside Gabe hardened, the urge to reach out and grab Pamela consuming him. He took a step forward, ignoring the growl that escaped from Marc behind him. Whether his oldest den mate warned him or growled at the *Cariboo*, Gabe didn't know, and he didn't fucking care. They were not going to take Pamela from him.

A smaller *Cariboo lunewulf* stepped around the older, larger *Cariboo,* leering at Gabe. The young punk was a piss-poor excuse for a werewolf, and Gabe instantly knew who he was. Blond hair greased back and his tall, lanky body only added to the wimp's disgusting appearance. No wonder Pamela had bolted during the night. A werewolf like that didn't deserve someone like Pamela.

The older *Cariboo* looked at Gabe, taking his time sniffing him out. Gabe didn't move, every muscle inside him so hard he could hardly breathe. There was no way he could curb his animosity toward the entire despicable scene, and he wouldn't try. Maybe Pamela's sire didn't think a real werewolf would speak for his daughter, but he was about to learn different. He had a hell of a lot more right to Pamela than that scrawny pup did. And they were all about to see that firsthand.

He took a step forward.

The older *Cariboo* spoke at the same time.

"Thank you for returning my cub to me," he said in a low roar, as if showing that for his age, he still could reign over his den.

"I'm not returning her." Gabe reached for Pamela.

"Get in the car, Pamela." The older *Cariboo lunewulf* moved faster than he looked like he could.

Reaching for his mate and cub, his large arm wrapped around the two of them.

"Father," Pamela froze, shaking her head at the same time. "I won't mate with him."

"It's done!" Her father roared so loudly that Pamela jumped.

He grabbed his daughter, throwing her toward the car. When she tried to regain her balance, Jordan Ricky reached for her.

"No. You've got to listen to me," she cried out, turning toward her sire and swatting at Jordan at the same time until he took a step backwards.

"You listen to me." Her sire took her by the arm, hauling her to his car while Pamela's mother hurried to get the door. "You disgrace your den and your pack. Now before you are shunned and howl alone for the rest of your life, get in the damn car."

Gabe lunged forward and felt uncontrollable violence rush through him when Marc grabbed him from behind, almost tackling him to the ground.

"Not like this," his oldest littermate hissed in his ear at the same time that the door shut. "Not like this," Marc said again. "You will have her, if that's what you want. But you will take her with honor."

Pamela turned, looking at Gabe as she leaned against the car door, the sadness surrounding her enough to crush him. "I won't be shunned, Gabe. I have to go…straighten this mess out. Don't forget about me." Her voice broke with her final words and then she climbed into the car, blocking her scent from him when she shut the car door.

Chapter Ten

Pamela hugged the side of the backseat of the car, staring out into the darkness. No way would she allow the tears that burned her eyes to fall. And no fucking way would she have a thing to do with the scum who sat next to her in the backseat.

All too aware of her sire's piercing gaze in the rearview mirror, she kept her arms crossed over her chest, willing the trepidation that threatened to consume her to go away.

Knowing her sire would endure the long drive back to the mountains without stopping, she allowed the fury in her to grow, stinking the car up, knowing they wondered what had her more pissed—being returned to Jordan or leaving the *Cariboo lunewulf* that none of them had the balls to ask her about.

Drifting off to sleep, her eyes fluttered open when she recognized the Kananaskis area. Her heart weighed heavy in her chest as she stared out the window at the glorious mountains she'd always loved and found comfort in while enjoying runs as a cub.

Severe cliffs and snow-covered tips surrounded them as they weaved deeper into the mountains. Mountains so regal and splendid, standing proudly with a calm domination that she'd always found solace in, now simply reminded her how far away she was from Gabe.

Pamela dwelled on her last moments with him at his den. Smashed between Gabe and Stone had been so fucking hot her pussy throbbed just thinking about it. She ignored her sire's frown in the rearview mirror when she filled the car with the smell of lust.

The hell with all of them. They wouldn't force her to do anything she didn't want to do. Somehow…some way, she would find her way back to Gabe.

Never had a werewolf seduced her the way he had. Making her crave him, crave his unique sexual behavior. She would have fucked both of them, bonding herself even more so with Gabe's den. Closing her eyes, she could feel their hands on her. Gabe stroking her breasts, caressing her skin until she burned to have him inside her. And Stone, holding her firmly in place, calm and quiet behind her but a strong reminder of what she would experience.

Their hard cocks had pressed against her, throbbing and virile, tempting her with what could happen. What could have, but didn't happen. Her heart ached and her breathing was heavy and slow as she ached inside to be with Gabe now, feel his hands on her, look into that confident gaze that was so dominating and in control.

And she would experience it. She would have Gabe, no matter what it took.

Hunching closer to the car door, and doing her best to block out Jordan's scent that wrapped around her like a dirty washcloth, she imagined how it would have been if Gabe hadn't made them leave his den. Her sexual experiences were limited, pretty straightforward and traditional in her opinion.

Gabe and Stone would share her. In a sense, she would be more a part of their den by fucking the two of them. In spite of the fact that she hadn't been able to get Gabe to say he would fight for her, that he would take on the challenge of making her his mate, she believed in her heart that he had it on his mind. No werewolf ever had such a protective, dominating scent about him like Gabe did. He wanted her. She wouldn't believe otherwise.

The oldest of their den, Marc, had told him, "Not like this." She'd heard the whispered words. They'd tickled her ears, sending chills rushing through her.

At that moment she'd known she would end up back here, her heart breaking. She carried those words in her heart as she focused on the mountains that now surrounded their car. Whatever the meaning behind them, she dwelt on the fact that his den knew what she ached to believe was true. Gabe would make her his mate.

As they cut off the highway before reaching Banff, heading toward the secluded area not inhabited by humans, there was one other thing Pamela knew to be true. She wasn't going to sit on her ass waiting for the werewolf of her dreams to come sauntering into her pack and announce a challenge. Such things were fairy tales.

While slowly plotting ways to escape once again, she watched her sire turn into the narrow drive that led to Jordan's den. A painful thud began in her chest while her stomach churned.

"Let's go," Jordan said, speaking to her for the first time during the long drive.

She glared at him, seeing none of the qualities that Gabe carried so naturally. Jordan was a lowlife, a nothing. Curling her lip, she let him know as much with her stare.

"I'm not going anywhere with you," she hissed.

Her sire let out an exasperated sigh. "This is getting old, Pamela."

"Yes. It is. And I don't understand why either of you would curse me with a miserable mating." She trembled and locked her knees together, knowing she needed to be strong.

Her heart raced so hard in her chest though that she could hardly catch her breath. Never had she spoken to her parents so boldly. Always trusting their judgment and doing everything to make their den happy after losing her brother.

But she wasn't a cub any longer. No matter his backward way of thinking, he needed to see that staying with Jordan would destroy her. In spite of his determination to mate her to Jordan, she just couldn't believe that her sire truly wished her unhappy.

When her father bolted out of the car, she almost yelped. There was no way she could take off running and escape the two of them in her fur. Not with them so close to her. But thoughts of it entered her mind. Her sire was outraged, obviously out of his head, refusing to see how he destined her to live with such a disgusting *Cariboo lunewulf*.

Her sire loved her though. And she knew her mother did also. The only way to make them see what this was doing was to stand up to them.

She jumped out of the car, meeting her sire head on. "He isn't the *Cariboo* for me," she said, pointing at Jordan, who stood on the other side of the car, looking disgusted by her behavior.

"The deal is done," her father barked, muscles in his chest stretching his shirt.

His outrage filled the air around them but Pamela wouldn't stand down.

"I won't mate with a liar and a cheat. He forged papers, told the pack leader in Prince George lies. Is that the kind of *Cariboo* you would tie to our den?" she yelled at him.

When he grabbed her arm, almost dragging her away from the car, Pamela's mother jumped out, the smell of worry clinging to her when she ran over to them.

"Jon. No!" Pamela's mother rushed over to them.

Her sire ignored her. His hand pinched her arm and never had Pamela seen him look so outraged. She fought the nerves that rushed through her. It didn't make sense that he would be so mad when she announced she wasn't happy here. He'd been a good sire to her when she was a cub, always spoiling her, taking care of her. His behavior now didn't add up.

"Dad," she said quietly, trying to calm him down.

"No. You listen to me." His voice was a harsh whisper.

She swore even the wildlife grew quiet at the sound of his tone. Large and dangerous-looking, Jon Bordeaux was a *Cariboo lunewulf* to be reckoned with even at his age. Pamela sucked in her breath, straightening to show him respect. No matter how wrong his actions were at the moment, she would hear him out.

Then she would set him straight.

"You had your little fun running with a few werewolves. Now it's time to settle down. We have a deal here, and I'll be damned if you mess it up."

"Running with a few werewolves?" Her temper would get the best of her. "I find a werewolf and fall in love and you call it running with a few werewolves?"

"Oh, Pamela," her mother cried, reaching for her.

Her mother's compassion had always been like a warm blanket, and it was just like that now. So soothing, so tempting to cuddle into except that her sire still held her arm.

Pamela looked down, her sire's grip relaxing just a bit. Had she fallen in love with Gabe? She hadn't given love a thought until that moment. He offered security, incredible sex. But did she love him?

Her sire sensed her hesitation. "There's a big difference between love and lust. Forget about that *Cariboo lunewulf*. There is no life for you in Prince George. You belong here, in the mountains, carrying on our heritage and building our land."

She looked up at him, and Jon Bordeaux let out a sigh. "You won't run again. Jordan Ricky is a good *Cariboo*. He may not offer all of the excitement that you've found, but trust an old werewolf. Those *Cariboo lunewulf* who run willingly with a bitch are out for only one thing. Jordan won't treat you wrong. The Bordeaux land will remain strong and intact for werewolves. What matters most here is that we continue to grow, breed and keep the mountain for ourselves."

"So that's what this is all about." Pamela pulled away from her sire and surprisingly, he let her go.

She stared at him, and then at her mother. "You bid me off so that you could assure the land stayed in our family. Is that all I mean to you, Father?"

"Bid you off?" Her sire looked like she'd slapped him.

For a moment his lip curled, as if he'd retaliate. Without giving it thought, Pamela slipped her hand into her mother's. She straightened, staring dead on at the *Cariboo* who'd given her life, raised her, taught her right from wrong. That werewolf didn't stand before her now. Something dwelled in her sire's eyes, something she couldn't label. But as she stared at him, she sensed more existed here than was apparent.

"Pamela," her sire said, looking down at her like he so often had when she was a cub and he tried to explain something difficult for him to discuss. "You are a grown bitch, beautiful, a catch for any *Cariboo lunewulf*. Yet you turned them away. I have the right, the right passed down through generations and upheld in all respectable packs. You now have a mate. Jordan Ricky now owns the rest of the mountain. Your mating to him will give us right over the entire mountain, making us stronger. It is done. And you will honor it."

This was ridiculous. Her sire was blinded by maintaining the strength of their den, of their pack. He'd made her a tool in achieving his goal. Talking to him would accomplish nothing.

Letting go of her mother's hand, the cool tender flesh her only assurance that love still existed in her den, she turned from her parents.

Jordan Ricky leaned against her parents' car, his arms crossed over his chest, looking almost disgusted with the entire scene. He stood, puffing his chest out when she approached him. She wanted to puke.

He cocked his head, throwing his arms back slightly, as if trying pathetically to look like a bad ass. He was bad, and making an ass of himself, but that was about it.

Walking toward him, letting him smell her repulsion, she stared into his beady blue eyes.

"You're going to regret the day you agreed to this pathetic arrangement," she whispered, glaring at him.

He looked down at her, his hands fisting. There was no way he would lay a hand on her in front of her sire, but she almost wished he'd try.

"Don't threaten me," he whispered in return.

"Trust me. You're not worth threatening. You're going to regret this."

Walking past him, she kept her head held high, her emotions under check. None of them would smell her fear, her trepidation. She would have to endure staying at Ricky's den. Her parents wouldn't take her home. That much she didn't doubt. Running again would be a tricky feat.

That left only one thing she could do.

Somehow, she needed to call Gabe.

Facing the door to the small cabin where Ricky had recently moved, she kept her back to all of them while her parents got in their car and left. Jordan's boots crunched the ground behind her. His slow pace made her heart race even faster. If he touched her, she wasn't sure she'd be able to keep her cool. And right now, at least until she got him to fall asleep, she had to convince him she wouldn't run.

"Don't think I'm thrilled that the pack thinks I bought you," he told her, unlocking the cabin and then standing to the side so she'd enter.

"You gave my den money? I thought you jumped on the land that you'll get if you mate with me."

Jordan snorted, shutting the cabin door behind him. Her stomach lurched when she heard the bolt lock.

Pamela stood in the dark, the smell of Jordan thick around her. That and dirty clothes, unwashed dishes and a stale musty smell told her that he'd left his den in shambles and now they had the treat of returning to it stinking worse than a pigsty.

He walked past her, turning on a lamp next to the couch. "Don't think for a minute I'm thrilled about having a bitch I have to chase across the country." He turned around, untucking his shirt as he glared at her. "What I did, I did for the pack, to keep us strong. Now you need to quit being a spoiled cub and start thinking about someone other than yourself. You run again, and you'll be shunned. And don't think that Gabe McAllister will have anything to do with a shunned bitch."

He turned again, walking into the only bedroom the small cabin had. She watched light suddenly flood from the room and then listened as he entered the adjoining bathroom and water started running.

Glancing toward the door, she licked her lips, staring at the padlock that had her trapped in the cabin. Two windows had curtains closed over them. She let out a sigh. More than likely they hadn't been opened in ages.

She wasn't going to run. Nibbling her lip, she glanced again toward the bathroom. At the most she had minutes. Her own nervousness smelled so strongly around her that her stomach turned.

Her hands were clammy when she reached for the phone. Just hearing the dial tone had her letting out a sigh of relief. Punching in the numbers, she prayed she had the number right.

"Hello?" The familiar voice made her heart explode in her chest.

"Stone?" Her voice cracked and she gulped in a breath, her hair tingling on the back of her neck.

"Where are you?" He yelled into the phone so loudly she jumped, worry flooding through her when she heard the water turn off in the other room.

"Come get me. Please."

Jordan's footsteps made the wooden floor creak.

"I can't talk. I'm outside of Banff." Then she put the phone down but didn't hang it up.

As long as Jordan didn't notice his cordless was off the base unit, this just might work. That and assuming she could keep her nervousness down to a dull roar. Hopefully he would think the raunchy smell of her emotions came from her displeasure at being forced to stay there—which was more than true.

Walking away from the phone, she moved to the window, pulling the curtain back. Her hands shook so hard that her muscles hardened, blood rushing through her veins like a wildfire.

"Those windows haven't been opened in years." The smell of toothpaste and nauseating cologne didn't cover the too sweet smell of lust.

She fought the bile that quickly rose to her throat. The urge to run, to let the change rush through her and jump through the window, made it hard to think straight. Praying the line was still open on the phone, her heart thudded in her chest, pumping blood through her human veins way too fast. Turning to face him, she glanced quickly at the phone that rested on the small table next to the couch.

"Don't think for a moment that you're going to touch me." Somehow she needed to let Gabe know exactly where she was. "I'm in this small run-down cabin with you isolated on the side of this mountain with Banff a good ten kilometers from here. Unless you want me to humiliate you again, then you go into the bedroom and I'll sleep on the couch."

"You fucked that *Cariboo lunewulf* and for all I know his entire den. You should have no problem getting me off." He moved closer, his lust swarming around him. "I never knew you had that kind of kink in you. We could get another bitch up here. I'd have a damn good time watching both of you on your knees."

Pamela almost choked. Jordan probably already had a girlfriend, someone he'd rather be with, yet for whatever reasons motivated him, he'd agreed to this ridiculous mating.

"As many times as I was with Gabe, I'm more mated to him than I am you." She walked closer to the phone.

Somehow imagining that Gabe was at the other end, listening, his hand gripping the receiver in angered anticipation, while powerful muscles bulged throughout his body in rage, she gathered strength to take on Jordan. "If you want two bitches, you go find them. Go howl with any bitch you can find. I couldn't care less who you fuck. Just know that it will never be me."

Jordan laughed, moving even closer, touching the side of her head. His fingers tangled in her hair, rough and cold, yet his touch was awkward, lacking that brutal confidence that flowed through Gabe. Everything inside her went rigid.

"Nice try, you untamed bitch. But if you think I'm going on a run without you on a leash next to me, you can think again."

"And would you run me south to Banff, or north to Lake Louise?"

Jordan pulled her hair, forcing her head back. "Damn, you're one kinky bitch. Once I have you tamed, this ridiculous deal might turn out to be a decent trade."

Pamela closed her eyes, repulsion running through her so thickly that her teeth threatened to grow, pressing against her lips. Allowing the sweet pain of the change to course through her would be the only way she could take on this *Cariboo*. It would be so much fun to lash her claws through him, teach him a quick lesson in how to treat a lady.

"Get your fucking hands off of me," she hissed before she could stop herself.

Jordan threw her, making her land on her hands and knees on the couch. She stared at the phone, resting on its side on the end table. Gabe had to be at the other end of that line. He just had to be listening. He had to be there. Pamela needed him more than she needed to breathe. There was no way she could stomach being with Jordan, not one day, not for a week, not at all. There had to be a way out of this nightmare.

Jordan stood over her. "Fine. Take the couch. Just know that you're mine. Nothing and no one is going to change that. The deal is done, approved by the pack and your den. You might as well get accustomed to it."

She didn't move as he walked toward the bedroom, not daring to breathe. No sooner had he disappeared through the doorway, then she grabbed the phone.

"Gabe?" she whispered.

Her heart about broke, sinking to her gut, when she heard a dial tone.

Chapter Eleven

ജ

Lake Louise, Alberta, was a quaint town and mostly human.

"We're going to have to hit the mountains in order to find her," Stone said, standing next to the truck downtown after they'd strolled the shops and most of the restaurants and hadn't found a single werewolf.

"And with all these mountains, it's going to be harder to get an Internet signal." Marc sat in the passenger seat of the truck and shut the laptop he'd been trying to use. "We can also try that connection Heather mentioned who works at the Banff newspaper."

Marc nodded, sniffing the fresh mountain air that was completely polluted by the smell of humans around them. He'd be willing to bet there wasn't a damn werewolf in this entire town. Having grown up not too far north of here, it didn't surprise him too much. *Cariboo lunewulf* kept to themselves for the most part, living in the mountains and enjoying a more wild existence than many city werewolves did.

"You sure there aren't any sites on the Net for any packs out this way?" Gabe waited for Stone to climb into the truck and then slid behind the steering wheel.

It had been a tight fit with him and his littermates in his truck all the way out here. But Gabe hadn't been too surprised when both of them insisted on tagging along. He was going to get his mate, and this was a den affair. Nonetheless, if he'd been alone, he would simply change and take on the mountains, the hell with whether it was day or night.

The longer he was away from Pamela, the more time she had to spend with that asshole. And thinking about that made his insides harden with a fury he knew he'd never experienced before.

By nightfall, Gabe thought he'd climb right out of his skin. The need to change rushed through him with a vengeance that pushed dangerous. Images of Pamela, her sultry blue eyes, her long, flowing blonde hair fanning over her full, ripe breasts, distracted his thoughts.

After driving into the mountains and parking at a camping lodge, waiting for the sun to set took an eternity. Cold mountain air did nothing to soothe the fiery rage that simmered inside him, threatening to boil over if he didn't keep his emotions in check.

"We've got word out to most of the packs between here and Prince George," Marc reminded him as Gabe paced the length of his truck. "If she ran, we'd know by now."

"It's been almost twenty-four hours since she called," Gabe snapped at him. "How the fuck would you feel?"

"Like killing someone." Marc didn't hesitate with his answer.

"That's the plan." Gabe didn't either.

Ever since the other night, when Stone had answered Pamela's call, he'd been kicking himself for not taking Jordan down when he'd been in Prince George. He'd been a fool for thinking he would have more time to get to know Pamela, for the two of them to have more time to run together, learn more about each other. And all along he'd known deep inside he didn't want her to get away.

Just because prior to meeting her he hadn't given a thought to setting up his own den, he'd hesitated, and now Pamela was gone. Anger rushed through him so hard, making the more primal, raw, emotional side of him dominant.

It was time to get Pamela back.

"We've waited long enough." Gabe pulled his shirt off, the mountain chill doing nothing to soothe the burning need that rushed through him to find Pamela.

"We stick together," Marc ordered, turning to Stone, who leaned against the front of the truck watching some campers hike up toward the lodge set back off the parking lot.

"I'm ready." Stone moved to the other side of the truck and then stripped.

At the moment, Gabe realized he'd never been so eager to see a bitch again. Just to know she was okay, and that that bastard had kept his paws off her. Although whether he'd touched her or not, Ricky would die.

Marc and Stone kept an eye out for humans and when there were none around, the three of them changed and then raced off into the thick growth of trees surrounding the parking lot.

Emotions changed once he was in his fur. Senses fine-tuned, allowing Gabe to sniff out the nearest werewolves. And they weren't too far away. No longer feeling the cold mountain air, or disabled by limited vision, the evening dusk faded while his vision grew more acute.

Stronger muscles and keener senses made it easier to travel. No longer limited by his human form, Gabe leapt over rocks and moved easily around trees as the three of them moved up the mountain with ease.

Mountains familiar to all three of them. Growing up in the Canadian Rockies, each of them had the stamina to climb, to adjust to the thinning air, as they sniffed out the nearest group of *Cariboo lunewulf.*

After taking the phone from Stone the night before and listening to Pamela talk to Jordan, they had little to go by. But hearing that she was in an isolated cabin on the side of a mountain between Banff and Lake Louise, they'd plotted out where to start looking. Gabe hadn't wanted to hang up. More than anything he'd wanted Jordan to discover the phone was off the hook, to pick it up, so that he could warn the bastard that his life was about to end. Gabe had craved telling him that making a deal so horrendous, of forcing Pamela to do something against her will, made him the poorest excuse for *Cariboo* that he'd ever known.

But giving the asshole any warning would have made it harder on Pamela. So they'd hung up the phone, knowing then if Jordan had discovered it off the hook, it would have gone easier on her.

Now the plan was simple. Find the cabin or find the pack leader. Once they did that, he would be able to put his plan into effect. And Pamela would be his.

After climbing the mountain for almost an hour, the sun had dipped low enough that darkness loomed around them. In his fur, with his acute vision, images were gray and shadows ran deep, the smaller creatures of the night obvious as they cleared out, fearing for their life. The three of them weren't out for a kill this evening though. All creatures were safe from the deadly werewolves, shy of one.

When a cabin came into view through the trees and undergrowth, buried so deep on the side of the mountain no human could possibly get to it, Gabe's insides tightened with anticipation. His heart pumped with an energy more dangerous than even a *Cariboo lunewulf* should possess. The urge to leap at the door, tear it down with a single swipe of his paw and demand entrance, surged through his blood. His thoughts were controlled with the raw need to conquer and possess.

Stone and Marc slowed, growling at each other and snapping at him. The warning was clear.

Keep your head until you know who is inside.

Gabe fought the basic instincts that ached to control every muscle in his body. Growling at his littermates, baring his teeth, he let them see the fury that consumed him. They were here with him, but neither understood the craving he had for Pamela.

They didn't feel the pain that had eaten away at his heart ever since she'd been hauled off. Stone and Marc had no clue what it felt like to miss the opportunity to fight for the bitch that he loved.

And that was the simple truth that he understood. He loved Pamela. They had found each other under extreme circumstances. And the circumstances would be extreme in getting her back. Nothing would stand in his way.

Marc lunged into him, knocking Gabe into Stone. He was wired with adrenaline enough to take both of them on. And they knew it. But that would waste his energy.

Marc let the change flow through him, slowly straightening until he stood on two feet. "Stay where you are," he ordered quietly while unbundling his clothes that had been tied around his neck.

Gabe didn't give a rat's ass about his brother's orders. Pain coursed through his veins as he closed his eyes, fighting to control the amount of energy that filled his body, controlled his mind and breathed through him. Fire raged throughout his soul. It was an energy too strong for his human frame. Yet he forced the change anyway. This was his battle and he'd be damned if his littermate would give the orders.

They'd barely allowed the change to go through them when the den inside the cabin opened the door. Gabe pulled his clothes from the knapsack around his neck, dressed quickly while his brothers did the same.

A stout *Cariboo* walked into the night, several cubs hovering at the door. That sight alone told Gabe they didn't have the right cabin.

"Direct us to your pack leader," Gabe said, deciding to sway from formal greetings.

The less anyone knew about their reasons for being there, the better.

"What's your purpose here?" The *Cariboo* was instantly on his guard, glancing warily from one of them to the other.

A female appeared in the doorway behind him, and his arm went out to block her from view of the three of them.

"We'll discuss that with your pack leader." Gabe smelled the suspicion coming from the werewolf facing the three of them.

His hackles were up and Gabe didn't blame him a bit. Three strange *Cariboo lunewulf* approaching his den in the evening would put any werewolf on guard.

"His den is up the road." The *Cariboo lunewulf* nodded toward the side of the cabin.

Gabe didn't see any road but didn't question the directions. They would find it.

"Who should I tell him is paying him a call?" he asked.

"Tell him Gabe McAllister from Prince George," Gabe said, "and good hunting to your den."

The *Cariboo* took his time looking at each one of them. "You'll honor our pack and wait while I notify our pack leader of your arrival."

He turned and disappeared into the cabin, shutting the door behind him. Gabe didn't doubt for a minute that a run was quickly being organized.

"I would have preferred this be kept quiet," he admitted under his breath.

"You'll bring her honor approaching her pack in the traditional manner." Stone looked at him, his blue eyes still streaked with silver as his blond hair looked a mess around his face.

Gabe didn't doubt he looked much the same way. "Pamela has always had honor. Nothing this pack could do to her would disgrace her."

Stone nodded, and in the dark Gabe was pretty sure Marc nodded as well. His human vision hindered him, but the smells of the night were still acute in his system.

And something was stirring in the mountain.

Glancing around, the night life had picked up a nervous chatter, birds suddenly hurrying from tree to tree while the rodents scurried for protection, announcement of a more primal, predatory beast claiming the night.

The *Cariboo lunewulf* had notified his pack. Gabe knew that before the werewolf reappeared at his door. Reinforcements were being called out. Speculations were being drawn. If his name meant anything to anyone, and he had a feeling that it did, then word would travel through the night quickly that a challenge was about to be made. No werewolf would miss this.

The *Cariboo lunewulf* filled the doorway when he opened it, his mate behind him, touching him quickly as if bidding him to be careful.

Gabe and his brothers stood solemnly, none of them needing to discuss the fact that they would show respect to this pack. There was only one werewolf who would die tonight.

"I'll escort you to our pack leader," he told them and pulled his shirt off and then handed it to his mate.

"We're honored with the courtesy," Gabe nodded, and then stripped as well.

He welcomed the more carnal side of him as it tore through his system. Muscles bulged and stretched almost before he could get his clothes off. His teeth ground together as more primitive emotions rushed through him, adding to the fire of the change.

Dropping to all fours, he let out a howl, roaring at the night as adrenaline pumped through his body.

Instantly the other *Cariboo lunewulf* grew skittish, and Marc and Stone fell to all fours next to him, quickly growling and snapping at him.

Gabe fought for control, the desire to attack, to tear through the werewolf who had stolen his bitch, overwhelming him. In his animal form, it was harder to control the more primal instincts. Claim and possess. Make her his. Nothing else mattered. The predator in him overruled all other senses.

They leapt up the mountain, clearing boulders and tearing through undergrowth surrounding the pines. The *Cariboo* turned when he reached the top of the mountainside, where a small clearing laid the way to another cabin, buried among trees. He growled at the three McAllisters, showing long deadly white fangs. His large muscular body, covered with thick white fur, blended in naturally with the snowy surroundings.

Raw energy soared through Gabe with such intensity that the run up the side of the mountain barely curbed it. He danced sideways, unable to stand still, while they waited to be announced to the pack leader.

The large *Cariboo lunewulf* took his time changing into a large man with much weight on his body. He pulled on his pants and, remaining bare-chested, walked through the cold night and rapped on the door to the cabin.

Gabe didn't see who opened it, but the *Cariboo* disappeared inside, leaving the three of them out in the cold. Not that Gabe felt a bit of the chill. Distracted by the night coming to life, the thick woods around them radiating with an energy as other *Cariboo lunewulf* moved toward them, he moved sideways around Stone and Marc, his ears twitching as he heard the large beasts race toward them.

Marc was the first to let the change run through him once again. Pulling on his clothes, he turned on Gabe and Stone.

"The pack leader is in his human form. We'll honor him by appearing the same. Change!" he barked, his mouth still too large to be completely human.

The pain was stronger than ever when Gabe forced the change to his human form. He no sooner had his clothes on him when the cabin door opened, the *Cariboo lunewulf* who'd escorted them up the mountain appearing with another *Cariboo*.

"What is this?" the *Cariboo lunewulf* that Gabe guessed was pack leader asked, sounding annoyed. "Who are you to disturb my evening meal?"

An image of Pamela being raped and abused by Jordan Ricky came without bidding. Gabe wanted to rip the pack leader's face off for giving such little concern toward the bitches in his pack. Having grown up in these mountains, and the *Cariboo* blood running through him with a vengeance, he knew how these werewolves were.

Walking across the unkempt yard, stepping away from his den, he kept his hands relaxed at his side as he appraised the pack leader.

"I've come for Pamela Bordeaux," he said, staring the werewolf in the eye, a man of about his age.

It didn't surprise him that the pack leader of these *Cariboo lunewulf* would be young. Challenges were commonplace in the mountains. *Cariboo* were a hot-blooded sort, dominating and aggressive. In these parts, werewolves often didn't live to see their fiftieth birthday.

Gabe had no doubts he would live through the night. And he had no doubts that he would walk away with Pamela, with or without this pack leader's consent.

"She's mated." The pack leader turned, as if the discussion were over.

"I'm here to challenge her mate."

The pack leader turned, watery blue eyes narrowing on him. He glanced at the *Cariboo* who'd brought them to him, and then past Gabe at Marc and Stone. Turning to the werewolf next to him, he whispered.

"Go inside and contact the Bordeaux den. Prepare a small run, a handful of the older werewolves, to go the Ricky cabin."

Gabe didn't move, knowing the words weren't for his ears but also aware that the pack leader knew they would be able to hear the whispering. A werewolf's hearing was easily acute enough to hear the quietest of voices under normal circumstances. Gabe's senses were on overdrive. He would have heard a nut fall from a tree by a careless squirrel right now.

After the other werewolf shut the cabin door behind him, the pack leader strolled closer to Gabe, walking slowly around him, giving him the once-over. Just as in their fur, male werewolves would size each other up, even in human form.

"And who are you to think you can take one of our bitches, mated or unmated?" the pack leader snarled, looking at Gabe as if he found him lacking.

Gabe wasn't daunted. "Gabe McAllister, *Cariboo lunewulf* raised in a pack not too far north from here."

"And these two with you?"

Marc stepped forward. "Marc McAllister, and this is the youngest of our den, Stone McAllister."

"Tip Rochester, pack leader of the Kananaskis pack." The pack leader nodded to the three men, accepting the introductions. "Where is your pack?"

"We're in Prince George now, have been for almost five years." The social chitchat did nothing to soothe Gabe's nerves. His blood boiled for the fight, to challenge and take what would be his. He had proper breeding, though, and would honor the pack leader with conversation. "So the packs have united, have they? All of the Kananaskis territory is under your jurisdiction?"

"Yup." Tip straightened, appearing proud of the fact. "We're over a hundred *Cariboo lunewulf* scattered throughout the mountains. I have overseers here and there, but they report to me."

The cabin door opened, light flooding through the natural setting surrounding the wooden structure. The faint smell of coffee filled the air when the older *Cariboo* joined them.

"It is done," he said quietly.

The pack leader nodded.

Chapter Twelve

Pamela did her best to ignore the dull throb on either of her temples as she sank onto the floor, reaching for the thin newspaper. Losing herself in the crosswords would hardly be enough to clear her mind. But it was something to do—anything other than spend time with Jordan.

"Hard to lay my kill at your feet when your feet aren't in the kitchen," Jordan muttered, scratching his stomach as he stood in the kitchen staring at her.

"I'm not hungry." She sat cross-legged on the floor, taking her time flipping through the paper until she reached the crossword.

"Well, I am."

"Fix a frozen pizza." It had given her warped satisfaction while being at the store earlier when she'd refused to buy anything that required any prep time in the kitchen.

"If you aren't going to cook for me, then you sure as hell better start putting out."

She didn't even bother to look up. He would get neither, and it would serve him right. Her stomach twisted in knots and she couldn't decide if the thought of food or of fucking him was less appealing.

A car rumbled to a stop outside, its tires crunching over the gravel. Pamela looked at the door, instinctively sniffing the air. Ever since the other night when she'd tried to let Gabe know where she was on the phone, the slightest noise outside had her hoping it was him. Visions of him forcing the door down, grabbing her and sending Jordan's scrawny ass flying filled her mind.

It had been almost twenty-four hours though since she'd placed that call. If he were coming, he'd be here by now. No matter, she still cocked her head, listening as a car door opened and shut. Then there was another car. Her heart skipped a beat. They'd had no visitors since her parents had left. Not that she'd been surprised to be left alone. Who would possibly want to visit the most miserable den in the mountains?

"What the fuck?" Jordan's nervousness filled the small living area as he walked to the door.

Pamela watched as he pulled it open. Cold air quickly filled the cabin and a chill rushed through her. She smelled anger before she could see anyone.

"Ricky. Tip Rochester sent me over."

Pamela recognized the voice of the older werewolf who spoke, although the opened door blocked her view of the outside. She dropped the newspaper, standing so that she could see.

"What the hell for?" Jordan had no manners.

And she had no desire to apologize for his behavior. There couldn't possibly be a member in the pack who didn't know their situation. *Cariboo lunewulf* loved to gossip almost as much as they loved the mountains.

"Hi, Mac," she said, nodding to the older werewolf that she'd known since she was a cub.

Always a friend to her den, the pudgy man had raised a good-sized litter and had a good mate. He nodded to her, squinting as he gave her the once-over.

"Well, if you haven't turned into the stunning young bitch," he said cordially. "Hard to believe you're all grown up."

She smiled, although she smelled the stiffness in the air. This wasn't a social call. Mac Fortone hadn't stopped by to see how her new den was going. She didn't doubt he already knew she was here under protest.

Two more car doors closed, and Pamela looked past him, stunned to see her parents hurry to the den.

"Pamela. Are you okay?" Her mother's voice full of concern.

"Not now, Maria." Her sire put his hand on her shoulder. "Mac, I assume you were sent to announce the challenge?"

Mac nodded, and Pamela watched Jordan take a step backwards. "What challenge?"

Pamela's heart skipped a beat. She held her breath as she looked anxiously to each of the werewolves standing just outside the cabin. She was scared to ask. But her expression had to show that she ached to hear that Gabe had come for her.

"It's been formally announced." Mac's expression turned serious, and he puffed out his chest, the messenger of official pack news. "I've been sent to get you. You're being challenged for the mating of Pamela."

"I'm already mated." He swung out his arm, turning to look at her and then tried to reach for her.

If he thought for one damn second she would give the impression they were a happy den, he could rot in hell. Pamela stepped away from him, her attention riveting to her mother.

"Challenge?" she asked, her voice cracking. "Mama. What's happening?"

She knew she had to be glowing. The older werewolves studied her, their seriousness almost outweighing the sudden fear and anger that wrapped around Jordan. Pamela was scared to jump for joy. She had to hear it though. She had to know that Gabe was here, with her pack leader, awaiting the word to be sent so that he could properly claim Pamela.

"A *Cariboo lunewulf* has arrived from Prince George with his den. Name is Gabe McAllister." Mac shifted his gaze from her to Jordan. "Do you know him?"

"Yes." Pamela couldn't stop the grin that spread across her face and finally remembered to breathe again. "Yes, I know him very well."

"We had a deal, Bordeaux," Jordan scowled. The nasty smell of his temper filled the room. "I gave you rights to my half of this mountain for this mating. You'll lose it all if I lose Pamela."

Jon ignored Jordan and entered the cabin, making the small living room look even smaller with his large physique and overwhelming presence.

"I want to talk to you." He reached for Pamela, taking her arm although his grip was gentle.

Immediately she noticed he wasn't angry. Concern filled her nostrils, and she glanced from him to her mother, who hurried in around him and pulled Pamela into her arms.

Pamela sank against her mother, so excited that Gabe was actually here, calling for her, that she couldn't stop from trembling.

"Is this the werewolf who brought you to us in Prince George?" her mother whispered into her hair.

"Yes, Mom." Pamela felt tears threaten at the edge of her eyes. So many emotions flooded through her at once, she could hardly think straight. "I haven't been able to quit thinking about him since I've been back."

"What the fuck is this?" Jordan hissed, trying to grab her from her mother's arms. "You're my bitch. The deal is final. No fucking challenge is going to happen."

"The challenge is pack approved." Mac's calm tone was music to her ears. "I've been sent to come get you and take you to the meadow south of Lake Louise."

"And what if I refuse?" Jordan put his fists on his hips, glaring at the lot of them like the stupid idiot he was.

"Well, if you surrender without a fight," Pamela couldn't help grinning, "then I guess you can live through the night."

"Pamela," her father scolded. "You'll honor your mate. Properly bred young bitches shouldn't show so much excitement over a challenge."

"You know I never wanted him as a mate." She kept her arm wrapped around her mother, her heart beating so hard with happiness that she didn't care who noticed.

"Let's go." Mac crossed his thick arms across his barrel chest, seeming completely indifferent to her excitement and focusing on the chore he'd been sent to carry out.

Jordan puffed out his chest, any fear he'd had initially now settling into the salty smell of anger. "Don't go getting so damned excited, Pamela. I'll kick that *Cariboo lunewulf's* ass. And you're going to watch me take him down."

Pamela shook her head, knowing more than anything that Jordan wouldn't stand a chance against Gabe. Wishing him dead wasn't the issue here. The ways of her pack were set in stone, and she didn't question them. In a challenge, there would be only one survivor. Before the night was out, Jordan would be dead.

"You shouldn't have agreed to such a terrible deal." She looked from Jordan to her sire. "Forgive me, Father, but using me to gain land was wrong. And Jordan, your stupidity will be your downfall tonight."

Jordan snarled and then turned, storming into the bedroom, and slammed the door. Mac rocked up on his toes, content to wait for the werewolf to come back out.

Jon Bordeaux turned to her, taking her from her mother's arms and holding her at arm's length.

"Promise me one thing," he said quietly. "I want your word that you will stay in the mountains."

Pamela realized that her sire accepted the fact that this mating would end. Gabe would claim her. It was a done deal aside from the formalities.

"I won't promise anything without discussing it with Gabe first," she answered solemnly.

The smell of excitement tinged the air when she arrived at the designated meadow for the challenge. Oftentimes used for ceremonies, Pamela knew the land had been owned by *Cariboo lunewulf* as long as they'd roamed the mountains.

A star-filled sky hung low overhead as they parked. She climbed out of the back of her parents' car, more than happy over the fact that she hadn't had to drive out there with Jordan. He'd left with Mac and had almost looked green the last time she'd seen him. Watching him walk to the older werewolf's car, she had a hard time feeling sorry for him. He would die tonight, or he would surrender. Although refusing the challenge would bring him shame. Nothing would surprise her with Jordan though. She had a feeling he'd try anything to manipulate his way out of the predicament he was in.

"You're glowing the way a young bitch should when she's about to be mated," her mother whispered, snuggling next to her as they stood outside the car.

Other cars had arrived, the event probably pulling in most of the pack. Pamela nibbled her lip as she searched for Gabe's car. A knot twisted in her stomach, the ache growing by the second as she prayed she would see him soon.

"He's a wonderful werewolf, Mom. You'll like him."

Her mother took her hand, stealing her attention for a moment.

"I know you think what your sire did was wrong," she said, concern in her soft blue eyes.

Pamela had always thought her mother beautiful, her long lean body and the elegant shape of her nose giving her such a regal look. In her fur, Maria Bordeaux was like a goddess, elegant and shapely. And even in her human form, she still turned heads among the pack.

"You need to understand how he thinks though," Maria continued. "Your father fears the growing bond between humans and werewolves. They aren't to be trusted, and Jon realizes they will take us down if given the chance. Strengthening the pack is all we can do. Making that arrangement with Jordan was hard on you, but it assured the land would never fall into human hands."

Pamela didn't agree with his methods or with his fear over humans. But she smiled at her mother, seeing beyond the words.

"You love Father very much."

Her mother nodded, glancing past Pamela at Jon before returning her soft gaze to her daughter. "And I always have," she said, smiling. "Just the way I see that you love your werewolf."

"I wish I knew where Gabe was," she admitted, once again scanning the growing group of pack members.

None of them approached her, but she smelled their curiosity, their excitement over the challenge, and their whispers tickled her ears.

"I'm sure he is with our pack leader." Maria nodded toward a group of men, huddling along the other side of the meadow.

With her human eyes there were too many shadows to differentiate who was who at such a distance. Her heart pounded in her chest. More than anything she needed to see him, feel his reassuring touch, be in his strong arms. Every inch of her ached for him. As she stared at the men, her pussy began to throb, anticipation getting the better of her.

Before the night was out, she would be with Gabe. Need swarmed through her with a vengeance. Never in her life had she craved a werewolf the way she craved him.

"I've got to go see him." She couldn't wait another minute.

"No. It's not right for a bitch to talk to the challenger. You are mated. Remember that."

"I've never…" She almost said "fucked Jordan", but then curbed her words in front of her mother. "I've never done anything with Jordan. Seriously, Mom, I'm hardly his mate."

"It's down in the books. What's happened, or didn't happen, in the privacy of your den doesn't matter."

"It does to me."

Her mother smiled, understanding, and wrapped her arm around her daughter. "I hope you will honor your sire's request."

Pamela knew her mother wanted her to stay in the mountains. Gabe's den was in Prince George though. And she had no doubts she would go wherever Gabe wanted to go.

The energy changed in the air, and she straightened. Her mother turned her attention toward the others as well. The werewolves around them slowly began to move closer to the group of men who huddled at the other end of the meadow. Pamela couldn't stay still. Dragging her mother with her, she started walking in that direction too. The hell with traditions and pack laws. She had to see Gabe.

"As is the right and tradition of our laws," Tip Rochester began, and the crowd in the starlit meadow silenced, giving him their attention. "We honor the right of our matings. But as it is known, when a mating is challenged, and grounds are given that we accept and confirm, the mates will be brought before the pack, the challenger allowed to speak."

Pamela realized she'd never seen a mating challenged before. Tiny hairs prickled over her flesh, a sudden nervousness setting in. She was about to be put on display for the entire pack to judge.

Gulping in a deep breath of cold air, she let go of her mother's hand. Whatever it took to be with Gabe, she would do.

And then she saw him.

Standing with the rest of his den, watching her with a piercing stare that penetrated right through her, Gabe stood toward the edge of the group of werewolves. The powerful predator, muscles stretching the simple T-shirt that he wore, his thighs bulging against his jeans, and long legs adding to his persona, made him stand out among the others. Pamela's mouth went dry. Suddenly there was no one else in the meadow. All she saw and focused on was Gabe. She had to be with him.

"You can't go to him," her mother called out from behind her but Pamela ignored her.

Her body had a mind of its own, and suddenly she was hurrying across the field, needing to be with him.

Gabe took a step forward, and Pamela watched as his oldest littermate grabbed his arm.

Her heart raced. He'd come all the way out here, found her on the side of a mountain and spoken out for her. No pack law or tradition would stop her. She broke into a run, every inch of her aching to be in his arms.

"The bitch disgraces me," Jordan called out, his harsh accusation breaking the hush that had fallen over the pack. "She runs to him like a slut. I demand that she is shunned. Not only does she discredit me and her den but all of the pack."

Discussion and comments quickly filled the meadow. Several hands grabbed Pamela, although she didn't notice who at first. Gabe had moved closer to her, shrugging off the attempts of his den to keep his distance from her. His dark brooding stare never left her as he yelled over the disrupted pack.

"She was never yours to begin with," Gabe yelled at Jordan. "You stole her from me. My entire den is here as witness. And tonight you will die for your crimes."

Gabe ripped off his shirt, tearing the material from his body. Pamela couldn't take her attention from him. Even as strong hands pulled her back, and the surrounding pack members put in their two cents about the accusations that the two werewolves had made toward each other and Pamela, she watched Gabe.

Stripping out of his clothes, tearing them from his body as if they were made out of nothing more than paper, a sharp throbbing need began pulsing through her body.

"His accusations are false," Jordan managed to yell over the crowd. "He wishes to steal her and all the mountain that will come with her. Do we want an outsider stealing our land?"

This comment brought more turmoil among those around her. Emotions clogged the night air, while angry comments, spreading through the pack, created a moment of confusion.

Suddenly strong arms grabbed her. Gabe had moved so quickly she didn't realize he'd lifted her in the air until his rich scent filled her senses.

Touching him, feeling his power, his confidence, his assured domination, made blood rush through her fast enough to trigger the change. She fought it off long enough to wrap her arms around him, wishing more than anything that this terrible night would end, and she could just be alone with him.

"Will you have me?" he whispered in her ear.

His breath tortured her flesh, sending chills rushing through her.

"Oh, hell yes," she said quickly, turning her head so that she could claim his mouth.

His taste sank through her, filling her with a need so raw, so out of control, that she would have fucked him in front of God and everyone if given the chance.

"The whore!" Jordan screamed from not too far away, and more than anything she just wished he would disappear, be gone from her life.

Hands were on both of them, pulling them apart, and still she felt his touch, his strength, his scent wrapped around her, assuring her that all would be okay.

"You will follow the laws." It was Marc McAllister who hissed at his littermate, holding him fiercely when Gabe fought to be freed.

"Where is the asshole?" Gabe snarled, and then let the change ripple through him.

Everyone around her began stripping, the challenge to be honored in their fur. Tradition merited most ceremonies be conducted in their more pure state. Quickly Pamela stripped, ignoring the slap of cold air that attacked her human body. A heat more powerful than anything she'd ever experienced coursed through her. The harshest of mountain air wouldn't soothe it.

Feeling her blood pound through her body, her muscles change and grow, while her body changed, taking on its more carnal form, she fell to all fours. As those around her fell to the ground, fur covering their human flesh, a howl started, growing in volume as the blood continued to course through her veins.

Energy charged through her, filling the meadow, surging from one of them to the other. She jumped back in spite of herself when Gabe charged, screaming in the night, as he rushed into Jordan.

The pack quickly formed a circle around the two deadly werewolves. Jordan screamed when Gabe charged into him, sending the two *Cariboo lunewulfs* tumbling over each other as fur flew and bodies crashed into each other.

Pamela danced around her mother and sire, energy coursing through her, making it impossible to stand still. One of them would die tonight because of her. No matter that she'd understood and never questioned this tradition as long as she'd lived, suddenly watching it seemed too much to endure.

Jordan was an ass, a poor excuse for a *Cariboo lunewulf*. Without the challenge she would never be able to be with Gabe. Yet suddenly it seemed too harsh that Jordan would die because of it. She barked her protest, which was ignored and seemingly not even heard as the pack growled and barked, encouraging the two fighting werewolves on.

Gabe, show him mercy. This isn't right.

No one heard her. No one paid any attention to her.

The snarling grew louder. Blood stained the grass that the two werewolves rolled over. Interlocked and aggressive, the two mighty beasts tore at each other, large fangs and deadly claws ripping at each other's flesh.

Never for a moment had it crossed Pamela's mind that Gabe might not win. Her thoughts flew to her sire's comments earlier in the cabin. Even he had assumed Jordan would die. Her tummy flip-flopped, her muscles clenched as apprehension made her sick to her stomach. Gabe had to win. He couldn't die. She wouldn't be able to live without him.

At the same time, she realized he was willing to murder to be with her. What kind of creatures were they? This wasn't right. There had to be another way to resolve this. Yet as long as she'd lived, she'd never heard of a werewolf divorcing.

This was their way. Primitive and barbaric as it seemed. Watching the two of them rip flesh, blood splattering, bones crunching as they tore into each other, Pamela knew nothing she could do or say would stop this terrible fight. A fight to the death — and all because of her.

The urge to lunge forward, scream at the two of them, took over with more power than she could control.

Don't kill each other because of me. I'm not worth it!

She must have hurried toward them, because large paws pounced on her while a strong mouth clamped down on the back of her neck, pinning her to the ground. There was too much weight on her for her to turn or even move. She was trapped, her face on the ground, forced to watch while one man died fighting for her.

Praying Gabe wouldn't be the one, her insides crying when her eyes could shed no tears, she watched while the two of them continued to roll each other over, roaring and screaming as they ripped through each other.

When she was sure they would both die, leaving her a widow before she was ever truly mated, Jordan broke free of Gabe's hold. Barking furiously, Gabe lunged at him, but Jordan dodged the deadly blow.

Then, much to her surprise, Jordan turned from Gabe, running toward her with too much speed. She was pinned to the ground. Unable to move, she screamed, closing her eyes as she feared the worse.

A sudden eruption of barking filled the meadow and she realized she hadn't experienced an impact.

The weight lifted from her, and she looked around her quickly, realizing that Gabe now stood in the middle of the circle alone.

Jordan had run for his life.

The coward. He ran from a challenge.

Pamela looked around in confusion as the pack continued to bark, turning to look in the direction Jordan had run.

A howl started, silencing the commentary from the pack, as Gabe moved in on her. She turned quickly, her gaze darting over him, wondering how much of the blood that soaked his coat was actually his.

The challenge is ended. Her pack leader pranced into the circle, barking in a high pitch to grab everyone's attention.

Slowly those around her silenced, backing away out of respect.

All except Gabe who strutted toward her, his virile energy stealing her breath. Silver eyes glowed triumphantly as he pressed against her.

Mine! For all to see. You are mine.

Pamela fell to the ground. Relief swarmed through her that the ugly event was over. Half stumbling, her mind vaguely aware of tradition as happiness and need consumed her, she rolled over on her back, offering Gabe McAllister her belly.

I am yours – forever.

Chapter Thirteen

❧

Gabe could feel the cuts and bruises throb throughout his body, but he couldn't have cared less. Pamela's tender touch, as she dabbed at the cuts with a damp cloth, made him feel like he'd died and now was in paradise.

He sat at a kitchen chair in the Bordeauxs' kitchen as Pamela and her mother washed his cuts and wrapped bandages around his arms and chest.

The way Pamela leaned over him, her ripe breasts gently brushing against him as she tended to him, made his blood drain straight to his cock. Focusing on preventing a hard-on in front of her mother distracted him from the pain of his wounds.

Not that any of the pain would be there tomorrow. With a good nap, preferably with Pamela tucked in next to him, he possibly would be healed before midday tomorrow. Werewolves had a different metabolism than humans, and as hard as his heart was pumping right now, he wouldn't be surprised if he were better before daybreak. And if she kept touching him the way she was now, he'd forget he was ever wounded and it wouldn't matter when he healed.

The front door opened, and the mood of the den changed instantly. Both bitches straightened, acknowledging the sire of the den, Jon Bordeaux, as he walked with a heavy foot into the kitchen.

"They found Ricky," he announced, and Gabe stood, facing the large werewolf. "He ran to his parents' den, more than likely to complain of the unrighteous treatment he'd endured."

"He endured?" Pamela challenged, standing close enough to Gabe that her arm brushed against his.

Hairs stood on end over his flesh, aching to be closer to her.

Jon gave Gabe the once-over. "These women have you wrapped up enough?"

"I'm fine." Gabe smelled the tension pouring from Pamela's sire. There was something on his mind, and Gabe would hear it.

Jon nodded. "Let's go. There's business to discuss and I'm not a werewolf to put matters off."

Pamela reached for him, her warm fingers wrapping around his wrist. Gabe wasn't sure at this point if the pack leader would consider them mated or not. What he did know was that she was his, no matter what the law might say. One look into those pretty blue eyes and he knew her heart belonged to him. And damn it if she didn't own every inch of his soul.

"I'll be back. I promise," he told her quietly, taking her hand and giving it a squeeze.

"You better be," she told him, and then moved closer, obviously not caring that her parents stood alongside them.

Leaning into him, she placed a soft kiss on his lips, proper and chaste, and promising so much more later. The glow in her eyes made his blood boil. Damn it to hell. He needed to be inside her—and soon.

"She's not going anywhere," Jon announced. "Let's go."

There were still a few hours left to the night when Jon Bordeaux dropped Gabe off at the cabin where his littermates were being put up for the night. He learned a lot about the *Cariboo lunewulf* over the past few hours, and although he doubted Pamela would agree with him, he saw how much the werewolf cared for her and wanted the best for his den.

Granted, his methods had been extreme. Bordeaux believed in werewolves for werewolves. Somehow her sire believed forcing Pamela into mating would ensure the mountain would remain exclusively for their pack. Gabe ran his hand through his hair, staring after the *Cariboo* as he changed and raced down the mountain, disappearing while Gabe stood naked in the cold night, his clothes still bundled in his arms.

The cabin was quiet and isolated, and he entered into the darkness, the smell of a smoldering fire in the fireplace dominating over the other smells. His littermates' heavy breathing let him know they both slept, but Gabe wasn't sure he'd be able to sleep. Too much weighed on his thoughts, and he ached to see Pamela.

For a few minutes he thought he wanted to be with her so bad that he imagined her scent wrapped around him. His heart and mind were heavy with the discussion he'd had with Bordeaux, though. If he could only see Pamela right now, he just knew time spent with her would make it so much easier to think straight. He plopped his pile of clothes down on the table that sat in the middle of the cabin. Then a twig snapping outside the cabin alerted him.

Standing silently inside the dark, warm cabin, he closed his eyes, focusing on the sounds outside. There was definitely someone out there. If Ricky thought he could sneak up on Gabe and get the best of him, he could think again.

He glanced at Marc and Stone. His older denmate crashed on the couch, while Stone spread over several blankets in front of the fire. He wasn't sure where they thought he'd sleep.

Footsteps sounded outside the front door. Pamela's scent saturated his senses. It wasn't Ricky outside the cabin. Suddenly he didn't give a damn where he slept.

Gabe pulled the door open quickly and silently, and Pamela jumped from the unexpected action. "What are you doing here?" he hissed the moment he opened the cabin door.

Pamela stood before him, nibbling at her lower lip while she adjusted a sweatshirt she'd obviously just put on. He could still smell the night air on her, and the way her hair had no part, but looked almost windblown, gave her a wild, irresistible look.

Her gaze traveled slowly down his naked body, and his cock stood to attention, eager to be noticed.

"I think that would be obvious." She looked up at him, her gaze on fire with lust.

When she touched his chest, her small hand sent fire rushing through him. Need for her consumed him so greatly that he no longer cared how she'd managed to get out of her den. No matter that her parents would look for her here before anywhere else.

Pamela's simple touch washed all thoughts of the promise he'd given her sire. The conversation he and Bordeaux had no longer weighed heavily on his mind. All that mattered now was that Pamela be his.

"You're a little troublemaker." He couldn't help but smile at her.

"I don't see anything little about you," she teased, her hand strolling down his chest. "And you know I couldn't stay away. You fought for me and it's time you had your reward."

"Oh, I definitely plan on enjoying my reward." He felt all blood rush from his head when she grabbed his cock, her gentle touch the worst torture he'd ever endured. "Come here."

Pulling her inside the cabin, more than aware that his littermates' heavy breathing had stopped, he ignored both of them and pushed her up against the cabin wall.

Her sweet scent turned richer as she hurried out of her jeans, shoving them down her long slender legs. He couldn't wait for her to undress.

A low growl rushed through her when he turned her around, her jeans wrapped around her ankles. Pressing his cock against her sweet ass, he pushed against her flesh, his cock swelling while he nipped at the sensitive spot at the edge of her shoulder.

Pamela stretched against the wall, turning her head so that he could see her run her tongue over her lips, moistening them. Lust swarmed around her, the most wonderful scent he'd ever smelled. Her long hair streamed down her back, and she arched with a sultry ease when he ran his hands up her side and then cupped her breasts.

She couldn't spread her legs since her jeans kept them trapped together. Gliding his cock between her thighs, he felt humidity move through him from her hot little pussy. Knowing she was confined in her movements was so fucking hot he could hardly breathe. Pressed against the wall, and indifferent to Marc and Stone, who, if they had half a brain, were enjoying the show, made his blood boil in excitement.

More than anything he knew at that moment that Pamela was meant to be part of his den. Her uninhibited excitement, regardless of the fact that his littermates were in the room, was enough for him to know that she was meant to be his bitch. Her craving for him went to the length of knowing how he was. For him, for his littermates, sharing what meant more to him than anything else on earth was simply bonding closer with his den.

Although Marc never played as large a role, Gabe and Stone had always offered the best of their belongings to each other since they were cubs. It was an agreement they'd made at a very young age, a way of saying, "I'll always protect you if you share what is most dear to you". As they'd grown up, that had meant sharing their bitches. And now, his gaze wandering down Pamela, he knew beyond a doubt she was definitely his most cherished possession. She wanted him and wanted to belong to him. Her lust filled the air with its intoxicating scent, while her actions spoke louder than words.

The heat that surrounded his cock when he slid into her wet pussy about undid him. Pamela let her head fall back, stretching her arms over her head as she leaned into the wall.

"Please. Gabe, please," she said on a breath, doing her best to spread her legs while her jeans prevented it. "I need you so bad."

And she accepted that the others were there. She didn't beg him to run off somewhere with her. Pamela knew that Stone and Marc were her den now too. He'd truly found his soul mate. She accepted them and craved him. Happiness flooded through him so hard he was lightheaded with need to be inside her, to enjoy what truly was his. More so than because he'd made a challenge and won the right to her, more so than because he'd spoken with her sire, Pamela was his because it was how it was meant to be.

His cock buried deeper and deeper into her hot little cunt. The thick aroma of her cum soaked the air while her muscles clamped against him, threatening to suffocate the life out of him.

Gripping her hips, he loved how she stretched against the wall, her arms raised high over her head while her adorable ass curved toward him.

So tight—so fucking tight. He would burn alive inside her and die a happy werewolf.

He built the momentum, knowing there would be time later for hours of lazy sex. Right now she shouldn't be here, and his blood thickened when he realized his need for her exceeded what he knew was right. Her pussy muscles contracted while her fingernails scraped the wall. Chills rushed down her body and she shook her head from side to side. In the dark he saw her bite her lip and knew she tried to be quiet.

Gritting his teeth, he thrust harder, a more carnal and primitive side of him aching to hear her scream his name. Let everyone know she howled for him, that Pamela was his bitch, that she'd come to him, needing him. His lust swarmed through him, consuming all rational thought.

There was no one for him other than Pamela. And with a final lunge and a growl starting from deep inside him, he released all he had inside her, once again claiming her and marking her as his bitch.

He collapsed against her, wrapping his arms around her while the two of them hugged the wall. The smell of their sex hung heavily in the small cabin. He breathed in her scent, burying his face in her hair.

"Gabe?" she whispered, reaching behind her so that her hands hugged his hips.

"Hmm?" He was content never to move.

"I love you."

For a second he couldn't breathe. The air in the cabin seemed to seep out through the walls. Still locked inside her, it suddenly seemed impossible to stand up straight.

Staggering before he could stop himself, he held on to her as he stumbled backwards.

"Oh shit." She reached out, unable to find anything to grab on to.

Her jeans were still tangled around her legs, making it impossible for her to maintain her balance.

He managed to hold on to her so that neither of them would be hurt since he was still locked inside her and couldn't pull out in time for either of them to keep from falling.

"Gabe!" She cried out his name, but it wasn't from awesome sex.

Unable to stop himself, they fell backwards. He reached behind him, managing to keep one of the chairs at the table in the middle of the cabin from collapsing. He landed hard on his ass, the boards underneath them protesting loudly with awkward creaks.

His cock impaled her and she let out a yelp, her nails digging into his outer thighs. Humor and embarrassment filled the cabin suddenly with a sour smell stronger than freshly cut lemons.

"Holy shit, Gabe," Stone muttered in the dark. "Fucking tell her that you love her too."

Pamela started giggling, which was enough to relax his dick so it could slide out of her and for her to fall forward, collapsing in a fit of giggles.

"I didn't mean to shock you," she said, turning and giving him a toothy grin.

With her tousled hair, and her face aglow from a good fucking, she looked absolutely radiant.

"I love you too," he whispered.

He'd just made a fool of himself, but in front of the bitch he loved and his littermates, it didn't hurt that bad. She'd voiced with simple words what he'd been thinking. That embarrassed him more than falling backwards. But that would be something he would share with Pamela at a more intimate and private time. Stone and Marc didn't need to know that.

"'Bout time," Marc mumbled.

"Sorry we woke you." Pamela fumbled with her jeans, managing to pull them up her thighs.

She lifted her ass off the floor and then zipped and buttoned them.

"I can think of worse ways to be awoken," Stone said.

His twin stood and swatted him on the side of the head before extending his hand to help her to her feet. She accepted the offer, and then let go of him to comb her hair with her fingers.

"You're going to be missed." Gabe stood as well, surprised her sire hadn't already come through the cabin door looking for her.

More than anything he wanted Pamela with him when he slept. And with sunrise not too far away, he needed to crash. But he would see her home to her parents' den first.

"You fought for me. You know as well as I do what pack law says when there is a forfeit."

"We don't have word yet from your pack leader. The law states the forfeit will be announced, so we wait on Rochester. And I don't trust Ricky. He might try to argue that he didn't lose you because he is still alive."

"He never had me," she said, pursing her lips.

Her irritation filled the small area quickly. And Gabe didn't blame her a bit for feeling that way. He stood and pulled on his jeans, then pulled Pamela into his arms. She collapsed against him with a heavy sigh. The smell of sex on her was intoxicating. He ran his hand over her hair and stared over her head at Marc and Stone.

Marc sat up on the only bed in the small cabin. The glowing logs in the fireplace were beginning to go out, making it harder to see expressions in the almost completely dark room. Gabe relied on other senses to tell that his oldest littermate was concerned.

"You were with Bordeaux all night and never learned word if the pack leader deemed you victor in the challenge?" he asked.

"We talked about other things." Gabe moved over to the fire.

Adding one of the few logs next to the fireplace, he had a blazing fire going in no time. Instantly the temperature rose in the cabin, and firelight made it much easier to see with his human eyes.

Everyone looked a bit tousled and all eyes were on him, expectation and curiosity blanketing their faces.

"Bordeaux basically offered me the same deal he'd given Ricky."

"What?" both of his littermates said at the same time.

"And what exactly was that deal?" Pamela asked, her arms crossing over her chest.

He'd planned on discussing this alone with Pamela, but Marc and Stone had a right to know everything also. He might as well tell all of them at once. This was a den decision, and everyone in this tiny cabin was involved.

Gabe reached for Pamela and then sat her down in a chair at the table. He began pacing in the small space in front of her.

"Jon Bordeaux is a good *Cariboo lunewulf.* I want you to know that I gained a lot of respect for the werewolf while we were together earlier tonight," he began.

Pamela nodded. "Go on," she prompted, knowing she was about to learn what had plagued her ever since she'd run.

And Gabe didn't blame her a bit for running, not after what he'd learned tonight.

"Bordeaux worries that with humans knowing about werewolves, they will slowly infiltrate the packs — push their laws upon us."

Marc straightened, and Gabe glanced his way, knowing the werewolf/human issues affected him more than did most. He'd left his mate at their den to come out here with them — his human mate. Gabe wouldn't mince words on his behalf though.

"Bordeaux owns a large amount of his mountain. The other half belonged to the pack's territory. Ricky's den had money, and Jon convinced them to legally buy the other half of the mountain in exchange for his daughter."

"What the hell?" Pamela stood, but Gabe put his hand on her shoulder, making her sit again.

"The sale went through a bank in Banff, but there was a problem with the closing. The Ricky den blamed the Bordeaux den and claimed the mating wouldn't be valid until the land was secured."

"So Ricky didn't want me any more than I wanted him?" Pamela ran her hands through her hair, looking at the floor as if trying to make sense of all of this. "Then why did he come after me?"

"Your sire told me he would come up with the cash to secure the land if Ricky brought you back to the pack. So Ricky came after you. If he had you, he would have ownership in the entire mountain. That's a lot of clout in a pack to own most of the territory."

"I don't care about any land," she mumbled, shaking her head. "No wonder Ricky ran from the challenge. This whole ordeal wasn't worth losing his life over."

"I think he accepted the challenge to save face in his pack. But the real victor would be your sire. When Ricky ran, Jon risked losing the money needed to buy the mountain."

"Let me guess, so now he's propositioned you?" Pamela looked up at him with wide, blue eyes glowing with a mixture of emotion.

Gabe let out a sigh and nodded slowly. "He told me since the challenge needs to be resolved by the pack leader, and the pack leader is a good friend of his, he convinced Tip Rochester to hold off in announcing his decision until Bordeaux talked to me. Your sire said I could have you for a mate if I agreed to stay here, live on the mountain and take ownership in it. He's already convinced Tip of the terms — so they stand."

A heavy silence fell in the small cabin, the popping and crackling of the fire the only noise as the four of them looked at each other.

Gabe reached for Pamela, and she stood quickly, cuddling into him.

"Pamela," he said quietly. "I don't agree with what your sire did. But I will live anywhere if you'll be my mate."

"As far as I'm concerned, I'm already your mate," she told him, and then leaned into him, stretching and then kissing him with a heat that matched the fiery need that rushed through his veins.

"We can pull the law into this," Marc suggested, sounding almost as if he was talking to himself.

Gabe took his time with the kiss, barely hearing his oldest littermate. Pamela was so soft, her body a perfect fit against his. The fullness of her breasts, her wonderful enticing scent, made it hard to think about anyone or anything other than her. Bordeaux's offer earlier had meant little to him. Where he set up a den with Pamela would be their decision and not altered by the overbearing wishes of her sire.

Chapter Fourteen

෨

Not more than a week later, Pamela stood at the wooden cabin, complete with the front porch she'd asked for. The entire pack had put in their sweat and blood to help build their den. And she knew that strong bond was what her sire was so proud of.

"Something those humans don't have," he'd told her. "They lack the unity that we have and will never lose."

In spite of his actions in getting her a mate, Pamela couldn't stay angry with him.

"If I hadn't run, I'd never met Gabe," she'd told him earlier that day.

Standing now in the yard that would be theirs, with the morning sun shining down on them, she cuddled against Gabe, happier than she'd ever been in her life.

"It's perfect. I can't believe it's all ours." She looked up at him, and he grinned down at her.

Then with a quick motion, he scooped her into his arms. "And now that we're finally alone, it's time to make this den truly our own."

Gravel popped behind them and Gabe turned with Pamela still in his arms.

Stone parked the truck and then strolled toward them, grinning with complete satisfaction.

"Hell of a den you got yourself here." He ignored the fact that she was in Gabe's arms and stood next to them, crossing his arms as he stared at the cabin.

The fresh wood they'd had shipped out from the land where Stone and Gabe worked made the mountain air smell even sweeter.

"Not sure this pack would have been able to build it without our help," Stone added, his pride filling the air around them. "You going to invite me in too?"

He looked at Pamela, and warmth spread through her when Gabe glanced down at her too. Licking her lips, which suddenly were too dry. Her heart started pounding, a mixture of excitement and nervousness flooding through her.

"You're part of our den. You can come in." She swallowed, knowing what would happen.

And she wanted it. It made sense to her that Gabe loved her so much he would want to share her with his twin, with the werewolf who would do anything for him—for her.

Gabe pushed the cabin door open with his foot as he carried Pamela over the threshold. It was the first time they'd been there without half of her pack being there, without *their* pack being there.

Gabe had made her sire so happy when he'd agreed to join her pack, set up his den on the other side of the mountain from where Ricky had kept her. They'd spent a day running over the mountain, searching for the perfect site for their den after they'd agreed to live there. The way the sun flooded through the large living room, she knew they'd picked the perfect spot.

Stone shut the door behind them as Gabe continued through the living room, carrying her into the bedroom. The large bed, a mating gift from her den, was in the middle of the room, so large it almost filled the room. He sat her down on the bed, and then stroked her hair away from her face.

"I'm the luckiest werewolf," he whispered, his grin matching the warm scent that filled the room.

Stone entered the bedroom behind Gabe, his lust for her making her breath come quickly. Just the thought of both of them fucking her had her pussy throbbing. She wasn't sure what to expect, but trusted Gabe.

"I think I'm the lucky one." She reached up, feeling the hard muscles that bulged against his shirt. So much power soaked through her fingers. She could hardly breathe touching such raw carnal strength.

Her body ached to match that strength, her blood rushing through her veins too fast for her human body to handle. The urge to change grew strong and she fought it while she worked to slow her breathing.

"Do you want this?" Gabe asked her, crawling on the bed over her.

"More than anything." She knew taking Stone into her bed too would bond them as a den that no distance could conquer.

Gabe had always lived with his twin, and he'd agreed to move to her pack to be with her. For the first time they would be parted. More than anything she wanted this bond, because she loved Gabe, because she cared for Stone.

Wrapping her arms around Gabe's powerful neck, she pulled him down over her. He impaled her mouth with his tongue, making love to her mouth. She melted against him, fire rushing through her out of control.

Gabe pushed his hand under her sweater, breaking the kiss and nibbling his way down to her neck. He rose over her, lifting her sweater and then pulling it over her head.

"She's so beautiful," Stone breathed, his voice garbled, his own lust affecting his human body.

"Sit up," Gabe told her.

She trembled with need as she did what he bid. Both of them kneeled on the bed next to her. They helped her undress, their strong hands raking over her feverish flesh. She let her eyes flutter shut, enjoying how they touched her, their hands stroking her skin as her heart pounded with anticipation.

Their movements around her were too much to resist. She didn't want to miss a thing. Her breath caught in her throat when she opened her eyes to see both of them stripping. Muscles bulged around her, adrenaline mixing with lust in the air.

"Dear Lord." She reached out, her hands shaking as she touched both of their chests. Their heartbeats pounded against her palms, matching beats that pulsated through her. "Twice the perfection. What have I done to deserve this?"

"You love me," Gabe answered, without hesitating.

She smiled up at him. "You're right about that, wolf man."

He kissed her again, but this time Stone's hands were on her too. Strong like his twin, with a confident touch, he spread her legs.

"Oh shit," she cried into Gabe's mouth, when Stone kissed her pussy.

She convulsed against him and both of them held her in place.

Two mouths on her, adoring her. The pressure built inside her, pushing against a dam of lust that, if broken, would put her over the edge. She couldn't slow her breath, couldn't stop her heart from pounding in her chest, the need to come rushing through her with more intensity than she'd ever experienced before.

Gabe applied gentle kisses to her cheek, and then neck, before tracing a wet path with his tongue to her breast. Nipping at her nipple with his teeth at the same time that Stone thrust his tongue into her pussy, Pamela cried out, gripping their bedspread as her first orgasm rippled through her.

"Damn, she tastes good." Stone's breath against her feverish cunt added to the sweet torture as she exploded, the rich smell of her cum filling the room.

He pressed his face between her legs while his hands gripped her inner thighs. Sucking her juices from her cunt, he drank from her like a parched werewolf, eager for drink after a hard run.

Gabe nibbled at her breasts, his hands cupping and tugging against her swollen and tender flesh. Never could she have imagined two werewolves making her feel this good. Twice the attention, twice the energy surging through her while both of them loved her.

The pressure began again, stronger than her first orgasm, making her muscles harden painfully as a more primitive side of her ached to surface.

"I can't take it any longer," she managed to utter, speech becoming more of a challenge as she thrust her head from side to side.

They had the rest of her body pinned, and the more she tried to buck against both of them, the stronger their grips on her were.

"I want you to enjoy her first," Gabe said, his voice deeper and harsher than usual.

She looked at him through blurred vision, his cock swollen and thrusting toward her.

"Turn over," he told her.

She glimpsed down at Stone, who'd straightened, his body so similar to Gabe's, so hard and perfectly sculpted with a perfect spray of body hair covering rippling chest muscles. Stone's cock thrust toward her as well when he moved to his knees, helping her to roll over and then holding her while she moved to her hands and knees.

Gabe's rich scent robbed her senses when he cupped her cheeks and guided his cock to her mouth. She eagerly sucked it in, the growl that ripped through him feeding her as her lips stretched around his swollen cock.

She choked, gagging when Stone thrust his cock into her soaked pussy, feeling so much like Gabe yet so different at the same time. He filled her, thrusting with so much power that she almost swallowed Gabe's cock.

"Fuck." Stone pulled out just as quickly and then stabbed her again with his huge cock.

Her pussy soaked his cock, gripping it while her orgasm tore through her without her bidding. Stone had made her come just by entering her, his raw and aggressive way of fucking her making her come so hard that her head spun from its strength.

Lapping at Gabe's cock, forcing her muscles to harden as she managed to stay on all fours, she imagined the more pure sense of fucking, in their fur. There was no doubt these two would be as rough, as raw with their fucking as they were in their flesh. She'd definitely died and gone to heaven.

Gabe held her face, his fingers tangled through her hair so that she couldn't move her head as he moved in and out of her mouth.

"God, you suck cock so damn good," he said, his grip hardening while he thrust his swollen cock against her throat.

She gagged again, tasting his pre-cum. Managing to run her tongue over his shaft, she felt the veins that throbbed around his cock. Her body throbbed while her own veins bulged with blood that rushed through her with amazing speed.

Stone pounded her cunt, showing no mercy while he created a feverish heat that she doubted could ever be doused. She could fuck these two forever and know pure and total pleasure. She was positive no other bitch had ever experienced such ecstasy.

When Gabe pulled out of her mouth, she cried out, her breath coming so hard that her muscles altered, tightening around Stone's cock furiously.

"Holy shit," Stone said, gripping her ass. "Calm down, sweet little bitch."

He pulled out of her, leaving her cunt throbbing along with her entire body. She crawled around the bed, panting while her hair fell around her face.

"Fuck me, wolf man," she growled, offering her swollen and feverish pussy to Gabe.

He grabbed her rear end, dragging her over the bed while he positioned himself behind her. His cock was so like Stone's yet he managed to hit an all new spot when he impaled her. She collapsed on the bed, letting out a sigh as she came again. Torrents of cum rushed through her, her inner thighs soaked from her cream.

Stone wiped her hair from her face, an oddly gentle touch when she felt so wild with need. She didn't want gentle right now. She wanted it rough, hard and quick.

"Come here," she told Stone, managing to push herself up as she straightened her arms.

Stone's cock was covered with her cum, making her crazy as she lapped at her own cream while Gabe fucked the shit out of her.

She sucked him in deep, swallowing her own cum as his swollen cock filled her mouth.

Gabe showed no mercy, giving it to her just the way she wanted it, pounding her cunt with enough speed that the fever in her cunt rushed through her entire body.

"That's it, sweetheart," Gabe told her, hitting that spot deep inside her that only he could hit. "We're going to fill you with our cum. Are you ready for that?"

She nodded her head vigorously, groaning as her mouth stretched over Stone's cock.

"She's going to suck the life out of me," Stone growled over her head as his hands tightened on either side of her face.

"Give it to her," Gabe said.

Their voices drifted around her, both of them fucking her so hard she knew she'd collapse if both of them didn't have such a hard grip on her.

Stone's cock grew in her mouth, cum dripping into her mouth just before he pulled out. Hot cream spilled over her lips, burning her cheeks, as he exploded. She brushed her tongue over his swollen cock head, tasting how salty he was while his satisfaction filled the room.

Gabe moved quickly, turning her around as he lay on his back and pulled her over him. She straddled him quickly, eager for his cock to be back inside her. When she would have ridden him, he grabbed her hips and thrust upwards while a shit-eating grin spread over his face.

"Damn it," she screamed, collapsing over him while he slammed into her cunt, pounding her with intense satisfaction while his heat pounded furiously against her chest.

When he exploded, it was like fire surging through her, his cum soaking her pussy, filling her like he never had before.

She had experienced perfection, pure heaven, and she wasn't sure she'd live through it.

Collapsing over Gabe, his body glistening with moisture, he wrapped his powerful arms around her, hugging her soundly while he kissed her hair.

"There's no way it can get better than that," she whispered, more content than she'd been in her entire life.

Stone stretched out on the bed next to Gabe, closing his eyes and looking very content.

"I love you, my sweet mate," Gabe whispered.

"Love you too," she whispered, relaxing on top of him, content to stay there with his cock nestled inside her for the rest of her life.

Challenged

ဆ

Trademarks Acknowledgement

The author acknowledges the trademarked status and trademark owners of the following wordmarks mentioned in this work of fiction:

Bronco: Ford Motor Company

Chapter One

ജ

Stone McAllister hadn't been to Banff this much since he was a cub. And the town sure had changed. Human tourists from all over the world made the air thick with smells of polyester, cigarette smoke, and stuffed stale emotions. The small town nestled in the mountains was nothing like the cozy haven he remembered as a cub.

That was just like humans though. Find a beautiful paradise and they all flocked there until it lost its isolated wonder.

He parked the truck in a rather empty parking lot on the edge of town and headed toward the large wooden structure—The Last Howl. A rather corny name for a werewolf tavern, but he wasn't looking for anything classy, just a cold beer and maybe a loose bitch or two who would put out a piece of tail.

His cell phone rang as he reached the large wooden door to the tavern. Standing outside the place, a faint smell of beer lingering through the seasoned wood, he pulled his phone from the belt and glanced at the number on it.

"Yup," he said, idly looking around the lot and then up at the surrounding mountains.

"You headed home?" Marc McAllister, his older littermate, broke up from a lousy signal on the phone.

"Yeah." Stone felt an empty pang sting his gut and pushed his way into the tavern. "I'll head toward Prince George by nightfall."

The barmaid ran a heavily bleach-scented cloth over the top of the bar, giving him the once-over the way a bitch always did the first time she saw him. This one was worth looking back at. Maybe he would get lucky before heading back across country to his den.

It had been over two weeks since he'd arrived in the Kananaskis territory and helped his other littermate, and twin, Gabe, secure his mate. After helping Gabe build his new den, a cozy cabin up the mountain, Gabe and his new mate, Pamela, had left on a run into the Canadian Rockies, more than likely fucking day and night.

Nothing kept him here, yet he hadn't returned to his pack in Prince George yet.

"Are there problems there?" Marc asked.

"We've got a bad connection. And there's no problems." Stone had no intention of letting anyone know that going home to an empty den was about as appealing as spending a day with humans.

Marc laughed. "We figured you were just going through every bitch in the pack out that way. But we'll see you when you get home."

Stone hung up the phone and gave the barmaid the once-over. "How about a shot of whiskey?"

The barmaid nodded, reaching beneath the counter and then pouring the dark amber fluid into a small glass. She stood with bottle in hand, watching him, as if anticipating that he was more than a one-shot werewolf.

"I don't know you." She cocked her head, curiosity the overwhelming scent on her.

"Would you like to?" He slid the shot glass toward her and she promptly filled it again.

"Yes." Her lack of hesitation should have drawn caution. "Are you new to the pack?"

"Nope. Just passing through." He took his time sniffing her out.

Blonde hair streaked with red highlights layered around her face. She was young, in her early twenties he'd guess. Her clothes were too tight, just the way he liked them on a willing bitch. More than likely her attire got her a fair amount of tips, and a roll in the meadow after-hours too.

She had a smell of innocence about her, yet her actions belied that. Either she was a tease, or her youth still clung to her in spite of her willing attitude.

There was only one way to find out. The little bitch didn't know she messed with a professional. He slid the glass to her again, and then leaned forward onto the counter as he stared into her sapphire eyes.

"A lone werewolf," she whispered, her eyes sparkling with interest. "Where is your pack?"

"Prince George." He let his gaze drop, the shirt she wore cut low enough to show off a fair amount of cleavage.

Stone was willing to bet she wasn't as built as her clothing implied. The right bra pushed everything up and showed it off nicely. A bitch as young as she was seldom had cleavage like that.

"You're a long run from home, wolf-man," she drawled, leaning forward against the counter to give him a better view of what he stared at.

Stone shrugged. "All depends on how fast you are."

When she smiled, her eyes sparkled like rare jewels. His insides hardened as a more carnal side of him surfaced.

"I imagine you're mighty fast."

The door to the bar opened and daylight flooded the dimly lit establishment.

"Ali, my dear…a sight for sore eyes," a voice boomed behind Stone. "Line us up with a few beers. When does Cook arrive?"

"The same time he does every day," she said, laughter in her tone.

Stone adjusted himself on the barstool so he could watch Ali take several beers to the werewolves who'd just arrived. She wore tight jeans that displayed an ass tight enough he knew he'd explode the second he got in her. Damn.

Her jeans were black and her leather, vest-like shirt was a soft brown. Accentuated with that blonde hair that tapered just past her shoulders and had streaks of red that he bet she'd added from a box, she had a bad bitch look about her. And damn it if he didn't like them on the wild side.

The tavern slowly filled as the afternoon wore on. Apparently "Cook" had a reputation in this town. An older werewolf, salty around the edges with a sour attitude, prepared some of the best burgers and steaks Stone had seen in a long time.

Pack members pushed their way through the door, rubbing sleep from their eyes. Most werewolves enjoyed a good hard run at night, and napped when they could around working hours. The best life was one Stone had, working for another *Cariboo* who understood that a workday shouldn't start before noon—allowed plenty of time to sleep off the carousing from the night before.

Looking around the bar, he noticed the older werewolves, their unshaven faces and their potbellies. Their body odors and appearance told him one thing. None of them would get a better-cooked meal at their den.

He turned back to face the bar, his mood souring. He would end up like the lot of them.

Like hell he would.

"I get off in thirty minutes. Take me somewhere nice?" Ali's breath sent the hairs on the side of his neck into a full salute.

It wasn't the only part of him that jumped to attention.

She was off and running, carrying more beers to waiting customers before he could respond. He'd switched to beer, and nursed his second glass, not wanting to leave there drunk. But the alcohol had wound him up, and a roll in the meadow with a hot little bitch like that might be just the pick-me-up he needed before heading back to Prince George.

He turned to watch her bend over, her back to him, giving him an awesome ass shot, while she delivered an order to a table. Her laughter was melodic, her body a perfect ten. Those black jeans hugged long slender legs, and her hips were slender, her tummy flat. Typical tight little body for a bitch her age. Except for those tits. Full and round, they were so much more than a mouthful. What he wouldn't do to rub his cock between them, watch that perky little mouth open and try to suck him in.

When she turned toward the bar, she winked at him. Damn it if this fresh young bitch didn't want him bad. Letting his gaze stroll down her, he enjoyed watching her cheeks flush a beautiful pink as she disappeared into the kitchen behind the bar.

God, he swore it was a helluva lot longer than thirty minutes before another barmaid strolled in the door, older, a bit more street-smart in her appearance, and nothing compared to Ali.

The two females chatted amiably at the end of the bar. Noise came from all directions now, the locals filling the place with open talk of runs, and pack business. It hadn't been too many years ago that werewolves couldn't enjoy such open discussions in public. Humans knowing they existed had its good points too. This place wasn't all that different from Howley's back home.

Home. He'd been in Prince George for five years. Prior to that, these mountains had been his stomping ground. He could see why it hadn't been hard for his twin to set up his den here. Home was where there was happiness, a good bitch, something to call his own and be proud about it. Going home to that empty den, where no one waited for him, made his gut ache. He didn't want to do it.

Finally Ali strolled up to him, nibbling her lower lip. She smelled of beer and fried food, which hid her natural aromas. But those large sapphire eyes, not blinking as she moved to stand next to him, staring up at him with a look of wonder in her expression, told him enough.

He was a curiosity to her, the all-knowing werewolf out on the prowl.

"You better not be teasing me," he warned her under his breath.

Better to let her know up front what his intentions were. If she wanted to bail, he'd allow her that before he even left with her.

"I'm not teasing. I really do want you to take me somewhere nice." She grinned way too sweetly, suddenly looking even younger than she probably was. "At least somewhere nicer than this. By the way, what's your name?"

She took a deep breath, letting him know she was nervous and trying to hide it. He placed his hand on her back, escorting her outside to the truck he'd been driving since his littermate had left for time alone with his new mate.

"Stone McAllister at your service," he said, opening the truck door for her.

"Stone?" She crossed her arms, pressing those large breasts of hers closer together. "Your mother named you Stone?"

He let his gaze drop to her plump exposed flesh, his mouth suddenly too dry to speak.

"Well, I'm Alicia Bastien," she continued. Outside the tavern, her own scents grew stronger in the fresh mountain air. "Where are you taking me, Stone McAllister?"

"How about into the mountains where we can enjoy a private run?"

She cocked her head, amusement mixing with wariness, a pleasant smell on her.

"I had something nice in mind, like a restaurant where we could chat. Is that not in your budget, wolf-man?" She was challenging him.

"You're too young to be a gold digger. Get in."

She moved closer to him, needing to brush past him to climb into the truck. Glancing up at him, her slender frame making her appear petite when she was right next to him, her bright blue eyes sparkled with defiance.

He noticed her scent change, her hackles going up at his comment. What he saw now was a wild bitch who was trying her damnedest to appear high-class. There was no way he'd let her read him, but kept his expression blank as he stared down at her. The first thing they would establish was that he was in charge here.

"I'm not too young to be anything," she told him, and climbed into the truck.

He shut the door, then walked around to the driver's side, pondering over her comment. All it told him was that he'd judged her accurately. Little Miss Alicia had found a new werewolf on the prowl and thought she might have some fun with him. Well, fun was a two-way street.

Chapter Two

❧

Ali adjusted herself in the passenger seat of the truck. Watching Stone McAllister strut around the front of the truck, she knew she'd never known a more wild and dangerous *Cariboo lunewulf*. Her heart picked up a rapid beat while she sucked in an extra breath. Rubbing her damp palms against her jeans, she worked to calm her nerves. Her apprehension would fill the space of this small cab if she didn't calm down. This was an adventure, and she only lived once.

Stone opened the driver's side door and climbed in, cranking over the engine and then glancing at her. "You really hungry?"

She doubted she could eat a thing. "I'm starved."

The look he gave her, a long and slow assessment while he probably sniffed out every emotion and thought going through her… She was so out of his league.

"Well, no offense, but you smell like fried food and beer. If you want top of the line, you're getting a shower first."

Oh damn. More than out of her league. She wasn't even in the same district. The only way she could shower first was if she took him to her den.

Ali clamped her hands together in her lap, looking down while she watched her knuckles turn white.

"Now if we find a quiet area to take a run, I won't require that you shower first," he said quietly, his baritone racking her senses.

She licked her lips and then nibbled at her lower one, hoping she appeared to be pondering her choices.

"My den isn't far from here." She focused on the large mountains that confined the town to the small valley as Stone followed her directions to the small house where she'd grown up.

"This is it?" Stone asked, staring at the small house, freshly painted by her uncle, and her nephews rocking on the porch swing.

"I have a large den," she said, and gripped the handle to the truck door, wondering if she would be smart to just tell him thank you for the ride, and let him go on his way. No way. This was a once in a lifetime chance and she wasn't going to run from it with her tail between her legs. "Is your given name Stone?"

He smiled when she looked at him, a charming expression crossing his face while relaxed confidence filled the air in the cab. It smelled a lot better then her nervousness.

"My mother named me Frederic McAllister. The name Stone came soon after because I'm so hardheaded and always managed to get what I wanted."

He reached for her then, surprising her with his quick strength as he dragged her across the bench seat into his arms. "You'll do well to remember that. There will be no games. Do you understand?"

All she could do was nod. Stone let his gaze drop, possibly to her lips. Her breath caught in her throat when she thought he would kiss her. What her nephews wouldn't do with that news. They'd be howling that sweet gossip to all the neighboring dens before she could get out of the truck.

Stone surprised her by opening his side of the truck and then pulling her out on his side.

"You're being paranoid." She fought to sound worldly, not let him manipulate her simply because she was so young.

She slid to the ground, her natural instinct to protect herself making the hairs on the back of her neck stand to attention, while her muscles hardened.

But this was the old Ali. For twenty-two years she'd fought every werewolf who approached her, disgusted by their inability to measure up to her dreams. Nothing about Stone disgusted her.

Placing her hands against his chest, she felt warm muscles, hard and well-rounded, against her flesh. His pulse beat through him, solid and confident just like the rest of him. Stone was a powerful werewolf. Just touching him she sensed his strength.

Instead of hesitant lust, she sensed his cocky arrogance, smelled his all male scent.

The smell of lust came from her.

Ali took a moment, staring at her fingers, dirty from a day's work, spread over his firm chest. Then slowly her gaze traveled up him. Broad shoulders blocked her view of anything but him. And he had a neck, which was more than most of the brutes around here. His Adam's apple moved slightly as she ached to run her fingers over him, exploring him in full.

When she looked up at him, blue eyes sparkling with defiance, which added to the male smell that surrounded him, bored through her. Bangs barely reached perfect blond eyebrows that narrowed the longer she stared at him.

"I'm never paranoid," he told her quietly, resting his hands on her hips. "Just know that I won't be toyed with. You run with me, it's all or nothing. Do you understand?"

She couldn't move, could barely breathe. And for the life of her, she wasn't sure at all that she understood. What it sounded like, was that if she went out with him this evening, he expected some damn good sex, or he would leave her home.

Managing to swallow, she nodded, damned if she would sit at home another night, allowing the excitement life had to offer to pass her by.

"Good. Now go shower. I'll wait for you here."

When she would have protested, let him know her den would never allow him to simply stand and wait for her to come trotting back out to him, he turned her toward her den, giving her a swift swat on her ass.

A yelp escaped her, and she felt like a cub, nervous and excited all at the same time as she almost skipped inside, praying she wouldn't have to deal with anyone inside and could simply shower and escape again unnoticed.

"Who's that *Cariboo*?" her thirteen-year-old sister asked.

"My date." Ali hurried past her, knowing the questions would fly if she didn't hit the shower quickly. "Go find something to do, Janie Lynn. Don't be a pest."

Her younger littermate, one of four in her den, pranced after her, curiosity and jealousy filling the air when she followed Ali into her room.

"I've never seen him before. If he's not part of the pack you'll get a beating for going out without Papa's permission."

Ali hurriedly looked through her clothes hanging in her closet, none of them impressing her. She grabbed one of her sweaters that she'd received more than one comment on in the past, and then pulled clean jeans from her drawer.

"I'm a grown bitch. Who I see is my own business."

"Not as long as you are part of this den." Janie Lynn mimicked their sire, putting her hands on her hips so that she stood just like him.

When Ali turned, her other littermate, Jason, stood behind Janie Lynn.

"Who's that *Cariboo* out there?" At the age of seventeen, his hormones were on overload and filled the air as he puffed out his narrow chest. "Papa isn't here. Should I go talk to him?"

Ali hid her sigh of relief as she pushed past her curious littermates and hurried to the bathroom. "And that's why he's waiting outside." She had no problem hiding the smell of her lie in front of her younger littermates. "It wouldn't be proper to have him in when our sire and Mama aren't here."

She prayed Mom was with their sire.

"Well then, it's only proper for me to go question him," Jason said as she shut the bathroom door on them.

Ali had no sooner stepped out of the shower, wrapping the towel around her, when the bathroom door opened, steam escaping out the door as Jolene crossed her arms, scowling at her.

"Where did you find him?" Her fifteen-year-old littermate pouted.

"Jolene. Not now." Ali hurried to dry off, and then slid her still damp legs into her jeans.

"Well, you better find out if he has a younger littermate. He's definitely worth howling over." Jolene's immature lust swarmed around her developing teenage body.

Ali bent over, towel-drying her hair and then straightened so she could give her younger littermate a reprimanding look.

"We don't howl over any werewolf. That only gets you a reputation as a piece of tail."

Jolene studied her painted fingernails. "Well then, I guess you know all about his den then, don't you? And have Papa's blessing?"

When she looked up, she gave Ali a "gotcha" look.

Ali pulled her sweater over her head and then brushed out her hair. Bending down she pushed items out of the way in the cabinets under the sink until she found the hair dryer.

"His den is in Prince George. He's visiting our pack and helping a littermate settle into his den. Satisfied, smarty pants?"

Ali turned on the hair dryer, aiming it at Jolene and blowing away the smell of her defiant emotions. Jolene turned around, tossing her long blonde hair over her shoulder. Ali could guess she would go outside, if she hadn't been out there already, and flirt with Stone until Ali chased her off.

There was no way she could make her hair dry fast enough. Deciding the damp look would have to do, she straightened her hair with her hand, making a face in the mirror at her streaks of red, a gift from her birth sire, a werewolf who hadn't managed to stay around long enough for her to get to know him.

Wiping the steam from the bathroom mirror with her hand so she could see better, she stared at herself in the bathroom mirror. Her sweater hugged her too-large breasts, and her nipples puckered against the fabric while she watched. Stone would definitely like the view. Turning so she could see how her black jeans, her favorite color, hugged her hips and ass, she decided her attire would have to do.

Stone had probably had his fill of her littermates by now.

Hurrying out her front door, she groaned when she saw the youngest of their littermates, Joseph, jumping up and down on the bed of the truck. Jolene and Janie Lynn grinned and fought to out-flirt each other as they talked at the same time to Stone. Jason noticed her at the same time that Stone did. Her littermate strutted over to her, his tough guy attitude making the air around him spicy…like pepper.

"You'll be home by ten," he informed her, his voice deeper than usual.

"You'll be asleep before I'm home. And you'll keep an eye on your littermates." She patted him on the head, an action she knew he hated, and he dodged the sentimental touch, curling his lip at her.

Ignoring him, she smiled as she approached Stone, more than aware of his powerful gaze taking her in.

"Get Joseph out of the back of the truck," she told her sisters.

Her littermates pranced away from the truck, and Joseph jumped to the ground, running to the house and entering before the others.

Stone placed his hand on her back, his firm touch burning through her sweater as he reached for the passenger door.

"You clean up pretty damned good," he whispered, his breath torturing her flesh, sending chills through her as she climbed into the truck.

He'd pulled away from the curb and turned, heading back toward the center of town without saying anything. She clasped her hands in her lap, and then ran them down her jeans, wishing he would say something. Maybe already he regretted bringing her to her den. Her littermates had probably annoyed him, or reminded him that she was still young enough to live in her sire's den.

"Do you come from a large den?" she asked, desperate to break the silence before she broke out in a nervous sweat.

"I've got two littermates." He turned toward downtown and then slowed when they hit the main road. "My older littermate is a cop in Prince George, and my twin just took a mate and set up his den in the mountains."

"You're a twin?" Just the thought of another *Cariboo lunewulf* as sexy as Stone sent a rush of heat burning through her.

Stone pulled the truck into an empty stall and turned off the truck. "And we've always shared everything."

"Oh really?" she asked, his steady gaze when he turned and looked at her twisting her tummy in knots.

"Oh yes, really." He opened his truck door and then took her hand, forcing her to slide over the seat and get out on his side.

This time when her feet hit the ground, his arm wrapped around her, pressing her against that virile body. He cupped her cheek and then nipped at her lip.

A gasp escaped her, and she stared up at him when his mouth took hers. Demanding and very much in control, he ravished her, his tongue pressing past her lips.

Lust wrapped around them with its rich sweet smell. He nipped at her mouth again while tangling his hand through her damp hair. The slightest taste of blood from her lip sent a rush of raw energy coursing through her. Leaning into him, she wrapped her arms around his neck, suddenly feeling more alive than she had in ages.

He licked at the part of her lip that he'd nipped, growling into her mouth when he tasted her blood. Stone tightened his grip on her, muscles cording through his arm, his strength turning her on as much as his actions. Her breasts smashed against his steel chest, her nipples getting so hard that tingles shot through her straight to her pussy.

A new kind of heat, creating a pressure deep inside her, made her womb quicken and she could hardly breathe.

"Stone," she cried out, and pressed against him until he allowed a few inches of space between them.

There wasn't enough air to breathe that wasn't full of his scent.

"You are hungry," he growled, running his hands over her hair and then gripping her shoulders. "And I can't wait to feed you."

Her stomach twisted in anticipation. Ali had taken on more than she could chew. At that moment, while her heart started racing in her chest, she knew there was no turning back. If she wanted to see this through, she had to be strong, not let him smell her hesitation.

And she did want to see this through.

She made a show of looking around her. "Where are we going to eat?"

There was no doubt in her mind that a restaurant was not what Stone had in mind when he told her he couldn't wait to feed her.

Stone tapped her nose and then let his finger stroke down to her chin, and then down her snug sweater. Creating a line that ran between her breasts, his finger stopped at her stomach. For the life of her, she couldn't look away from him. His alluring touch sizzled through her, sending her insides into bursting flames.

"You wanted something nice," he told her, his mouth turning up slightly as if he found her request amusing.

She didn't smell amusement on him though.

Sliding his hand around her, placing it on the small of her back, he led her down the sidewalk to the well-known steakhouse in Banff.

Pushing open the large wooden door to the restaurant, he allowed her to enter. Instantly her tummy growled at the rich scent of steaks cooking on the grill. The lighting was dimmed, and the service outstanding. Ali couldn't remember when she'd last had such an awesome treat.

"Are you old enough to drink?" Stone asked her after glancing at the menu for a moment.

"I'm twenty-two." She wrinkled her brow, taking the blow personally. "How old did you think I was?"

"Young." He showed no sign that he knew he'd offended her but scanned the menu further and then looked up when the waiter approached. "Two steaks, rare. Baked potatoes. I'll have a beer and bring the lady a glass of wine."

He answered the waiter's questions and Ali just stared at him. Not once did he ask her what she wanted.

"Do you always order for your dates?" she asked, after the waiter left.

"Not always."

"I do know how to think for myself." She wouldn't have him thinking just because she was young that she couldn't think for herself.

"I'm aware of that. The challenge is to let go and allow me to lead." He leaned forward, taking her hand in his. "Do you think you can do that?"

The tips of his fingers scraped over her flesh, lust mingling in the air with anticipation mixed with the slight edge of fear. Goose bumps raced over her skin, while she stared into those strong blue eyes.

"Why would you want to control me?" she managed to ask, although her mouth was suddenly parched.

The waiter brought their drinks, and Stone released her hand, glancing at the human but then returning his attention to her.

"Try your wine," he said instead of answering her.

She sipped, the smooth alcohol barely taking away the dryness in her mouth. Another sip and she felt better as the light vapors slowly moved through her, helping her to relax.

"It's good," she said, and meant it. "But you didn't answer my question."

Stone took a long slow swallow of his beer, the hops filling the air with their sweet aroma. When he licked his lips her pussy swelled, the act more enticing than she expected it to be. Heat rushed through her and she sipped again at her wine, enjoying the smooth, almost sweet, taste.

"You asked the wrong question." He took her wineglass from her hand, his fingertips once again scraping over her flesh, sending fire rushing through her.

"What is the right question?" He was confusing her.

The tip of his mouth rose, again that half-smile snagging her insides, putting her on the defensive and curious to know more at the same time.

"There is a difference in being controlled, and submitting to trust." Stone leaned back against the bench seat on his side of the booth.

His long legs stretched under the table, brushing against the outside of her jeans. She moved her legs, unable to resist rubbing against his legs. His blue eyes lightened, the slightest slivers of silver streaking through them while she watched.

"You think I'm the one who needs taming, wolf-man?" she whispered, a sudden rush of daring surging through her. "When's the last time you submitted to trust?"

His eyebrow shot up, and she fought to hold on to her bravery. His look reminded her of how her sire or one of his friends might react to one of her questions — an almost reprimanding look.

The waiter showed up carrying a large tray and placed their food in front of them, agreed to bring more drinks, and then left.

"Enjoy your meal." He never answered her question, but instead unwrapped his silverware from the cloth napkin. His eyes still glowed with a silver hue when he gestured at her with his fork. "After we eat, we shall see how well you trust."

Chapter Three

ಬಿ

Stone slowed down when the truck hit a tight curve in the narrow mountain road. Ali's scent had grown stronger since they left the restaurant, so sweet and enticing it was making it hard for him to think.

She kept quiet once they'd started their trek into the mountains. He reminded himself it was this little bitch who'd come on to him, flirted with him, and asked him to show her a good time.

Well, he was going to do just that.

They pulled in front of the den that his littermate Gabe and his mate would be returning to in the next week or so. A small cabin, but solid—he'd help build it himself.

"Is this where you've been staying?" Ali looked out the windows into the darkness around them.

Only headlights offered a glimpse of the mountainous surroundings around them. Stone put the truck into park, and then cut the light, blanketing them in darkness.

She reached for him before he could take her hand.

"You aren't scared, are you?"

"Of course not," she snapped quickly.

He pulled her out his side of the truck, smelling her hesitation and fear mixed with her curiosity. Allowing the change to creep through him just enough to heighten his senses, he stared down at the pretty little bitch who looked wide-eyed around her.

"We can leave our clothes in the cabin and then enjoy a good run. You been up this mountain before?" he asked her, folding her soft little hand into his.

"With my den, a few times." Her pace was slow at first, but then it was as if she gained sudden conviction and took longer strides.

She reached the cabin first, looking up at him with a playful smile when he unlocked the door. Her hesitation had faded. The spark in her faded blue eyes, with hints of silver, matched her sudden change in scent.

"You were afraid and now you aren't?" he asked, watching her enter the dark living room.

He hadn't planned on returning to the cabin, and had put everything in order so it would be ready for Gabe and his mate when they returned home. There wasn't any reason to start a fire at this point. After a good run, they would be plenty warm. And fucking the shit out of her sweet little ass would definitely keep the chill away.

She turned around in the dark room, looking like she couldn't decide whether to cross her arms or leave them at her side.

"I was never afraid," she told him defiantly, her chin sticking out adorably with a stubborn look.

"Then you trust me," he said quietly, moving toward her slowly.

He ran his hands down the side of her head, tangling his fingers in her hair and then tugging.

"Why shouldn't I?" A bit of apprehension swam around her, but her sudden quick breathing when he snapped her head back let him see her lust as well.

"Because my dear sweet little bitch, I can smell your virginity."

She puckered her lips, and made an effort to free herself from his grasp. "You can't smell virginity. Hell, even a cub knows that."

With a quick move he slid his hands down her head and gripped her arms, squeezing them together so her breasts pressed together under her sweater and her nipples hardened.

"Then how many werewolves have you fucked?" he asked, his mouth getting wetter the longer he stared at those large breasts.

She wasn't wearing a bra. He'd noticed that in the restaurant and the knowledge that her breasts were actually that large had him envisioning all kinds of ways he'd like to play with them, torture them sweetly until she cried out his name.

"That, wolf-man, is none of your business."

He let go of her arms, reaching for her sweater and sliding it up her waist. She stiffened for a moment.

"Let me," he whispered.

He had to see her naked, enjoy her for just a minute before they changed into their fur.

She swallowed hard. "Okay. But it's none of your business who I've fucked."

His cock raged to life as he pulled her sweater off and tossed it to the ground. Perfectly ripe breasts, so full and round, with large nipples, dark and hardened to peaks, bounced slightly as he disrobed her.

"You're a virgin," he challenged, cupping her breasts.

She put her hands on her hips as if his touch did nothing for her.

"I am not."

Beyond a doubt, at that moment, he knew she was lying. The pungent smell of it hung in the air as she stared defiantly up at him.

Her breasts were larger than his hands. He wrapped his fingers around them, tugging, pulling them upward toward him. Her nipples teased him ruthlessly, pointing straight up at him as he squeezed her plump flesh. He about drooled as she reached out, grabbing his arms, and let out a cry.

The emotions between them changed so drastically that the rich sweet smell of lust made his head spin. Every muscle in him hardened as something more carnal swept over him.

"Part of letting go and trusting is knowing that I'll know the truth once I enter you." He didn't give her time to let his comment sink in.

More than anything he had to taste her, suck those nipples, feel her climax while she stood before him half-dressed.

"Oh shit," she almost screamed when he raked his teeth over her nipples, and then suckled one of them into his mouth.

Her fingernails dug into the flesh on his arms when he ran his tongue over the hard, puckered flesh, his fingers stroking those large mounds. Moving quickly to the other nipple, he nibbled and sucked on it, wanting more than anything to pound his cock deep into her tight little cunt.

The little bitch could barely handle what he did to her. Her body quivered while she held on to his arms for dear life.

"Stone. My God. What are you doing?" She almost collapsed against him, but instead stumbled, crying out as he made her come.

Never had an orgasm smelled so sweet, so fresh. His saucy little bitch might not have any intention of teasing him but he knew now she had never experienced what he'd just offered her.

Straightening, he looked down at her flushed cheeks, her hair that stood more on end than it had moments before, her teeth, which had grown enough to press against her sweet mouth. She gasped for breath, staring up at him as if he'd performed some feat never accomplished before.

Well, if no werewolf had ever made her come before, it was because she hadn't allowed it.

He let go of her, backing up and pulling his shirt over his head. Best to get out of his clothes before his muscles grew to the point where they would tear from his body.

"Let that be your first lesson in letting go," he told her, tossing his own shirt over hers and then reaching for the top button on his jeans.

She frowned at him, but didn't say anything. He knew she was out of her league with him, a novice who wanted to play with the big bad wolf. He'd go easy on her, but damn if he wouldn't enjoy the ride. After all, he reminded himself again, she was the one who wanted this. He hadn't seduced some virgin out to go on a run without an escort.

By the time he'd pulled off his boots and shed his jeans from his already too muscular body, she stood naked in front of him, holding her arms over her chest to shield the cold.

"I'm going outside. It's too cold to be in our skin." She started the change as she spoke, dropping to all fours before she'd walked through the door.

Stone followed her, watching as her long white tail grew between her legs until she dropped to all fours. Then, allowing the burning pain to surge through him, heighten his senses, he felt his blood boil through his veins. Bones stretched and popped while muscles grew around them. His mind altered, taking on more alert senses, becoming more in tune with his surroundings.

Leaping out of the cabin, he jumped over Ali, making her duck, as the change consumed him, ripping through him with an eager hungry power. The rush of being more alive, more powerful, the other half of the whole of his being taking over, he embraced the night, quickly claiming it his.

He turned and barked at her. *Stay by my side.*

A second look at the foxy little *Cariboo* bitch by his side, her silky white coat glistening with the slightest hints of red, her slender body just a bit more than half his size, and thoughts of running left his mind.

A more primitive instinct, raw and unharnessed, tightened through him, taking over and having him prancing up to her.

Ali lowered her head, baring her teeth as she let out a low growl. *Lead the way, or I will*, she demanded.

Everything inside him demanded he fuck her. And if it weren't for the fact that *Cariboo* were so much more than animals, so much more than human, he wouldn't have been able to stop the urge to take her right there.

Even more in her fur, he smelled her youth, her precious innocence that he wouldn't take on such casual terms. Ali craved adventure, excitement. Like she'd told him when he'd asked, she'd been up the mountain with her den, more than likely hauling her younger littermates along, snapping at their paws to keep them with her and from getting lost.

Ali was a beautiful, sultry bitch, with a fire burning in her to have more, experience more, take on the world. She'd seen him coming and she'd latched on. Stone saw the picture for what it was. And he'd give her that excitement, indulge her with an adventure, but he would have to keep his actions in check, not go too far.

After all, he would thrill her this evening, then be gone tomorrow, back to his life in Prince George. And little sweet bitch Ali would find her perfect werewolf who would lay his kill at her feet.

He let out two harsh barks, once again ordering her to stay close, and then leapt forward, allowing the pent-up energy inside him to burn free as he raced up the mountain. Ali did her best to keep up, managing with her shorter legs to almost match him as they jumped over rocks and ran around thick droves of trees.

The night belonged to them, thick and rich with smells of the trees and animals. The sky blanketed them, thick with stars so bright and close, Stone was sure he could leap into the air and grab one with his teeth.

More than once they let out barks, howling and growling at each other as they relaxed into the run, releasing energy that had built with their brief foreplay and exerting it instead on their run.

He wouldn't let her tire too much though. He had plans for his sweet little bitch once they returned to the cabin.

Ali hesitated when a new scent crept toward them. Slowing and growling, she turned to head down the mountain when Stone realized other *Cariboo lunewulf* were out enjoying a run in the mountains on that clear night.

It didn't surprise him. It was a perfect night for a good run. And he knew there were quite a few *Cariboo* up this way. What did strike him as odd was that Ali apparently didn't want anything to do with them. She'd already turned, hurrying back down the mountain, running away from him, before he realized it.

Damn the little bitch for disobeying him.

He tore through the undergrowth, digging into the ground with long, powerful claws, as he raced to catch up with her. They'd almost reached the cabin again when he burrowed into her, toppling her over. He'd told her to stay by his side, and no matter how brief their encounter, she would obey him while they were together. He would demand it.

Nipping at her fur, burying his teeth into her enough to get her attention, he let out a fierce growl. *Little bitches don't take off running by themselves*, he snapped, letting her see his irritation.

She slid out from underneath him, almost falling the rest of the way toward the clearing where the cabin was. The change surged through her when he would have leapt on her again. But she quickly straightened, standing on two feet now, and hurried into the cabin.

"What the hell was that all about?" he growled, the beast still swarming through his blood and garbling his words when he stormed into the cold cabin.

Ali turned around quickly, putting her hands on her narrow hips while her large nipples pointed at him, making his blood boil even harder.

"Is there a crime in not wanting to see anyone else?" Something crossed over her face, an emotion he couldn't detect.

It fogged the air between them as well, smelling a lot like worry. Stone forced himself to ignore it. They were alone in the cabin. And he hadn't smelled any of the other *Cariboo lunewulf* follow them back down the mountain. Closing the door behind them, he locked it, and then walked toward her.

Ali quickly crossed her arms over her chest, her hesitation more than obvious as her emotions filled the cabin. She was such an open book, an untried bitch who jumped back and forth between willing and unsure. That right there was the main reason he left the young ones alone. He preferred them willing and eager.

Turning on a small lamp on the side table next to the couch, he took her arm, pulling her to him before she could resist.

He impaled her mouth with his tongue, swallowing the gasp that escaped her. For just a few minutes he would enjoy her, relish what she had to offer, and then he would take her home and be done with it.

At first her body was stiff, taken off-guard. But it lasted a mere moment. She relaxed into him and at the same time her taste and smell changed. Those small hands brushed over his arms, gliding against his flesh. Every muscle that she caressed jerked against her, tightening and responding to her touch.

Stretching against him, her breasts pressed against his chest. She went up on her tiptoes, the sweet smell of her pussy drugging him as her legs spread. There was no way he could keep his cock in line. It jumped to attention faster than he could order it to behave, throbbing against her smooth skin.

And then her hands moved down him, between them, until she gripped his shaft, sending all blood rushing through him and making his cock swell to a dangerous point.

"Little bitch," he growled into her mouth.

She responded with a growl of her own, soft and deadly in an alluring innocent way. So fresh, suddenly so willing, she stroked his cock, building the fire that already coursed through him.

"I want you," she whispered, pushing against him.

Suddenly he didn't have the strength to stop her. Somewhere in his fogged sense of reasoning he knew there was a reason he should stop her. But damn it to hell, the way those soft fingers of hers worked magic on him, fondling and caressing him, there was no way he could figure out what that thinking had been.

Stone took a step backwards, pulling her down on top of him as he sat on the couch. Blood pulsed through him with such ferocity that moving forced a bit of reason back into his brain. And as much as he hated for it to end, it made her let go of his cock so he could think straight.

"You don't need some werewolf who's just passing through to take your virginity." That was what he needed to focus on.

There was no way this young bitch, barely grown, with no experience whatsoever, would out-seduce the king of seduction.

Ali slid down him, her skin like silk as she glided down his body, once again setting the fever raging through his body. Going down on her knees between his legs, she grabbed his cock again. Stone let his head fall back. When her mouth wrapped around his swollen cock head, the beast that had barely rested within him suddenly coursed through his blood.

Grabbing her head, tangling her hair around his hands, he thrust upward, her gagging sound the only thing that made him pull back from her sultry heat.

"Mmm," she growled, her tongue lapping at him while her blue eyes glanced up with him.

Streaks of silver coursed through them. At least her teeth were all human. Maybe she had some knowledge on this act. She was damned good at it. His vision blurred when her eyes fluttered shut and she stroked his cock with her lips and tongue.

"You are such a good little bitch. Where did you learn to do that?" He forced himself to keep a gentle grip on her head, allowing her to move up and down on his cock of own will.

She smiled around his shaft but didn't answer. Instead began moving faster, soaking his cock with her mouth while she closed her lips around him. She would suck the life right out of him at this rate, and he wouldn't be able to do a damn thing to stop her.

Every muscle inside him hardened into steel. Blood surged through his veins, while the heat of her mouth traveled throughout him. Pure instinct threatened to consume him. Pull her up and fuck her silly. Satisfy himself and break the agonizing pressure with his release.

He took slow, long breaths. There wasn't enough strength in him to make her stop doing what she was doing. But he wouldn't fuck her like this. It wasn't right. A bitch as young and sweet as she was deserved to be shown the true pleasures of life. Ali deserved to be given the same as what she offered.

"I ache," she whispered against his cock. "I'm throbbing and I know I can't make it go away myself."

Images of her trying only tortured him more.

She crawled up him slowly, climbing him on her hands and knees as if her beast coursed through her, controlling her. She straddled him, allowing her soaked pussy to brush along his shaft. Gripping the couch on either side of him, she looked down at him so that he could see the need burning through her in her fogged gaze.

"Fuck me, Stone. Give me what I need."

He wanted to shake his head, control her and the situation. She had him paralyzed.

"I'm leaving. You won't see me again." He wasn't stopping her though.

Damn it. Where was his strength to stop her?

"Fuck me," she repeated.

His cock throbbed so hard. Every ounce of blood in his body had descended into his shaft. It swelled with more need than he swore he'd ever experienced before. The forbidden fruit was dangling in front of him, caressing against him, holding him prisoner with his own need and lust. And he was just a werewolf.

Ali moved again, positioning her feverish cunt against his cock. And then she lowered herself. Somewhere in the back of his fogged brain he knew he should take over, at least make the positioning less painful for her. He knew he was good-sized, and her small tight cunt would stretch painfully taking him like this.

Ali sank down over him, her soaked pussy swelling around his cock as he entered her. He didn't dare move. Every muscle inside him hardened painfully as he forced himself still. She barely had him in her when she stopped, causing the fever inside him to burn past the boiling point.

Her eyes opened, her lips parting as she took a minute to get accustomed to him being inside her. He had to grab her hips when she pulled up, almost freeing his cock from her heat. He didn't push her back down. Damn it if he didn't want to. But he didn't.

"You don't have to do this." His words sounded foreign even to himself.

Damn her for putting him in this position. Stone wasn't a compassionate lover. He fucked with a vengeance, making his bitches scream for more. Stone was a wild *Cariboo*, a werewolf with a reputation. He fucked them and left them limp, soaked and satisfied, every damn time.

There was no way he could do that to Ali.

"I want this," she whispered, and then lowered herself over him again.

This time she moved faster, taking more of him quickly. Her fingernails dug into his shoulders when she cried out, almost collapsing over him. Her pussy muscles clamped down on him, tearing at the will that burned throughout his body.

He felt her pussy part, the small fragile skin that had been her youth tear free. Digging into the soft flesh of her hips, he lifted her slowly, and then lowered her, managing to create a rhythm for her to follow.

Her breathing came in gasps as she began fucking him, her orgasm filling the air around them with a raw sweet smell.

"More. More. I need more," she cried out. Her soft blonde hair, with its streaks of red, fanned around her flushed face. "Damn it, Stone. Fuck me."

He couldn't bear it any longer. Lifting her quickly, he laid her down on the couch and came over her. Ignoring every thought that struggled to come forth in his brain, he spread her legs open and dived into her tight cunt.

"God. Yes!" She was a bitch starving for cock.

Her slender legs wrapped around him and he rode her as hard as he dared. He didn't hold back, knowing she couldn't take it for long, and barely managed to pull out before his cock swelled, trying to lock inside her. Instead he came all over her flat tummy, watching her grin up at him with a look of intense satisfaction.

Chapter Four

ഇ

Ali shouldn't be doing this. It was the third day she'd trudged up the mountain, working her way to the small cabin isolated among the trees. Every time it was the same thing—an empty den.

It was the same way today. There was no one here.

The cold wind bit at her cheeks, carrying away the frustration that would have lingered around her.

"He told you he was leaving," she chastised herself.

Nonetheless, she couldn't stop the empty pang that made her stomach ache. It should be enough that she'd had an adventure, experienced something she never could have had with any of the local *Cariboo*. Thank God none of them had seen her that night. It wasn't anyone's damn business who she'd run with, or what she'd done. Her pack was pretty tight-knit, though. One word out of one mouth, and every den in Banff would have known sweet little Ali had gone and been a bad little bitch.

Well, she wouldn't have any of that.

Going down the mountain didn't take that long, and she managed to make it to the tavern before her shift started.

Hurrying behind the counter to drop off her purse, a couple at the corner table caught her attention.

It was Stone!

Her mouth went dry. At the same time her heart started pounding too hard. She couldn't think. She couldn't move.

And then she almost puked when he took the hand of bitch sitting across from him and nibbled on her finger.

"How dare he," she hissed under her breath.

Grabbing her order pad, she'd stalked up to the two of them, ready to scratch the bitch's eyes out. The couple looked up at her, their expressions relaxed and friendly.

Wait a minute.

Something wasn't right.

It wasn't Stone.

Ali knew she was staring, her mouth hanging open. She forced a breath, suddenly panicking that she was about to make a complete fool out of herself.

Holy shit!

Stone had told her that he had a twin. The twin had moved here to take a mate. The cabin she'd fucked Stone in was their den.

"What can I get you?" She knew her voice had to sound shaky.

Taking their order to memory—there was no way her trembling fingers could write down a thing—she hurried away from the table.

"Someone get out of line?" Cook asked, his scratchy voice matching his unshaven whiskers and abrupt manner. "One of those werewolves gets out of line, you just tell me."

"I need two steak sandwiches and fries," she told him, and then managed a smile. "And I'm fine."

She was anything but fine. Her hands still shook when she carried their drinks out to them.

"Your food should be out soon," she told Stone's twin, aching to say more, needing to know more.

Like where is your littermate? Did he go back to Prince George? How do I find him?

"I haven't eaten here in forever," the bitch said, grabbing Ali's attention. "I remember it being really good and told Gabe we just had to eat here."

The first thing Ali noticed was that the young bitch couldn't be that much different in age than she was. And Stone had accused her of being too young.

"Cook does a good job." She relaxed, the smile on the pretty young bitch putting Ali at ease. "But I haven't seen you around here. Should we know each other?"

"My den is pretty small." The bitch lowered her voice. Humans might know about werewolves, but none of them spoke that openly in public. It was just how they'd all been raised since cubs. "But I grew up in the mountains."

She smiled at her mate, squeezing his hand. "And now I have a den of my own."

"Well, I'm Alicia Bastien. Everyone calls me Ali." She didn't make it a habit of introducing herself to every pack member that strolled through the door. These two were her only connection to the werewolf she couldn't get out of her mind though.

"Hi, Ali. I'm Pamela and this is Gabe."

The tavern door opened then, gusts of chilled wind wrapping around her legs, as several others entered the place. Ali smiled at the two of them, forcing herself not to look too long at Gabe, even though she ached to note the similarities and differences between him and Stone. She didn't need some bitch challenging her for looking at her mate wrong.

"I'll have your food to you shortly," she promised them, and then forced herself to focus on her work.

By the time Cook had their food up, Ali was too busy serving drinks and meals to half the pack. All she had time to do was deliver their plates, and check on them once again before they were done. She watched them bring up their ticket, pay at the register, and then walk out the door, holding hands.

Damn it. She wanted the happiness that swelled around those two.

"I'll be right back," she told the other waitress before she could stop herself.

She didn't have a clue what she would say to them as she rushed out the door.

"Wait," she yelled, embarrassment already causing her cheeks to burn.

Pamela brushed her long blonde hair from her face when she turned around, her expression showing her concern.

"We paid our bill," Pamela said.

Gabe took his mate's arm, but smiled at Ali. "Let me guess. I remind you of someone."

Flustered embarrassment coursed through Ali so hard her mouth went dry. The smell of her awkwardness only made the matter worse.

"Never mind," she muttered, hating that she'd just made a complete ass out of herself.

"Oh my God," Pamela suddenly grinned like she'd just figured out a good joke.

That only made it worse. The joke was on Ali. She took an awkward step backwards, clutching her stomach, which had twisted into knots. Why couldn't she just leave well enough alone?

"You told me stuff like this used to happen to you and Stone." Pamela continued grinning as she looked at Ali. "Is that why you pranced up to me as if you were ready to challenge me in my skin?"

Now Ali would die for sure. Her humiliation soured the air around them. She looked from Pamela to her mate, Gabe. Soft red streaks ran through his blonde hair, something she hadn't noticed inside the dimly lit tavern. Stone was obviously the better-looking of the twins.

"I'm sorry," she mumbled. "I didn't mean to…"

Pamela let go of her mate, and touched Ali's hand, her fingers cool against Ali's flesh.

"Were you looking for Stone?"

"I…um…no. He's gone." If she didn't get away from these two soon, she would break down in tears.

Dear God. Could the embarrassment of this get any worse? This was part of Stone's den. They didn't need to see her like this.

Pamela nodded. "He went back to Prince George. You know that, don't you?"

Ali nodded. Her breaths came too fast. She had to get a grip. It was bad enough that they'd smelled her embarrassment. She'd be damned if they saw her as weak too. They could mention this to Stone, and she wouldn't have them telling him she was howling for him.

"Let him know Ali says hi if you talk to him." She straightened, managing a smile. "I need to get back to work."

"We'll be sure and do that." Pamela cuddled into Gabe, and the two of them left her, heading toward the truck that Stone had picked her up in on their one date.

She watched them walk away, once again catching herself comparing notes as Gabe helped Pamela into the truck. He was the same size as Stone, walked just like Stone, but his manner was different. He treated Pamela like a delicate flower. Stone was more rough, and a hell of a lot sexier.

Gabe turned and looked at her before climbing into the truck. The side of his mouth curved, just the way Stone's did. It was a cocky smile, a knowing smile. Embarrassment flushed through her again.

We share everything. The one comment Stone had made about his twin rushed through her without bidding. She covered her feverish cheeks with her hands, knowing they had to be glowing with the redness of her embarrassment. Turning, she hurried back into the tavern.

The house was quiet when she sat up quickly in bed later that night. Dreams, so vivid, still tormented her thoughts. Her teeth pressed against her lips. She brushed damp strands of hair from her face, her skin damp from a cool sweat that clung to her skin.

Everything she dreamed seemed so real. Stone, right there, touching her, caressing her. Damn it if her pussy didn't still feel stretched from his fingers.

Collapsing against her pillows, she let out an exasperated sigh. "This has got to stop," she commanded her thoughts.

Which didn't do a damn bit of good.

Stone's image, his sexy bare chest, muscles rippling against flesh covered with the perfect amount of chest hair, was branded into her mind's eye.

"What have you done to me?" she whispered, staring at the image conjured from her mind. "You won't leave me alone."

Or maybe it was that she wouldn't let him go.

Kicking her feet out from under the warmth of her blankets, the cold floor woke her up quickly.

Her long white cotton nightgown flowed around her as she left her bedroom, padding down the hallway while her den slept soundly in their bedrooms. Murmurs came from her parents' room and she hurried past their closed door, wondering if she'd ever find the happiness those two had.

Hurrying down the stairs, praying her sire was too occupied with her mother to hear her, she walked through the house as quietly as she could. Her senses were acute, aware of every creaking board, of every branch brushing against the house outside, of every breath her sleeping littermates took.

The wall phone hung in the kitchen, its cord twisted, hanging halfway to the floor. She touched the cold plastic, aching for the days when she could call one of her girlfriends, unload on them, talk out her problems until they didn't seem that big of a deal anymore. Or order a quick posse, round several of the bitches up in her pack for a quick run. Those had been the days when she and her friends would sneak out, enjoying the mountains and running neck and neck, barking and howling, daring anyone to find them.

Of course they scattered and hid at the first sight of any pack members. Running without an escort was seriously frowned on, primarily for unmated bitches.

And now all of your girlfriends are mated bitches, sleeping soundly, cuddled next to their mates.

Ali let out a sigh, leaning against the hard wall next to the phone. She turned and stared at the back door. If her sire found out she left alone during the night, she'd need a damn good story as to why she'd been out. And she absolutely sucked at lying.

Especially when she could smell her own lust still lingering on her. She'd never fucked a man before, and Stone had shown her a world she just didn't want to let go of.

Her thoughts lingered again on her dream—his hands had been all over her, rough and unrelenting, ripping her clothes from her body. There had been no words—there was no need for them.

She pressed her palms against the wall, dwelling on how she'd run her fingers over his bulging muscles, feeling the rapid pulse of his heart throb through her. His breath scorched her skin as he licked and nipped at her neck.

Ali touched herself, swearing her skin still tingled from his mouth. He'd scraped his teeth over her flesh, slightly sharp from the raw energy that pulsed through him, until he'd reached the top of her nightgown. Grabbing the thin material in his mouth, he'd yanked back, hard and fast, tearing the gown from her body.

She sucked in a breath a bit too loud, and then looked quickly around the quiet kitchen, focusing her attention on the hallway. For a moment she held her breath, listening to the quiet of the den. It would be hard to explain why she stood against the wall of her kitchen, panting while she filled the room with the smells of her cravings for a *Cariboo* who'd given her the best night of her life, and now was gone.

After three days, did he still think about her?

Ali shook her head, rubbing her forehead. This was unbelievable. What kind of stupid pup was she? Stone probably fucked a different bitch every night, entertaining every single bitch in his pack with dreams that he would pick her to be his mate. He led them all on a leash, and now he'd added her to his flock of aching women.

She focused again on the back door, sniffing out the scents of the trees, the dew on the grass, the fresh cold breeze that came down the mountains. Chewing on her lip until she tasted her own blood, her stomach churned at the thought that she didn't even have the nerve to walk through that door. The wrath of her sire, even though she was a grown bitch, was more than she could handle.

There was no way she could take on a worldly *Cariboo* like Stone McAllister.

And why did she want to take him on? Dear God. She didn't know anything about the werewolf other than he had given her the time of her life.

Fisting her hands, she hit the wall on either side of her, then paced the length of the kitchen. Her ears tickled annoyingly when whispers from upstairs grabbed her attention.

Damn it.

She paced the length of the kitchen again, knowing it wouldn't be hard to explain why she was in the kitchen—unable to sleep, wanting a late night snack, there were many believable reasons.

Footsteps sounded in the upstairs hallway, her mother's gentle steps, concern and curiosity that one of her cubs wasn't sleeping.

A cry from the far bedroom, her youngest littermate, letting out a yelp from a dream, distracted her mother. Then Ali heard the quiet reassuring tones that had often lulled her back to sleep as her mother went to soothe little Joseph. Taking advantage of the distraction, she hurried back up the stairs, slipping into her own room before her mother or sire appeared in the hallway.

Morning came too soon. Ali pulled her legs to her chest to avoid being trampled when Joseph leapt onto her bed.

"Wake up, Ali. You've got to see what we've got!" He leapt off the bed just as quickly, racing out of her bedroom, his small feet managing to sound like a pack of werewolves as he raced to the stairs.

She sat up, combing her hair with her fingers while sniffing the air. The usual morning smells, soap from showers, coffee brewing, anxious and eager emotions as her littermates hurried to start their days, slowly drifted into her room.

Would Stone be waking up alone? Did he have some bitch from his pack sleeping next to him as he stirred? Or was she already out of bed, hurrying to leave or possibly making him breakfast?

She gritted her teeth, the thought of him touching another bitch the way he had her making her bones harden throughout her body. Somehow she needed to get him out of her head.

No matter how cold she made the shower, the fever inside her didn't subside. She ached to feel Stone touching her again, grabbing her and making her do what he wanted. It ate her alive that no matter what she did, it made her think of him. Running the soap over her body, feeling the water pelt her breasts, ignited the ache in her that wouldn't die.

Thoughts of him standing in the shower with her, his hard body crushed against her backside while he pulled her hair, forced her hair back and enjoyed the view of her breasts while sudsy water rushed over them. Her pussy creamed with fresh desire as she arched into the water and rinsed her body.

"It's about time you joined the living." Audry Bastien walked through the back door into the kitchen and took Ali's hand. "Come outside and see what we have."

Ali yearned for coffee, but allowed her mother to lead her out to the backyard. The morning chill still hung in the air and dew clung to her shoes, seeping through to dampen her feet. She let go of her mother's hand and wrapped her arms around her waist.

"Dad, what have you done?" She couldn't help smiling as her father puffed out his chest and winked at her.

"I bought your mother a house on wheels, my dear. What do you think?" Her father's pride filled the air around them.

Ali stared at the trailer that had been backed into the driveway attached to his truck. Long, with several windows, and a door that was already open. Her sisters appeared in the doorway talking at the same time.

"Where are we going?"

"When are we leaving?"

Both Janie Lynn and Jolene spoke at the same time.

Another car pulled into the driveway, popping gravel grabbing Ali's attention. Two *Cariboo lunewulf* hopped out of the pale blue pickup truck. Ali's heart swelled to her throat making it hard to catch her breath. It was the truck Stone had driven. His twin, Gabe, strolled into the yard with Mickey Reginald sauntering by his side.

Mickey worked with her father building houses and had flirted with Ali in the past. Ali let her gaze travel down him, wondering what she'd ever seen in Mickey. He didn't hold a flame to Stone, and looked measly walking alongside Gabe.

"Welcome to our den." Ali's sire walked over to the two werewolves, extending his hand to Gabe McAllister. "I'm Jonathan Bastien."

"Gabe McAllister." He shook hands with her sire, and after releasing his hand, nodded to Ali and her mother.

She gave silent thanks that Gabe gave no indication that he'd met her before.

Ali's mother moved to stand next to her father. The excitement in the yard over the new mobile home diminishing as her littermates congregated around their parents.

"Sorry to bother your den so early in the morning." Mickey smiled at Ali, looking anything but sorry to be strolling into their yard. "I knew we had several contracts lined up, and Gabe here has experience. If you approve, we'll add him to the crew."

"You new to the pack?" Jonathan asked.

"Yup. Moved here from Prince George. Pamela Bordeaux is my new mate. We have a den up the mountain," Gabe informed him, his attention solely on Jonathan, showing his respect.

Her sire nodded, rubbing the whiskers on his chin as he studied Gabe. "I heard about that mating. Bit of a scandal around it, from what I hear tell."

"Pack gossip is exaggerated," Gabe said lightly.

Ali had heard how Pamela had run away from the mating her den had wanted, and then came back to the pack with Gabe on her heels. It had been such a romantic tale. She wondered if the craving to mate with a bitch ran thick through his den. Blinking, she frowned, turning her attention to her littermates who ran in and out of the mobile home. Stone wouldn't come sniffing after her after just one night of hot passion. She was too much of a realist to believe that.

"Gabe worked for a lumber mill back in Prince George," Mickey was saying.

He caught her attention and winked slyly before turning his attention back to her sire. Ali hated how he flirted with her so openly in front of her den, as if he already had her sire's approval or something.

Ali licked her lips, looking away from Mickey and glancing at Gabe. He looked so much like Stone, everything inside her ached to see his twin again.

"Paul down at the lumberyard told us you bought this trailer, asked us to stop by to help you measure for the new furniture you wanted inside it." Gabe glanced her way as he spoke, letting his gaze stroll down her.

Fire burned through Ali. She frowned and looked down at her feet. This wasn't right. She shouldn't feel anything from a mated werewolf.

Her sire started talking to the two werewolves about what his plans were for his new mobile home. The energy generating from everyone so early in the morning was too much for Ali. She needed coffee.

"Come help me get food ready," her mother said, taking her arm.

"Why did you buy the mobile home?" Ali asked her mother once they were alone in the kitchen.

"Your father thought it would be fun to do some traveling. All of you are getting older now, and traveling in a car to different packs would be cumbersome." Audry tucked a strand of hair behind her ear. "Besides, when he did the siding for the Millers, they couldn't pay for all the supplies. He got the mobile home in trade for labor."

Audry's once-blonde hair now streaked with gray, although her face still showed her youth in spite of all the cubs she'd birthed. Her blue eyes glowed as she spoke.

"Sounds like Dad," Ali said, pouring much-needed coffee into a mug then inhaling the rich scent of the hot brew as she turned to look out the back door.

"He's a good werewolf, always there for the pack." Audry didn't need to tell Ali that. She knew her sire had strong values.

And he'd given them to her too. He really had. Taking a quick sip from her cup, and then a bigger drink, she held the mug to her lips while watching Gabe's back. The werewolf reminded her too damned much of Stone. Just an inch or two taller than Mickey or her sire, muscles fine-tuned enough to stand out as stronger, bigger, tougher. Stone's appealing qualities were just as well-defined in his twin.

Damn it. Where were those redeeming qualities that were supposed to run through her bloodline?

She turned from the back door, sipping again at her coffee.

"Where would we go?" Thoughts of traveling to Prince George sounded damn appealing at the moment.

The back door opened and Janie Lynn skipped into the kitchen. "Mickey is asking Dad if he can take you out Friday night."

"No!" Ali snapped at her younger sister before she could stop herself. "I can't go out with him."

Mother and sister grew very quiet, both of them staring at Ali. She shook her head, turning away from both of them.

"Without making a scene," her mother began, using the tone she only used when what she had to say was very important, "go tell your father that Ali can't go out Friday night."

"Yes, Mother." Janie Lynn skipped back out of the kitchen, letting the door slam behind her.

Ali turned toward the coffee. Suddenly she desperately needed another cup.

"Is there something you want to talk about?" her mother asked.

Ali shook her head, not having a clue how she would bring up Stone to her mother. It wasn't like she could tell her that she allowed a werewolf who was just passing through to take her virginity, that she couldn't get him out of her head. And oh, by the way, his twin was out in the yard talking to her sire.

No. She couldn't say any of that.

"You were up last night. If I didn't know better I'd say you were howling after some werewolf. But since no one has come sniffing around, I'm clueless as to who it would be."

Ali turned, staring her mother in the eyes. She prayed she would have half her mother's perception when she finally birthed cubs.

"Mom. What would you say if I told you that I wanted to go to Prince George?"

Her mother puckered her lips, staring at Ali. She let out a sigh when she wasn't immediately accused of having lost her mind.

"Chasing after some werewolf?" her mother asked.

"Not exactly. How about if we call it a change in scenery?" Ali knew her mother wouldn't let her off the hook that easily.

"Tell me his name," her mother demanded.

"Stone. Stone McAllister. I met him at the tavern and he went back to his home pack."

"He's called for you?" her mother asked.

"No. Not exactly." Ali walked over to the back door, her attention immediately going to Gabe who had his back to her and was talking to her sire.

He had the same body as Stone's, large and so damned muscular. His broad back muscles tapered into a narrow waist and thick hips with tight buns of steel. It wasn't right to stare at a mated werewolf, but she wasn't really staring at Gabe. Her mind was envisioning Stone, and her body was screaming for him.

"I have to go, Mom." Just bringing it up to her mother made her realize how desperately true that was. "I can't sleep and I can't think. I have to go after him."

Her mother shook her head. "Lord knows how I chased down your sire." She shook her head, a sad smile appearing on her face. "I'm not sure we'll be able to talk your sire into permitting it though."

"There's got to be a way." Ali opened the back door, taking a deep breath of the cold morning mountain air and heading back over toward the werewolves.

"Someone's a lot more perky with a bit of caffeine in her," Mickey teased, ruffling her hair when she walked up to stand between her sisters.

"Hands off," she snapped, curling her lip at him. "I'll get a lot more than perky if you touch me again."

Mickey straightened, his ego obviously bruised. Ali didn't care.

Her sire was inside the mobile home and Ali decided it was time for her to take a look at the inside too. Stepping into the small living area, she was immediately drowned with the smell of male werewolf. Gabe and her sire stretched, reaching into a small hole in the ceiling while they fiddled with the wiring of one of the lights.

She wondered if Stone had the same skills, and somehow imagined that he did, capable of building and maintaining a den just like her sire and his twin. She let her eyes glide down Gabe, flat, hard abs visible against his close-fitting T-shirt. Well-worn jeans hugged muscular legs. Her mouth went dry, and she averted her eyes, a weird twisting in her stomach unnerving her. She had to quit staring at him.

God willing, her sire wouldn't have him working around here at their den. She would have to leave right away.

"This isn't so bad," she said, glancing around the simple mobile home.

Her sire grinned at her, lowering his arms and reaching for his toolbox. "Well, it looks good on the outside, but there's some things needing fixing inside."

Gabe straightened as well, pulling his shirt down and taking his time looking at her while her sire was busy sorting through tools.

"It wouldn't take too much time to build new furniture and cabinets." Gabe ran his hand over the cabinets above the built-in table. "My littermate and I worked at a lumber mill outside Prince George for a number of years. He's still there now. A project like this is pretty simple."

He never took his gaze off hers when he spoke. Ali suddenly couldn't breathe. Stone worked at a lumber mill outside Prince George. Gabe's scent suddenly seemed stronger, more rich, intense. When he winked at her, heat flushed through her, making her feel like a pup.

She scowled, crossing her arms over her chest. "If this is such an easy job, why don't you fix it up for us then?"

When he smiled, she almost believed Stone stood in front of her. She would absolutely go nuts with him working in her yard fixing up this damn trailer.

Audry called for Jonathan from outside and her sire walked over to the door. He stepped outside, although Ali smelled that he was just outside the door without looking. Gabe stepped closer to her, that crooked grin making her heart race in her chest.

"I talked to Stone about you last night," he whispered.

Chapter Five

෨

Stone navigated the huge flatbed truck into the lumberyard. The yard was a lot smaller than the one in Prince George. Mountains surrounded him as he jumped out of the truck. The fresh cold air filled his lungs, clean and crisp, reviving his brain. It had been a long drive.

Gabe walked up to him with a large, stocky werewolf at his side. The older man had gray whiskers and clear blue eyes. For an older *Cariboo lunewulf* he appeared in good shape.

Stone already knew who he was.

"You must be Jonathan Bastien." Stone held out his hand.

"Amazing." The older werewolf chuckled. "There are two of you."

"I'm the hardworking one." Stone grinned in return.

"Good. Then you won't need our help unloading," Gabe countered, which caused Bastien to break out into a deep laugh.

"Well, working with you two should prove interesting." He turned his attention to the load of wood that Stone had been asked to bring out.

Stone knew the *Cariboo* got a damned good deal on his supplies. Offering to bring the load out here had saved Bastien a pretty penny as well. But taking care of the sire of Ali had nothing to do with anything. Stone would make sure any *Cariboo* got the best deal.

It had been several days since Stone first talked to Gabe. After returning to Prince George, he'd dived into work, pulling long hours and spending nights in his fur running off pent-up energy. When Gabe and Pamela first called, telling them about their encounter with Ali, it had been all he could do not to return to Banff that day.

But he wouldn't go running across the country after some bitch. There were plenty of bitches in Prince George who wanted him. Sooner or later he would find one who would take his mind off that little spitfire.

Driving out here had nothing to do with Ali.

No matter that he'd never found himself comparing one bitch to another before meeting the young bitch. Each lady he'd met in the past had something intriguing about her. And Stone had always enjoyed finding that particular quality in each and every one of them.

Until recently.

And it was making him damn grouchy.

Somehow, returning to Banff had lifted his spirits. Just being around Gabe again had them both cracking jokes, laughing while they went through the inventory list confirming everything Jonathan had ordered was on the truck. The usually mundane job didn't bother him today.

Gabe and Jonathan smelled of sweat and contentment when they were done.

"You'll have to come by the den later," Jonathan told him, giving him a slap on the back when they were done. "Let the mate fix you up a good home-cooked meal before you make the drive back. You've saved me a bundle here. I won't take no for an answer."

Something tightened in Stone's gut. What would Ali do if he walked into her den and showed up to eat their kill?

"Hard to turn down a home-cooked meal." Stone looked at Gabe, saw the concern appear on his twin's face.

The smell of worry surrounded them quickly.

Jonathan misinterpreted what he smelled. "Bring the mate," he told Gabe. "I'll let Audry know we're having a houseful tonight."

Less than an hour later, Pamela ran from their small cabin, jumping into Stone's arms when he climbed out of the truck.

"I knew you couldn't stay away," she said, wrapping her arms around both of them as they walked into the cabin.

Pamela had put her touch on the place since he'd last been there. Colorful curtains hung on the windows, and fresh flowers were in a vase on the table. The place had a happy smell about it. Stone wouldn't be surprised at all to hear that cubs would be on their way soon.

"We've got a dinner invite to the Bastien den tonight," Gabe told Pamela.

Stone stripped out of his shirt, heading for the bathroom for a hot shower. He felt a lecture coming on, or worse yet, questions that he'd refused to answer on the phone. Neither of them sounded appealing.

"All of us?" Pamela asked.

"Yup. Stone, we have a right to know your intentions with Ali before we walk into that den." Gabe's tone matched his smell.

He was ready to defend the little bitch and he didn't even know her.

"There are no intentions so don't go filling the room with aggression." He didn't mean to snap so hard.

By doing so, both Pamela and Gabe raised eyebrows, their moods relaxing although turning curious.

The curiosity stemmed more from Pamela. His littermate knew him all too well to be curious.

"Tell us what you wouldn't tell us on the phone." Pamela's tone softened.

She walked up to him, running her cool small hand up his arm. He looked down into her soft, glowing expression. Her gaze wasn't too unlike Ali's—trusting, content, a good bitch.

Damn it. There he was comparing every bitch he knew to Ali.

He let out a growl which made her smile.

"During those brief moments when she thought Gabe was you at the tavern, she looked ready to bite into me with extended teeth," Pamela teased.

"That does it. I'm not going to their den." Stone turned to march toward the bathroom.

"Damn. That sweet little bitch crawled right under your fur, didn't she, Stone? You going to run from her with your tail between your legs," she taunted.

Stone turned on her, the urge to pounce and shake some sense into Pamela hitting him almost too hard. He glanced at Gabe, who stood silently in the living room. Calm and silent—and watching. Gabe would let his mate say what she wanted. This was her den after all. But Stone was no fool. He'd jump in a second if Stone lunged at her.

"There is nothing to run from," he said through clenched teeth, and stormed into the bathroom.

Coming here had been a mistake. He sensed that already. Granted, he'd been miserable ever since he'd returned to Prince George, but returning to Banff brought him right back to the problem.

Ali was here. That precious little bitch, barely a woman, who'd seduced the pants right off him. Turning on the shower and letting the steam quickly flood the small bathroom, he found little solace in the hard pellets of water when he climbed into the deep tub. No matter how hard he scrubbed, it was the same as it had been since he'd left here, he envisioned Ali.

That one night—restraining so he wouldn't fuck her, and her soft encouraging pleas. Bitches from many different packs had begged him before, seduced him, coerced him into taking them. He'd fucked each one of them, never giving it a thought once he'd left them, panting and satisfied.

Why the hell did it have to be any different with Ali?

He rinsed quickly and then shut the water off.

It didn't have to be any different. And it wouldn't be.

Turning down an invitation to dine at a den was bad manners. He would go, enjoy the food, and then get the hell out of there before the moon rose in the sky. It would do him good to run off some of the energy that had built in him over the past week. Maybe he should just go find the first available bitch and mount her under the stars. That would probably be just the attitude adjustment he needed.

"Well, sure. Don't they all?" Pamela giggled into the phone, lying on the couch when he strolled out to join them.

Gabe was standing over her, looking worried. Something wasn't right in the air. Gabe looked over his way, his gaze brooding, and that confirmed it. Stone adjusted his shirt over his slightly damp torso and moved in closer.

Pamela winked at him. "Blackened steak. Rare. I'm sure of it," she said into the phone. The little bitch looked damned proud of herself as she ran her bare foot over the top of the couch, stretching out nicely in front of the two of them.

Any other time he would have enjoyed the view. Pamela had a damn nice body. But her triumphant air was filling the room, and she didn't seem to mind a bit that both of them focused on her.

"Now you realize, anything you want to know, you can ask me." She'd lowered her tone, sounding suddenly conspiratorial. Then she giggled. "We guessed that you didn't know him that well. But I understand. Sometimes we just get feelings about these things. And of course, you should go with your gut."

Pamela laughed again. She grinned up at the both of them, looking more than pleased with herself at the moment.

"Next to my werewolf, I'd say he's the best out there. Of course I'll help you."

That was it. Stone stalked toward her, realizing at that moment that she was talking to Ali. The two bitches were scheming together and that was all he needed. If Pamela had called Ali, made sure that she knew he was coming, well, he wouldn't hold that against her. But the conversation had turned into a plot. The bitches were laying a trap. And he was the prey.

Gabe straightened, blocking Stone when he would have moved in on Pamela.

"End the conversation." Stone would warn his brother once.

Gabe stared at him for a moment, his gaze not faltering and his expression serious. Finally he turned around, looking down at Pamela.

"Tell her goodbye," he ordered.

Pamela sighed, her fun obviously being brought to an end. "I've got to go, Ali. We'll see you in a couple of hours."

She hung up the phone and jumped off the couch. When she snuggled up at him, he knew he was glaring, everything in him telling him to run, get the hell out of the mountains.

"You're a goner, Stone," she said, giggling, and then pranced around him into Gabe's arms.

"Who called who?" Stone asked, his mood darkening.

"Ali called me." Her hand snaked up Gabe's chest, while her eyes sparkled with humor as she smiled at Stone. "She is such a wonderful bitch, wanted to make sure all of your favorite foods would be there."

Stone envisioned Ali's large den, her littermates running around her while she talked on the phone. More than likely at least one of them would have known she'd called to arrange the menu. If that were the case, her sire or her mother would easily get word of it too. There would be questions. But—what would Ali say as the answer?

If she told her sire that he'd fucked her…

Stone let out a sigh. *Cariboo lunewulf* had some tough laws when it came to their virgins. Gabe picked up on the worry that raced through him.

"You've fucked her, haven't you?" Gabe said, more than asked.

Stone turned away from them, realizing it would only be fair to let them know what they would possibly be walking in on.

"It's worse than that." He ran his hand through his hair, staring through the pretty curtains Pamela had put up and out at the mountainous view outside. "She was a virgin."

"Stone." Pamela breathed his name, her concern sending a chill down his back.

He didn't like Pamela thinking he was less of a werewolf, for any reason.

He turned around, ready to face both of them as they judged him.

"So you fucked this young bitch and then just took off?" Pamela sounded more hurt than anything.

His brother's gaze was hard, his emotions in check, as he stared hard at Stone.

Quickly, he gave them an abridged version of what happened, the story they had wanted over the phone when they'd called earlier that week.

Pamela shook her head. "You're in deep this time. Pack law will be on her side if she even howls a minute about this."

"She's right." Gabe turned, running his hand through his hair the way Stone had just done. "I believe you that she wanted it. And if we were in a larger pack, things might go easier on you."

"We're in the mountains. *Cariboo* are more backwards than any other pack." Pamela crossed her arms over her waist, sincerely looking sorry for him. "You know as well as I do that many of us bitches run with a werewolf or two before we mate. Just don't let the pack find out about it. And here in the mountains…"

"Which is why we left the mountains," Stone interrupted her, and then looked at Gabe.

His twin had come back here for Pamela, to be with her, respect the wishes of her den and make their home here.

So why was Stone here? He didn't have any clearer answer several hours later, when they pulled up in front of the Bastien den. Anyone could have driven that load of supplies out here to Jonathan Bastien. Stone had jumped on the opportunity to come back to Banff. The reasons why didn't come to him easily. The more he dwelled on it, the more it brought a hardening pit to his gut.

The three of them sat in the truck for a moment, Pamela snug between the two of them with a covered dish on her lap. Cars lined both sides of the street, and the Bastien den seemed to be bursting with *Cariboo lunewulf.*

"It's a goddamned pack meeting." Stone didn't give a rat's ass if his mood soured the smell of the truck.

"Sure looks like it." Gabe sounded just as put out.

"Don't you two dare be spoilsports. Get out and show this pack what the McAllister den is made of," Pamela scolded both of them.

A pack of cubs came racing around the side of the house, hollering and carrying on. Several bitches followed in tow. But Stone only noticed one of them.

Ali wore a knit sweater, just as she had when he'd taken her up the mountain. From this distance he could tell she didn't wear a bra. Those large breasts pressed against the knitted fabric, stretching it, accenting how shapely she was. Instead of jeans, she had on a black skirt, with black hose that showed off those long slender legs. Flat black boots finished off the ensemble nicely. She looked sporty, sexy, and like food to a starving man.

He was out of the truck before he had time to think. With several long strides, he reached her, that fresh, sweet appealing scent of hers wrapping around him.

The other bitches with her seemed to disappear. She noticed him, stopped in her tracks, while a slow smile spread across her face.

"Stone," she whispered, when he'd reached her side.

"You look sexy as fucking hell." He reached out, taking a strand of her blonde hair and brushing it away from her face.

Her red highlights captured the gleam from the porch light. His fingers scraped over her cheek before he let his hand drop, reminding himself he was at her den and anyone could be watching.

Ali's blush made her blue eyes glow. "Thanks. You look damn good, too."

He realized then why he hadn't been able to get her off his mind. Ali wasn't like the many bitches he'd run with in the past. She wasn't a slut. The way she blushed when he praised her, then didn't come back with some sexy line added to her appeal.

She nibbled her lip, glancing quickly around her, while her hesitation in speaking brought out her pureness. That was what he liked about Ali. She'd been untouched, unspoiled, and he'd marked her.

He grinned, enjoying her moment of hesitation. "You throw this party for me?"

"Umm. No." She shrugged, drawing his attention to those large breasts of hers.

Suddenly he was hungry, damned hungry. And it wasn't for food.

"My sire decided to invite all the dens over who have werewolves who work for him," she explained, and then offered him an apologetic smile. "I didn't realize it would be this large."

Gabe and Pamela walked past him, both of them giving him sideways glances as several other werewolves surrounded them, leading them toward the backyard.

"The party is mainly out back," she added.

"Even more reason to stay up here with you." He ached to take her away from here, taste her one more time.

Her eyes glowed like sapphires, while lust filled the air between them. "I want to leave with you later," she told him boldly.

Yet another quality that appealed to him. Ali didn't play games. She didn't know how. Her innocence smelled so damned good it was all he could do not to haul her right out of there and fuck her until she screamed.

Damn it. He would have to do that soon.

The scent of another werewolf raised the hairs on the back of his neck. He looked over her shoulder when a *Cariboo* walked up to them, giving him an unsure look.

"Ali?" the *Cariboo* asked, frowning at him before giving Ali his attention. "They're pulling the steaks off the grill. I thought I'd come find you."

Stone got the sudden urge to punch the werewolf in the face. Straggly blond hair fell around his face and his face wasn't shaven. He had buckteeth that would be real easy to straighten with a hard blow to the mouth.

"Stone, this is Mickey Reginald." She placed a hand on his chest, quickly making introductions. "Mickey. This is Stone McAllister."

"I've met your twin. Passing through our pack?" Mickey focused on Ali.

His words had an impact on Ali. She took a step backwards, giving him a worried look while she nibbled her lower lip. If she expected an answer, she wasn't going to get one. Stone wouldn't be pressured into anything, not by her, or by this mangy werewolf.

"Is this your boyfriend?" he asked Ali.

If he sounded a bit bitter, he quickly dismissed it as being indifferent. Seizing his emotions, making sure he didn't litter the air with them, he glanced from her to the mutt.

"Better go get your food," he said before she could answer.

"Stone," Ali cried, running after him when he left her standing with the asshole. "He's nothing to me," she said quietly when she reached his side.

Her small hand on his biceps sent fire rushing through him. She'd used the same quiet tone when she'd begged him to fuck her, to show her pleasures she'd never experienced before. At least he had the satisfaction of knowing she'd never fucked the prick.

"He seems interested in you. Maybe you should go spend time with him." He needed to get out of there. His mood had grown much too sour.

And he knew it wasn't the realization that other *Cariboo* had an interest in her. Hell, he'd be surprised if the entire fucking pack didn't want a good roll in the meadow with her. Stone was no fool. He knew why his mood had turned from bad to worse.

The realization that Ali could make him jealous, make him want to claim her, make her his for her entire fucking pack to know — that didn't sit well with him.

Not one damn bit.

Chapter Six

୫୬

Never had more emotions raced through Ali harder and faster than they did at that moment. Stone was here. He stood right next to her.

Her heart raced. Even the early evening breeze sweeping down the mountain didn't soothe the heat that rushed through her. Damp sweat clung to her body, her palms, in between her breasts. Excitement and nerves made it hard to think straight.

Ali's sire glanced her way more than once. Her littermates, thank God, ran around with their friends and had decided tormenting her this evening wasn't at the top of their list. Only her mother's anxious looks kept her alert, and made her yearn for a way to sneak away with Stone.

He entered the backyard demanding attention. She immediately smelled the curiosity on the other bitches her age. The werewolves gave him a quick once-over, sizing him up, judging whether he was a threat or not. The single werewolves gave him a look of disdain.

As they should. No one here could compete with his magnificence.

If only he weren't being so indifferent toward her. Without as much as a glance her way, he walked over to his twin, joining him and his mate and the other werewolves chatting among them.

"Tell me you don't see something in that werewolf." Mickey was at her side again, his jealousy making him stink.

"He's ten times the werewolf you are," she snarled, glaring at him for being the cause of Stone suddenly ignoring her.

She walked away from Mickey, hoping she made a show of the fact that they were not together. But she had to admit, Stone's sudden change in attitude meant one thing. He was jealous too.

Careful listening earlier had confirmed that Stone had returned to bring a load of supplies for her sire. She'd overheard her sire mention that he'd offer the werewolf work if he was interested. Her sire always needed strong werewolves to help with work needed in the pack. Ali's heart had soared at the thought that Stone could possibly have reason to stay here.

After a week of dreaming about him every night, thinking about him all day long, she knew she needed to go after him. But now he was here. And she'd be damned if she let him slip through her paws again. Somehow she needed to snag the werewolf.

"Hungry?" her sire asked, winking at her as he stood in front of the grill, smelling of smoke and cooked meat.

Ali grabbed two plates, glancing over at Stone who still talked with a group of werewolves in the middle of the yard.

"Making my plate?" Mickey had managed to sneak up behind her.

"Hardly." She turned away from him, holding the plates out to her sire so he could put meat on them. "Make one of them the blackened steaks raw."

"Who is the plate for?" Her sire obliged, plopping two large steaks onto the plates.

"One is for Stone McAllister." She waited for his reaction.

Her sire squinted through the dark yard until he focused on the twins. As if aware he'd been made the object of attention, Stone looked their way. In the dark she swore his blue eyes glowed. He didn't smile, but kept his gaze focused on her sire, as if waiting for judgment to be passed.

"How do you know him?" She smelled the protector coming out in her sire.

"I met him at the tavern, papa. He's a good werewolf."

Her sire grunted. "Take him his plate and then go help your mother."

Her mother didn't need any help. And Ali had no desire to hang out with the bitches, listening to them chatter about cubs and their mates. She wouldn't argue with her sire though. It would get her nowhere.

She balanced the two plates, grabbed silverware, and then took a deep breath. Stone had turned his attention back to the group of werewolves around him. Darkness offered some protection, although she knew more than one curious set of eyes watched her as she took the plate to him.

Someone announced a group run, grabbing everyone's attention in the yard just as she reached Stone.

"Just the way you like it," she whispered, nudging his arm as the others surrounding him turned to holler back in agreement that a run sounded perfect.

"Yes. It is," he said, looking down at her as he took the plate. "Did you lose the prick?"

Ali smiled, enjoying how he didn't want other werewolves around her. "He'd get lost chasing his tail," she told him, which brought out that crooked smile that she'd dreamed about way too many times.

"He seems to know you fairly well. Obviously he doesn't get lost following you around." Stone's brooding stare bored right though her.

Heat swarmed through her so that she could hardly breathe. When she gulped in a breath of air, it tasted like Stone.

"I was born in this pack. We grew up together. You have nothing to worry about."

"Do I look worried?"

No. He looked anything but worried.

"Then you'll run with me tonight?" Her stomach twisted in knots at her boldness.

She had to be with him though. And just thinking about stripping under the stars with him at her side brought her insides to a boiling point. Her pussy throbbed as her gaze dropped, taking him in. More *Cariboo* than should be legal.

Stone laughed. "Your sire isn't going to let you run with me."

Her heart started pounding in her chest. Need rushed through her with enough fierceness that she couldn't think. One thing mattered. She had to be with him—and soon.

"Meet me behind the tavern at one." She bit her lip until it hurt, not daring to look away as he stared down at her.

"The run won't be over by one," he told her, although she smelled lust begin to swarm around him.

She drank in his scent like a starving werewolf. Not even the smell of the steaks between them drowned out the thick, rich smell of his sexuality. If the yard weren't so full of werewolves, she would dare to reach out, run her hand over his shaft. It had to be hard as a rock.

"Meet me there," she repeated, gripping her plate with both hands.

Her palms were so damp she couldn't have managed to tear a piece of the meat off with her fork if she'd tried. Not to mention the nervous flip-flops in her stomach would make eating a task she had no desire to take on at the moment.

"You're biting off more than you can chew, little bitch," he growled, and then gracefully managed to pull his own steak apart with his fork.

Holding the meat up on the fork, he brought it to her lips. Her mouth opened in spite of the fact that steak was the last thing she wanted right now. She watched him as he fed her.

"I wonder how much you can take," he added, and tiny slivers of silver appeared around his pupils.

Somehow she managed to chew and swallow the meat. A growl escaped him when she licked the spices from the meat off her lips. Her breasts swelled, the ache that throbbed throughout her responding to him.

It took her a minute to realize her mother called for her. More than likely warned by her sire that she played with fire. And damn it, she was definitely in the heat. Stone McAllister would burn her alive. And her need for him might take her out just waiting for one in the morning to arrive.

At quarter 'til one, she walked around the quiet building. Most of her pack members raced through the mountains, enjoying the cold night air. Her mother and sire hadn't gone, much to her disappointment. And she thought she'd die waiting for them to go to sleep. If they'd heard her leave the den, they hadn't said anything.

Her heart pounded in her chest so hard it hurt when she walked around to the back of the building. Sucking in the cold night air didn't help any. She stared up at the sky, so black and full of stars. All alone behind the building, nervous anticipation seeped through her. What would she do if he didn't show up?

"Feel like a fucking fool," she grumbled to her self.

Slow, deep breaths did nothing to calm her racing heart. And the lump growing in her throat made it hard to swallow.

"If he doesn't show, you're going to quit thinking about him." She wouldn't be able to handle the humiliation of being stood up.

But damn it. She needed him so bad. Every fiber in her body ached for him. She looked away from the stars. They were hardly distraction enough to keep her from mentally calculating each second, every minute that she stood in the cold, waiting.

Maybe changing, hiding in the bushes and trees, and watching for him that way would be better. A shiver rushed through her as she acknowledged how cold it was.

She jumped when a hand grabbed the back of her neck. Her instincts kicked in and she tried to turn quickly, make her aggressor let go.

He was stronger than she was. "And what have you been taught about running by yourself, little bitch?"

Stone's breath sent heat rushing down her body. His deep baritone made every muscle in her body shiver so that her legs suddenly were too weak. Adrenaline pumped through her from being snuck up on, and at the same time relief washed over her that he hadn't stood her up. Suddenly she was a whirlwind of emotions. They consumed her, making it hard to regain composure now that he was here.

Stone wrapped one hand around the back of her neck and the other hand covered her mouth. He pulled her backwards, pressing his hard body against her backside, his cock raging with hardness and pulsating against her ass.

Now she would surely die from need and being taken off-guard.

"You want something you can't handle," he told her, his tone sharp, almost sounding angry.

As her senses cleared she could smell the wild still on him. The musty smell of his beast mixed with alcohol and the aromas from the outdoors swarmed around her. She tried to turn around, but he wouldn't let her.

"I can fuck bitch after bitch. But you continue to torture my insides." He definitely sounded angry.

Ali struggled, not liking this. Just the thought of him pleasuring another bitch made her insides roar with fury. Putting on a little muscle of her own, she struggled harder under his grasp until he almost pushed her forward.

"And have you?" she snapped as soon as his hand was off her mouth.

"No." His expression was a war of emotions, many that she smelled in the air between them. "And that's probably the problem," he added, his brooding stare dark and predatory.

She straightened her sweater, ready to take him on. Maybe she was a fool, but he should be nicer to her. She hadn't done a damn thing wrong.

"So if I went out and fucked other werewolves, I would quit thinking about you?" She put her hands on her hips, watching as he grew in front of her.

He didn't wear a shirt, and in spite of the cold night air, sweat clung to his body, making it glow under the moonlight. His blond hair had some curl to it, damp from a hard run. Corded muscles rippled under tanned smooth skin. Just staring at him made her mouth go dry. He was right about one thing. She'd taken on more werewolf than she could handle. And the thought of it excited her so much she throbbed with need, with an ache so incredible it made it hard to think straight.

Stone let out a growl, pouncing toward her, grabbing her before she could turn away. Although part of her didn't want to move. She wanted his hands on her, rough or otherwise, she needed him touching her.

"You liked what I gave you so much you're going to turn into a slut, go fuck every werewolf who howls after you?" He lifted her off the ground, giving her a quick shake as he brought their faces close together.

She reached out, grabbing his hair, tugging against his roots as she tried to pull his mouth to hers. "I liked what you gave me so much that I want you to give it to me again."

His arms snaked around her, pulling her against him with such fierceness that all air left her lungs. Stone devoured her mouth. There was nothing gentle about him. His actions, like his body, were hard and rough. And it ignited a fire in her that had simmered for over a week now.

Raw. Hungry. Needy. She took him on with the same aggression he gave her.

Her fingers combed through his hair, tangling in it, feeling the softness of it, which countered the roughness of his actions.

When he let go of her mouth, it took a minute to catch her breath. Panting as she stared into his eyes, seeing the wild *Cariboo* that pulsed through his veins, her heart pattered against his chest.

She brought her legs up, wrapping them around his hips, and rested her arms on his shoulders, staring deep into the soul that had tormented her since she met him.

"What is it about you, Stone McAllister?" she asked.

"You got a taste of something you like." His voice garbled, his teeth pressing against his lips.

"That explains me then. But why did you come?"

She saw the emotions that she had smelled on him since he'd arrived war inside him.

Stone pushed her away. She hit the ground hard, but stabilized quickly. He turned, running his hand through his hair. There was no way he was walking away from her. He'd come to her. She'd seen the need in his eyes. Emotions tore through him that he might not wish to address, but he would, damn it.

Ali leapt at him, her heart swelling painfully when he turned from her. She couldn't bear him walking away, not answering her. She deserved more than that.

"Why, Stone?" She grabbed his arm, feeling his bulging muscles, that raw untamed strength. "You came to me. You came back to Banff. Tell me it's not because you want me."

"Damn it," he roared.

Stone turned on her with an expression so fierce it made her heart stop. Grabbing her arm, he half-lifted her off the ground. Well, if he wanted rough, she had it in her to play that way too.

But when she struggled to be free, he gripped harder, his eyes almost turning silver with the amount of emotion that swarmed through him.

"Don't try and trap me," he told her, his tone almost threatening.

"There is no trap." Her mouth was so dry she could hardly speak. But he wouldn't intimidate her. "What are you afraid of?"

"Nothing. I fear nothing," he told her, then grabbed her ass, his hand moving quickly under her skirt, and ripping at her stockings.

The fibers tore, tiny threads popping as he yanked the stockings from her ass. Cold night air rushed around her cunt and ass, suddenly exposed.

Ali gulped in air, looking at him wide-eyed, so stunned by his quick and fierce action.

"Be sure you don't learn to fear me," he added, doing anything but scaring her.

She guessed he was trying to show her his true nature—that he was too wild to tame. Even in her feverish and lust-filled state she saw that. Instead of revealing his emotions, sharing what was in his heart, he would try and send her running with her tail between her legs.

He was such a damn *Cariboo*.

"Bring it on, wolf-man." She was being too damned brazen.

Playing with fire was an understatement. Already his emotions bordered on hostile. *Cariboo lunewulf* could easily get violent if provoked. Being one of them herself, Ali knew that if you pushed her kind too far, the results were pretty damned ugly.

But even with that slight bit of rational thought seeping through her, she couldn't stop herself. Her own emotions bordered on something too carnal for her human thoughts to accept.

He gripped one arm, but with her free hand she touched him, gliding over bulging muscle and heat from his flesh. Touching him burned her skin, the fever rushing through him bordering on dangerous. But she slid her hand between them and ran it over the bulge in his crotch.

Stone growled, gripping her ass, pulling on her flesh, his fingers moving past her ass and running over the moisture coating her pussy.

Their act was dangerous, bordering on ridiculous. They were in the middle of town, humans everywhere. To be caught by a human would be embarrassing. To be caught by one of her pack would be worse.

Grabbing his cock, staring into those eyes that were almost completely silver, her human thoughts warred with the beast inside her. Her fingers trembled over his swollen shaft, the smell of his need for her making her drunk.

"Why me, Ali?" His voice was hard to understand.

She'd pushed him over the edge. Intense emotions he wouldn't identify, and extreme arousal had all but brought the beast out in him. Ali doubted he would change right here behind the tavern, but he was damned close. Not sure if he would understand her, his human side damn near buried with the beast that threatened to surface at any moment, she had to try anyway.

"Stone. Don't you see? You are the best. And that's all I want. The best." She panted while his fingers stroked her pussy, rubbing her cream over her exposed skin.

He reached for her sweater, letting go of her arm. For a moment she had her freedom. Reasoning with a *Cariboo* could be damned hard under the best of circumstances. Her own mind was in a state of flux, most of her crying out to tear her clothes from her body, demand he mount her and take care of the building urge that had grown over the past week.

"The best, huh," he muttered, and then yanked on her sweater.

The threads threatened to snap. Her clothes would be torn from her, leaving her naked. Already she stood in front of a man who wore no shirt. His muscles bulged under his flesh. She knew his bones craved to pop, to grow and distort so they could hold the weight of the growth threatening him. And if he changed, there would be no stopping him, no outrunning him. He would take her, without question, without reasoning.

His fingers thrust inside her, impaling her. He damned near lifted her off the ground with his hand when he thrust inside her.

Ali howled, her world suddenly tilting to the side as she threw her head back. An orgasm ransacked her body with more intensity than she knew possible. Wave after wave of desire rushed through her.

"Stone," she cried out, reaching for him, gripping his shoulders.

A car driving down the street, the faint sound of its engine as it drove past the building in front of them, brought her to her senses.

If the pack caught her back here with him, the repercussions would be serious. Her sire would demand he mate with her. Stone would be shunned if he didn't speak out for her.

Did she want him?

Oh hell fucking yeah, she did.

But she didn't want him forced into taking her.

And mating with him—well, she would want to know him better first.

"Stone," she said again, sagging into him as her orgasm still trembled through her. "We can't."

"We're going to," he told her, his whisper harsh and intense against her hair.

"Yes." She needed him more than she needed to breathe. "But not here."

"Are you scared of getting caught?" Suddenly he seemed more coherent, more in control than he had a minute ago.

His fingers twisted inside her pussy, stroking her soaked muscles, probing and pushing while she struggled to stand.

"I won't have my pack…" she stopped, panting, unable to catch her breath, "telling you that you have to mate with me."

"Little bitch. You need to learn to let go and trust me." He gripped her chin, while his other hand slipped out of her.

He moved to the front, again reaching under her skirt and sliding his fingers deep inside her.

"Do you trust me?" he asked, his long thick fingers gliding in and out of her.

She barely heard the question. Thick and strong, his fingers worked magic on her, taking away her ability to think.

"Tell me," he said, his hand cupping her chin, forcing her to look up at him.

"Yes. Stone, I trust you."

"Good. Then know I would hear someone before they saw us."

The pressure built inside her again, growing and spreading throughout her. He moved faster, harder, fucking her with his fingers while she dug into his flesh.

"That's it, my little bitch. Come for me."

She had little choice. Everything inside her was about to explode. Staring into his face, his eyes bright with lust and attentive as he studied her, she fought to keep from collapsing.

Speech left her. She panted in front of him, her insides hardening ruthlessly, bones threatening to pop, her heart pounding so hard. He would take everything, draw her life from her and control it with two fingers.

Harder and faster, those two fingers pounded her pussy. His jaw twitched while his teeth clamped together, his lips a straight line while his expression matched the thick lust hanging in the air around them. Her legs were like jelly, wobbly and no longer strong enough to hold her.

Scraping her fingers down his chest, she cried out, everything around her exploding as he made her soak his hand. She felt cum stream from her, coat her inner thighs, its fresh rich smell intoxicating.

Stone growled with enough ferocity that she wondered for a moment if he'd come too.

"You look so fucking hot with your face glowing from coming." That half-smile appeared on his face, and the silver in his eyes faded to blue.

She sucked in her lower lip. Her fingers still clung to him, holding on while her world slowly spun around her.

"I feel like I've just been fucked." Admitting that to him seemed so personal.

But somehow she didn't mind the confession.

"Your pussy is still virginal." He moved his hands, taking her and turning her toward the building. "Let's go. You need a rest before I fuck you."

Before he fucked her. He wasn't taking her home. Ali's heart beat so hard with anticipation that she barely paid attention to where he took her. Every inch of her pulsed with excitement. Her lust filled the cab of the truck. Stone remained silent, his large hands on the steering wheel. Whatever thoughts traipsed through his brain were a mystery to her. She glanced at him several times, adoring his perfect body, and that hard confident expression painted on his face. When they pulled up in front of the small cabin it took her a minute to realize where they were.

The moon cast its light over the trees, accenting them around the small cabin where she'd first fucked Stone. But it was more than being brought back to where she'd first been with him. This was his twin's den. And they were no longer gone. Last time this had seemed like an isolated cabin, somewhat abandoned, and a safe haven to enjoy Stone. Now it was someone's home.

"Where are Gabe and Pamela?" she asked, sudden nervousness making her feel shaky.

Stone opened the truck door, climbing out and grabbing her so that she had to slide across the seat to get out on his side. Blue eyes pierced through her, his look so damned predatory.

"Probably still on the run," he said, his gaze dark and possessive as he looked down at her. "Suddenly you're nervous?" he asked, obviously smelling the change in her scent.

"What if they walk in on us?" she sniffed the air.

For the moment, they were alone.

"Gabe and I don't keep secrets from each other." He pulled her out of the truck so that her feet landed hard on the ground.

He held her hand firmly, leading her to the cabin door and then continuing to hold it when he pushed the door open and took her inside.

We share everything. Remembering what he'd said about his twin didn't help her nerves at the moment.

There was a different air about the place from when she'd been there before. Familiar scents of baking and cleaning made this place smell more like a den than it had. Her torn stocking rubbed against her inner thighs as she walked into the small living room, her eyes quickly adjusting to the darkness. Her short skirt did little to make her feel covered. Her pussy was exposed, pulsing, nervous and excited energy filling the air around her.

"What about Pamela?" She walked over to one of the windows and fingered the curtains.

The cabin had the bitch's scent all over it.

"I heard you two talking on the phone. Seems to me you liked her fine."

"That's not what I meant." She couldn't turn around when he came up behind her, pressing against her while his hands moved under her skirt.

"Pamela is Gabe's mate." His breath tortured her neck.

And then the spot he'd just made ultrasensitive, he bit, pressing his teeth into her flesh. He touched her thighs, her nerve endings exploding, while he worked his way toward her swollen pussy.

"Have you seen him fuck her?" she asked, her heart racing, knowing it shouldn't be any of her business.

But damn it, she wanted to know everything about this *Cariboo*. She wanted to know what made Stone click, what thoughts went through his head.

Stone let go of her. He undid his pants behind her but she couldn't turn around. Instead her insides about exploded, need swarming through her, filling the air with all the emotions she couldn't contain.

"Yup. I've fucked her too. We share what we have."

His words hit her too hard. There wasn't a thing she could say to respond. Her mind just wouldn't work that quickly.

Stone lifted her skirt, pulling her back toward him. She slapped her hands against the wall, bracing herself when his swollen cock pressed against her sensitive flesh.

She was so wet that when he rushed inside her, filling her so quickly, she couldn't breathe, let alone think. He glided over her inner muscles, stroking them, while she contracted around him. His cock just about split her in two. So large…so thick.

Ali cried out, scratching her fingers against the wall while she let her head fall back.

"Damn it. Stone." She arched into him, wanting more but at the same time positive she couldn't handle it.

He pulled back, almost leaving her empty, before plunging in again, this time harder, with more intensity.

"Does that bother you?" he asked.

Did what bother her? Not a damn thing about what he was doing bothered her. Never had she felt better in her entire life. The smell of lust between them was enough to get drunk on. His hands gripped her hips, pinching her flesh while he drove his cock deep inside her, hitting that spot that sent her over the edge.

"What? God." She bucked against him.

What he was giving her was too much. Yet he held her firm, relentless while he built up speed, tearing into her harder and faster.

When she was positive she would collapse, completely pass out from the fucking he was giving her, he held her firmly. His fingers dug into her flesh, the sweet pain enough to trigger the beast within her. More than anything the urge to change, experience such raw, hard sex in a more primal form took over as she struggled to remain standing.

"Ali." Stone let out a growl so fierce that she was sure it shook the cabin.

He buried himself in her, his arms wrapping around her. "I'm going to come," he told her, exploding inside her at the same time.

Ali lost her grip against the wall. She collapsed, falling to the floor while he still held her, buried deep inside her. He prevented her from hurting herself when they fell, rolling her to her side while he remained inside her.

Her mind remained in a fog but the words he'd told her slowly seeped through her.

He'd fucked Pamela. Stone and Gabe shared their women.

What kind of *Cariboo lunewulf* were they?

What was she getting herself into?

Chapter Seven

ဆ

By the end of her shift the next day, Ali wasn't sure she'd make it another thirty minutes without a nap. Every inch of her body tingled, muscles ached, and sensations rushed through her that she'd never experienced before. It had made waiting tables through lunch and dinner quite the challenge.

She pulled her apron off, hanging it on the hook on the kitchen wall when the door opened out in the tavern. All day long she'd hoped Stone would stop in. Every time the bell jingled above the tavern door, she'd sniffed the air. And then she'd turned to look just in case her senses deceived her.

It wasn't Stone. It was Pamela.

"Ali, your mother is on the phone," Cook called from behind the grill.

She gave Pamela the once-over as the bitch moved to sit at the counter. Pamela smiled at her, her manner and scent showing no signs of hostility. Maybe the girl seriously wanted to be friends.

Get in good with his den and you can see more of him.

She gave her a wave of a greeting before turning to take the call.

"Ali, there was some trouble up the mountain just a bit ago." Her mother's worry alerted Ali.

"What kind of trouble?" she asked, trepidation seeping through her.

"I'm not sure. Argument over land your sire has been clearing for several new dens." Her mother paused, saying something to her littermates in the background. "None of them are back yet. I just wanted you to keep your ears alert and let me know anything if you catch word as to what is going on."

It wasn't an unusual request for Ali to be asked to listen to the pack gossip that went on in the tavern. Most of them straggled in after late afternoon naps to grab a bite before heading out for evening runs. The tavern was the source of most pack news.

"No problem, Mom. I haven't heard anything yet. My shift is over but I'll tell the night shift to keep their ears open."

"Is there trouble?" Cook asked after she hung up the phone.

"I'm not sure. Sounds like my sire ran into some trouble up the mountain." She eyed the steaks he was flipping, her stomach growling.

It dawned on her she hadn't eaten yet today. Walking back out to the counter, she nibbled her lip as she approached Pamela. There was a good chance that Gabe and Stone could be working with her sire. Pamela didn't smell tense or upset about anything though.

"I got bored up at the den all alone," Pamela confessed, her smile sincere. "Are you off work?"

"Yeah, I was thinking about getting food. Are you hungry?"

Pamela's expression lit up, her smile answer enough. Ali quickly put in an order for a couple of burgers with all the fixings.

"I can't reach either of them on their cell phones."

Pamela didn't mention names, but Ali guessed she meant Stone and Gabe. It would make sense that she would call Stone from time to time. She was his twin's mate. Nonetheless, Ali felt her tummy twist at the knowledge that Pamela could so easily reach out to talk to Stone. Ali had ached to talk to him all day. But she didn't even have his cell phone number.

"I got so bored up there that I decided to come into town. I'm so glad that I found you here. I don't have any bitches to run with anymore. Once the bitches I used to play with grew up and mated, they don't come around anymore." Pamela adjusted herself on her stool at the counter, crossing her long thin legs.

"Yeah, I know the feeling. Everyone I went to high school with is mated now. They run with their mates." And mated bitches could do things that single bitches couldn't, like decide to come into town alone when they were bored with their den.

Ali envied Pamela's happiness, and her freedom. The relaxed air around Pamela was incentive to continue her pursuit of Stone. He might not realize it, but she'd be the perfect mate for him. And he was definitely old enough to be settling down.

Ali jumped up when Cook rang the bell, letting her know their order was up. She placed two hot plates with large burgers and mounds of French fries in front of Pamela and where she was sitting. Then walking around the counter, her mind began churning of ways to land Stone.

Pamela munched into her burger and then gave Ali an appraising look. "Stone would be a tough *Cariboo* to get to settle down."

Ali held her burger in front of her, ready to take a bite but pausing. She met Pamela's gaze. The bitch didn't have any animosity coming from her. Her words seemed sincere, almost sympathetic.

"How long is he staying here in Banff?" Prying information from Pamela might not be that hard of a feat.

Pamela shrugged. "We didn't know he was coming back. Gabe thinks you might be getting under his skin."

Ali's heart soared. Stone's twin would know his thoughts if anyone did. She took a bite out of her burger. More than once he'd told her how close he was with Gabe, as if warning her, preparing her.

Close enough that Stone had fucked Pamela. She glanced again at the pretty bitch sitting next to her. Not much older than she was, with long blonde hair to die for. Any werewolf would go sniffing after her. But just thinking about how it could have happened, if Pamela had been excited to have Stone, made her stomach churn.

Pamela put her burger down and brushed her fingers over Ali's hand—a reassuring gesture. Obviously she'd misunderstood the emotions she smelled on Ali.

"He brought that shipment out here for your sire. He didn't have to make the trip. There were plenty of werewolves who could have driven those supplies here." Pamela grinned, and then poured ketchup onto the corner of her plate. "So whatever you're doing, keep doing it."

Whatever she was doing?

Ali sighed. "He's not letting me do anything," she confessed, except fuck him. "When he comes around, he just wants one thing."

"Well, he could get that anywhere. So it's a start." Pamela giggled, and then bit into her burger again.

Ali tried to enjoy her burger. It was damn good. Cook always made good food. The pretty and friendly bitch sitting next to her had enjoyed Stone. More than likely he'd made her scream just like he had with Ali. Pamela knew what it was like to be filled by Stone, pounded with that rock-hard cock.

But then, more than likely, Stone had mounted many bitches.

That did it. There was no way she could take another bite. Dropping the burger on her plate she let out a sigh.

Pamela looked at her, frowning. Even as her forehead wrinkled, she was still a stunning bitch. Stone had to enjoy the hell out of fucking her.

Damn it. If she didn't stop this, she would go nuts.

"Pamela," she said, her muscles cramping throughout her body as a wave of nervousness consumed her. "There's something I need to ask you."

"Sure. What is it?" Pamela continued frowning, slowly putting what was left of her burger down. "Are you okay?"

"Yeah." She bit her lip. There was no turning back now. She had Pamela's complete attention and if she didn't talk to her about this, it would make her nuts. "Stone told me something…about you…and him."

Pamela's frown disappeared. Her expression went completely blank and then she looked down before returning her attention to Ali. A rush of emotions filled the air, too many to identify. Ali's stomach lurched, her food suddenly not sitting well at all.

Pamela licked her lips. "Then I guess we have something we need to talk about."

The door opened behind Pamela and Mickey rushed in, his urgent expression grabbing Ali's attention.

"Ali." He hurried over to her, the smell of the mountains lingering on him. "You should probably go to your den now."

"You aren't my keeper," she snapped, but then her annoyance faded when she remembered what her mother had said, and smelled worry on him. "What is it?"

He didn't answer her but turned his attention to Pamela. "Your mate sent me to find you. They are all over at the pack doctor's. There's been some trouble."

"What?" Both women said at the same time.

"Up in the mountains. Some of them broke out into a fight. Gabe asked me to find you and tell you to go to him." He then turned to Ali, taking her arm. "I can give you a ride to your den."

Pamela was already jumping up. But Ali pulled away from Mickey. She grabbed both of their plates and was hurrying around the counter with them. Stone had been with them. She was sure he would be working with his twin. If there had been fights, and they were at the pack doctor, then he could be hurt. There was no way she was going back to her den.

"Pamela. Can I go with you?" she asked, placing the plates up for the dishwasher to take.

"Sure." Pamela pulled money out of her purse, throwing it down on the counter. "I figured you probably would."

"You really should go to your den," Mickey intervened, standing in front of Pamela.

"Mickey. Who all is at the pack doctor's?" If Stone was hurt... Her heart started racing. She couldn't bear the thought of him being attacked by anyone in her pack.

"Your sire is fine. I'll take you home."

She ignored him and hurried past him to Pamela. "You go to my den, Mickey. Tell them I'm helping out at the pack doctor's."

And with that she hurried out the front door, her own worry matching the smells that came from Pamela as they hurried to her car.

"Do you know how to get to Renee's?" Ali asked Pamela.

"Yes." Pamela was all business.

Mickey came up behind them. "I don't want you going over there, Ali."

Pamela reached a small silver car, dirty from climbing up back-mountain roads, and pulled open the driver's side door. Ali reached for the passenger door, her irritation toward Mickey growing by the moment.

"I've been to Renee's before, Mickey. You're being ridiculous."

Mickey's anger filled the chilly air with its spicy scent. "Fine. But I know what you're doing. Go chase after that *Cariboo*. You wind up carrying his cub, don't come crying to me."

Ali blinked. "Don't worry. I won't."

She was shaking when she climbed into the car, outrage consuming her.

Pamela's cell phone rang and she glanced down at it. "It's about time," she mumbled, and grabbed the phone. "Are you hurt?" she demanded when she answered the phone.

At the same time, she started her car, shifting quickly and heading out of the parking lot.

Banff wasn't a large town, and the area the werewolves populated was even smaller. Within blocks, Pamela turned the wheel hard and then slowed onto a side street.

"Okay. We'll be there in a minute." Pamela hung up the phone and glanced over at Ali. "Gabe wouldn't give me the details. But apparently there was a fight and a few of them got scratched up. Stone was one of them."

Ali looked at her, desperately needing more information. Werewolves could take quite a beating and mend quickly. But Stone wasn't part of the pack. And if the pack didn't approve of the fight…

"Who'd he fight?" If he took on someone with clout in the pack, Stone would be chased off.

They drove halfway down the street and Ali quickly recognized several cars parked in front of Renee's house. Gabe's light blue truck was parked across the street. Her heart tightened in her chest when she spotted her sire's work truck, and the brown Bronco that their pack leader, Tip Rochester, drove.

"Everyone's here," she whispered, unnecessarily.

"It'll be okay." Pamela squeezed her hand and then got out of the car.

They hurried up the path and inside the small house where Renee lived. Blood and sweat and the strong smell of male adrenaline hit Ali hard when she entered the living room.

She didn't notice anyone other than Stone, who sat at a chair at the oval-shaped dining room table in the adjoining room. Pamela said something to Gabe, who greeted them at the door. But Ali didn't pay attention. She walked up to Stone, who had two bitches hovering around him.

He didn't wear a shirt, and there were some deep scratches going down his chest and on his neck. The bitches, who were a bit older than she was, and whom she'd seen around but didn't know that well, were touching Stone a bit too much for her tastes.

"I'll take care of him now," she told both of them, stepping in front of one of them so she faced Stone.

He looked up at her with sharp blue eyes. She smelled his pain, and his frustration.

The bitch behind him caressed his shoulder. Her aroused look pissed Ali off.

Hands off. He's mine. She let her gaze drop to the sultry way the woman ran her fingernails over his shoulder, and then met her gaze.

The bitch's smile was anything but friendly. "I don't see your mark on him. Besides, you're just a cub. Let a grown bitch take care of this *Cariboo*."

"You don't see my mark on him?" Ali glared at the bitch, and then bent over and kissed Stone.

Dear God. What had come over her? In front of God and practically everyone in the pack, she leaned over Stone, and pressed her lips to his. Stone's mouth was hot, his tongue so wet as he returned the kiss, opening his mouth while a growl rose from deep inside him, vibrating through his body.

He grabbed the back of her head, turning her so that he could deepen the kiss. Taking what she offered, he demanded more, obviously not caring any more than she did that they were surrounded by so much of the pack.

Ali could smell when the bitches who'd been tending to him left in disgust. She broke off the kiss, but remained bent over him, staring into those deep blue eyes, which were streaked with silver. The smell of his pain was still there but it was the raw energy that coursed through him that grabbed her attention.

"Where does it hurt most?" she whispered, not wanting to straighten.

More than anything she didn't want to acknowledge anyone else in the room. Her sire was here somewhere. If he made a scene, lunged forward because his cub had just made a public spectacle of herself, she would die.

She didn't smell anyone but Stone now. For all she knew or cared at that moment, they could have been alone in the pack doctor's house.

"The only pain I'm feeling at the moment, you're going to take care of later," Stone whispered, and then pulled her face closer and nipped at her lip.

The sharp pain from his quick bite sent a rush of excitement through her. His words tortured her. Suddenly she couldn't breathe, wanted nothing else than to drag him out of there, demand that he fuck her now.

She sucked in a breath, finally straightening. A quick glance told her that Gabe and Pamela stood right next to them. They'd offered a shield preventing others from having seen her bold actions.

Ali licked her lip, returning her attention to Stone.

"You should see what the other werewolf looks like," Gabe teased, walking behind his twin and frowning as he looked at the claw marks going down Stone's back.

Ali took the ointment off the table that the other bitches had been using. Stone didn't move when she rubbed it into his torn flesh.

"He got everything he deserved," Stone said through gritted teeth.

"You going to tell me what happened?" Ali asked.

"I'd like to hear your version too." Tip Rochester had walked up to them, Renee right next to him.

"Rub that ointment in really well," Renee instructed Ali. She placed some large bandages on the table. "Put these over the deep ones. He'll be sore tonight but my guess is he'll be fine in the morning."

"Stone, this is our pack leader, Tip Rochester," Gabe said, quickly offering introductions.

Ali stepped back when Stone stood. She realized then that her sire had entered the dining room from the kitchen. He had a scratch over his forehead, but otherwise simply looked annoyed. He frowned when he noticed her.

"Stone McAllister," Stone said and shook hands with the pack leader. "You'll have to forgive me. I'm sure I get credit for starting the fight. But where I come from, werewolves don't beat up bitches."

Tip nodded and then looked past him at her sire.

"He's part of your crew, Jonathan?" Tip asked.

Jonathan stepped further into the room, watching Ali as she applied the ointment to Stone.

"Yup. His den is here." Jonathan nodded to Gabe. "Stone here is just passing through."

Ali met her sire's gaze, knowing the last comment was directed toward her. A sinking feeling hit her gut. Stone didn't say anything to counter her sire's statement.

Tip looked around at all of them and then patted Renee on the shoulder. "Well, it looks like they'll all survive. I'll take a drive up into the mountains, see how the dens are doing up there."

The large *Cariboo* turned and left the dining room, and a few minutes later left the house.

"Where's your shirt?" Ali finished putting the bandages on the deeper cuts on Stone's back then turned to look at the smaller cuts on his neck.

If the other werewolf looked worse, then Stone had to come close to killing him. Her sire couldn't be that upset with him if Stone had started the fight. She knew her sire detested werewolves who didn't treat their bitches right. Her heart still pattered in her chest when her sire walked up to them.

"I have the deepest respect for a *Cariboo* who insists on wholesome values in a den," he told Stone. "Don't lose my respect."

His last words were a mere growl, his gaze never leaving Stone's face.

"I don't plan on it." Stone straightened.

Even with the clean white bandages covering part of his torso, the muscles that rippled under his flesh were more than a distraction for Ali. Her mouth was suddenly too dry. Her sire and Stone stared at each other, male adrenaline filling the air with a rich smell. Her heart throbbed so hard in her chest she was sure everyone around her could hear it. Licking her dry lips, she glanced down and then gave Pamela, who stood on the other side of her, a quick glance. Concern covered the pretty bitch's face. Gabe's expression looked as hard as Stone's did. The two were so similar, yet so different.

Ali returned her attention to Stone, and then to her sire.

"I'll need to head back up the mountain." Jonathan followed Stone's actions when he turned and grabbed his shirt that had been hanging on the back of his chair. Jonathan didn't look at anyone else but the werewolf in front of him while Stone pulled his shirt over his head. "My daughter will be at her den by the time I get home."

Ali ached to help Stone with his shirt. She didn't dare move though. Her sire bordered on hostile. After half of them getting in a fight up the mountain, it wouldn't take much to set them off again. She could smell the tension that lingered in the room.

"Dad. I want to make sure Stone gets to his den," Ali said, unable to stay quiet.

She desperately wanted to be alone with Stone and the last thing she wanted to do was sit at home tonight listening to her littermates growl and snap at each other.

Stone held up his hand, looking down at her before returning his attention to Jonathan. "She'll be home. I'll see to it."

Jonathan nodded. He growled at her, letting her know he was serious, and then left the dining room.

"Give me the keys to the truck," Stone told Gabe when it was just the four of them at the dining room table.

"You sure you can drive?" Gabe asked, pulling the keys from his pocket.

"I can drive." Stone took the keys and then put his hand on the back of her neck, leading her out of the pack doctor's home.

Ali could feel her sire's gaze burning through her back as they left the house.

"Remind me to tell you what Gabe had to go through with my sire," Pamela told her as they walked toward the cars.

"This isn't the same," Stone growled at all of them.

"Of course not." Pamela ignored his scowl, grinning at him. "I saw Ali chase those bitches away from you."

Ali's face burned with sudden embarrassment, but she hurried after Stone when he picked up his pace and stalked over to the truck. Grabbing her arm, he pulled her around to the driver's side, then opened the door and pushed her into the cab.

"Don't tell me you're suddenly mad that I got those sluts away from you." She adjusted herself in the cab, praying he wasn't planning on driving her straight to her den and dropping her off.

"They were just tending to my wounds." Stone started the truck.

He didn't look at her when he pulled away from the curb.

"They were hanging all over you. I didn't like it." She clenched her teeth together.

Granted, Stone had given her no indication that he was staying with this pack. But he'd come back. He came to her when she'd asked him to, and she knew it wasn't just because he wanted her for sex. Stone could get it from anyone. And Pamela had told her that Gabe thought she was getting under his skin. What worried her right now was that Stone would be stubborn enough to deny that he had feelings for her.

Stone looked at her and tingles rushed over her flesh. His expression was hard but she didn't miss that possessive look. He'd liked how she'd chased them away. She knew he had.

"You going to chase away any bitch who might be by my side?"

"Damn straight I am," Ali spoke before she could think about it.

She fisted her hands, turning toward him. Stone glanced over at her, suddenly looking amused. Ali realized at that moment that they weren't heading toward her den. Instead, Stone turned up the mountain. Her heart skipped a beat. He wasn't taking her to her den, but to Gabe and Pamela's den.

"And what are you going to do when I leave?" he asked.

Ali's heart sunk to her gut. "When you leave? When are you leaving?"

"Don't know." It was hard to tell but she thought she smelled amusement.

Stone pulled the truck in front of the small cabin and parked. When he opened the truck door, he didn't grab her and pull her out on his side. Ali scooted toward him anyway, wondering if he might be in more pain than he let on.

"Then why did you ask?" She climbed out, standing right next to him.

Stone looked down at her and then ran his hand through her hair, tangling his fingers and then pulling so her head fell back.

"Because, little bitch, you are digging your claws in deep." He didn't sound overly disappointed about that.

"You knew I was lying when I denied being a virgin," she began and he tugged harder on her hair. "I could have fucked at least a handful of werewolves before I meant you. None of them were worth my time."

"Don't be so sure that I'm worth your time." His grip pinched her hair at her scalp.

The slight pain he inflicted made her muscles ache to grow, to take him on for implying he wasn't worth the fight.

"Don't tell me a big bad wolf like you gets nervous about the thought of taking a mate."

His expression hardened and a muscle twitched next to his mouth. He pushed into her until she was pressed against the side of the truck.

"What makes you think I'm looking for a mate?"

She reached up, brushing his hair from the side of his face. Her fingers lingered over the strong pulse in his temple. Never had she seen a sexier, and more dangerous-looking, werewolf.

"Usually when you aren't looking is when you find just what you need," she whispered.

Stone leaned into her, pressing his weight against her so that the cold metal of the truck soaked through her clothes.

"You think I need you?" He nipped at her neck and then ran his tongue down to her collarbone.

"God. Stone." She couldn't pull her head forward.

He still had his hand clamped against the side of her head.

"There's a lot about me that you don't know," he breathed into her neck, sending chills rushing through her.

"I'll learn," she told him, her entire body turning into a pulsing nerve ending.

"Then what will you do when I strip you down and give you to Gabe?"

Her heart exploded in her chest, and then quickly rose to her throat.

Chapter Eight

🖎

Gravel popped behind Stone and he pushed away from Ali, deciding a moment for her to digest his direct question might do her some good.

Dreams had plagued him ever since he'd met this feisty little bitch. Sharing her with Gabe, watching her take both of them, turned him on more than it had with any other bitch. And in truth, other than with Pamela, it had only happened twice before. Each of them had found a bitch in their past, thought she might be the one, and then for whatever reasons, it hadn't worked out.

Damn if he knew why he was considering Ali. She was so young, had so much to learn. And he wasn't looking for a mate.

But he'd asked her, and even as the Bronco pulled up behind them, he could tell the question had rendered her speechless. She glanced up at him and then at the pack leader's truck.

"I'd do anything for you," she whispered, shocking him.

Ali straightened her clothes and turned her attention to the pack leader.

Tip Rochester got out of his Bronco, immediately sniffing the air. Stone turned to face him, show him the respect of his rank. If the pack leader had a problem with Ali being here, he would have it out with him now.

"Is there a problem?" Stone asked in greeting.

"I sure hope not." Tip looked past him at Ali. "You here because you want to be?"

"Of course I am, Tip." Ali crossed her arms over her chest, and glared at the pack leader. "Don't you go thinking anything bad about Stone here."

"I heard your sire, little cub. Don't get mouthy with me. If you're wanting a mating here, you won't get it unless I hear his approval."

Stone wasn't surprised to see that the pack leader would back anything that Jonathan Bastien had to say. The older *Cariboo* had struck Stone as an honest and hardworking werewolf. The fact that he was working for him, and that the werewolf was Ali's sire, wasn't going to change a damn thing.

"I'm not a cub," she said defiantly.

"Behave," Stone growled at her. He wouldn't have a scene blow out of proportion because his little bitch had an attitude. "What can we do for you?" he asked the pack leader.

"It's you I came to see." Tip faced Stone, putting his hands on his hips and sizing him up.

Stone didn't smell any aggravation, more of a curiosity scent. It wouldn't surprise him to be challenged though. This was the heart of *Cariboo lunewulf* country and Stone wasn't part of this pack. Unlike Gabe, who entered in by taking one of their bitches as a mate and settling his den here, Stone was an outsider, a drifting werewolf. The pack leader had a duty to check him out.

"Well, you found me." Stone had no problem dealing with the pack leader.

"You killed that *Cariboo lunewulf* up the mountain earlier today." Tip was a young leader, not surprising among *Cariboo*.

Cariboo lived hard and often died young. The good ones did at least.

"Hopefully the rest of that den doesn't beat their bitches the way I saw him doing it." Stone wouldn't show remorse for a waste of flesh werewolf, who had no idea how to treat a bitch.

Tip inhaled slowly, his barrel chest puffing out. He stood about as tall as Stone, and would be a hard match if they fought in their fur. Stone didn't anticipate that. He would hear the pack leader out.

"You stay out of that area up the mountain for right now. Is that clear?"

Ali edged closer to him, straightening. Her anger quickly made the air around them spicy. Tip didn't even look her way, his attention riveted to Stone. And damn it, if the little bitch got mouthy with the pack leader over this matter, he'd tan her hide as soon as he left.

"Understood." Stone knew the pack leader had to deal with many dens in the mountains.

Regardless of whether Tip approved of what had happened earlier or not, and Stone would be willing to bet the werewolf would back him if put on the spot, the *Cariboo* had a job to do. Stone respected him for that.

"Another thing," Tip added, his stance still alert. "How long will you be staying with this pack?"

Gabe and Pamela took that moment to pull up behind the Bronco. His twin jumped out quickly, approaching them with several long strides. Stone didn't give him the time of day though. The pack leader meant business, and he wouldn't have his name marred if the pack leader thought he didn't show the right respect. Gabe had made this pack his home, and Stone would make sure their name carried honor.

"Bastien says he has work for me. I thought I'd stay around for a bit."

"Is there trouble?" Gabe asked, and Pamela hurried to join him, locking her hand around his arm.

"Not yet," Tip told him, giving Gabe a quick glance and then nodding to Pamela. "Just asking your littermate here a few questions."

"Stone killed that werewolf who was beating his mate." Ali sounded so proud of him. Her small hands were cool when they wrapped around his arm.

But Stone couldn't have Ali interfering in this conversation right now. The little bitch needed training. Having her present at all right now was almost too much. But having her make comments, boast about him when they weren't even mated, was pushing it. He could tell by the way that Tip frowned that the pack leader agreed.

"Pamela. Ali needs to get home. Her sire wanted her there before he returned to his den." Stone took Ali by the arms and pushed her toward Pamela.

"I'm not ready to leave yet," Ali complained, twisting in his arms.

Stone couldn't stop the low growl that escaped from him. He glared at Ali. "Do as you're told, little bitch."

"Come on, Ali," Pamela said quietly.

"Fine." Ali put her hands on her hips, looking adorable as hell. "Tip Rochester. I swear if you send Stone out of this pack, I'll run after him. Don't you think that I won't."

Stone let out a loud sigh and watched as the bitches headed toward Pamela's car.

None of them said anything but just watched as the two turned the car around and headed down the narrow road. Finally Tip looked at the ground, letting out a sigh before giving Stone a hard look.

"I've known the Bastien den most of my life," he said quietly. "They are good werewolves and Ali is their oldest. She's taken to you, and if you do her wrong, it will be more than her sire that you have to deal with."

Stone didn't take well to being threatened. He straightened, fighting to keep his temper in check. This was Gabe's den, and he would honor that. At the same time, he'd be damned if he'd be cornered into a mating. He hadn't done anything to Ali that she hadn't wanted—hell, begged for.

Tip nodded once at his silence, and then turned toward his Bronco. "I'll give you a week. By that time, you either ask to join the pack, or let me know you're headed out."

Stone turned toward the cabin before the pack leader had gotten into his Bronco. Damn it to hell, the last thing he wanted was someone laying down an ultimatum. The urge to pack up and run before nightfall hit him hard.

"You've gone and done it this time." Gabe wasn't going to help matters any.

But he didn't need to show Gabe any respect. "Shut the hell up."

Gabe followed him into the cabin, indifferent to Stone's attitude. "What brought him up here?"

"I killed a werewolf." Stone walked over to the refrigerator.

Reaching for a beer, he pulled the tab and downed half of it before giving Gabe his attention.

"Well, I can't say the asshole didn't have it coming to him. He was beating the crap out of that poor bitch." Gabe shook his head, and pushed past Stone to grab his own can. "You're going to have to watch your tail for a while."

"It'll be fine." He wouldn't let any pack leader bully him around.

Gabe popped his can of beer open and gave Stone a hard look. Stone hated that compassionate scent that got on his brother when he worried about him.

"I'm not sure this time." He used that quiet tone that he knew got under Stone's skin.

"Well then, you just watch and find out. No one is going to tell me how to run my life, or who I can run with." Stone gulped down his beer then crushed the can.

On an afterthought he tossed it in the trash instead of putting it on the counter. Pamela kept a clean den.

"You've run wild way too long." Gabe got in his face. "And don't tell me that you didn't come back here because of Ali."

"She's a piece of tail." His heart hardened.

No matter that images of her pretty face, her defiant attitude when she defended him and made it clear to anyone in her pack that she wanted him, grossly distracted his thoughts. No bitch had ever spoken out for him before.

"Like hell she is." Gabe scowled at him. "Wake up, asshole. She loves you."

"So what if she does?" He opened the refrigerator to grab another beer, but then slammed it shut. Getting drunk wouldn't take his mind off her. "She's a cub. There will be better werewolves sniffing after her and she'll drop me cold."

"You are such a fucking jerk." Gabe smacked him on the side of the head. "Why won't you admit that you have feelings for her?"

Stone smacked his brother's hand away, hitting it hard enough that flesh smacked against flesh, creating a loud crack between them. He glared at Gabe, anger and frustration riveting through him hard enough to make it hard to focus. Slamming his twin against the wall right now sounded pretty damned good.

The spicy irritating smell of his negative emotions swam through the air. Gabe grunted at him then turned his back, walking into the living room.

"You know she mentioned something to Pamela about both of us fucking her?" Gabe said, standing at the front door, which was still open.

Ali had stared at him so wide-eyed when he'd mentioned it to her just a bit ago. There had been no fear, no repulsion. But he'd planted a seed, given her something to think about. If the little bitch wanted him so damned bad, she would have to take him as he was.

"How did Pamela react to that?" he asked.

Gabe turned around, fisting his hand in the air and then letting it drop, shaking his head. "You're a damn smart werewolf. I know you are. But sometimes you are more dense than a rock."

"Yeah, well, that's how I got my name, remember?" Stone sneered, suddenly leery that Gabe would throw something in his face that he didn't want to hear.

A run in the mountains was sounding pretty damned good at the moment. The hell with what that pack leader said.

"Pamela knows I love her. She knows that if you took a mate there would be friction if that mate knew you'd done Pamela and I didn't do your mate. She will go along with whatever you and I want." Gabe put his hands on his hips, his back blocking the sunshine that tried to stream through the doorway. "You try and tell yourself that you don't want Ali, yet you are thinking about offering her to me."

Stone already knew this. He'd given more thought than he wanted to admit to making Ali his mate. But damn it, he wasn't ready to settle down. Just having a pack leader try and tell him where he could go, or trying to force him to make decisions about what pack he would belong to—none of that sat well with him. None of it at all.

"I'm getting out of here. Maybe I'll head to town and find a little slut to put out for me." Stone shoved Gabe out of the way, wishing more than anything he could do just that.

The second he'd mentioned it though, the only bitch who came to mind was Ali.

"You're going to the Bastien den, aren't you?" Gabe didn't even give his comment the time of day.

"Why should I go there?" He lunged out of the cabin, heading for the truck.

Gabe was on his heels. "Because you need to make sure your job is secure. And because you can't think about any bitch other than Ali."

Stone turned on him, raising his fist to strike. "How the hell do you know what I'm thinking?"

Gabe grabbed his fist, the two of them locked in midair while adrenaline pumped through both of them and their faces hardened. They glared at each other, their faces close enough that they could feel each other's breath.

"Because, twin brother," Gabe said through gritted teeth. "I'm in love also. And I'd kill for Pamela without giving it a thought."

Stone yanked his fist out of Gabe's grasp and pulled open the truck door. "I'm not in love, damn it."

"Like hell you aren't," Gabe muttered and then turned and walked into the cabin.

An hour later, Stone had to accept the fact that beer wasn't going to affect him tonight. He sat at the tavern, hunched over at the counter, his mood darkening with every gulp of the cold brew.

"Stone McAllister." A werewolf stood next to him.

Stone didn't like the way he said his name. Looking up, he straightened when the werewolf he'd seen pawing Ali at her den put his hands on his hips and glared at him.

"What do you want?" Stone stood slowly, sizing the werewolf up quickly.

He could take him out with one blow.

"I want you to stay the hell away from Ali Bastien." Mickey Reginald had tension swarming all around him.

This asshole was the last thing he wanted sniffing around him right now. Stone grunted, not even wishing to acknowledge the werewolf.

"Another beer," he barked at the bitch behind the counter.

He saw the uneasiness in her gaze as she glanced from him to Mickey. What the fuck ever! He was damned tired of werewolves trying to tell him what to do.

Mickey grabbed his arm, forcing him around on his stool. Stone came off the stool too fast for Mickey to react. The werewolf stumbled backwards, stopping before he toppled onto a nearby table.

"You don't want to touch me like that," Stone sneered.

"And you won't touch Ali again. Is that clear?" Mickey came back at him, proving he was a bit stronger than Stone had originally guessed.

"The only thing clear here is that you're about to get your tail whooped in a public place." Every muscle inside Stone hardened.

"Just because you can take out some lame-ass excuse for a werewolf up in the mountains doesn't mean you'd stand a chance against me." Mickey wasn't just a jerk. He was stupid too.

The older werewolf who cooked back in the kitchen moved around the counter faster than Stone thought possible. Although a good paw's length shorter than both of them, the older werewolf jumped in between them, not a bit of fear on him.

"I won't have any fighting in my place," he sneered at both of them.

"It's okay, Cook," Mickey said, smiling so that he showed off his buckteeth.

The werewolf was one ugly motherfucker. He'd be doing Ali a favor by sending this guy running with his tail between his legs.

"I've said what needed saying." His smile looked more like a sneer when he met Stone's gaze.

The room had grown quiet. Stone didn't smell any humans in the place, and he knew every pack member watched and waited to see what would happen next.

"Sounds to me like you need to talk to Ali, and not me." Stone turned away from the werewolves and sat on his stool.

The bitch behind the counter had brought him another beer. He held it up to her in a silent salute and then downed a good portion of the cold brew. Every muscle inside him had hardened while the acute pain of the change surged through his blood. Too much anger, too much frustration rushed through him.

"I saw you groping her at her den. Ali is barely a bitch. She don't need some no-good werewolf like you messing with her head." Mickey still stood behind Cook, who hadn't moved from his stance between them.

Stone looked the two werewolves over when he turned around, beer still in hand. He put the glass down when muscles cramped inside him. He'd crush the glass if he kept holding it.

"Ali is no longer any of your concern." He'd had about all he could take.

"I'll see to it that she's my concern. I'm in good with her den. You're not even a member of this pack." Mickey turned toward the door but then spun around, pointing a finger at Stone. "If you go near her again, I'll kick your ass."

"Might as well do it now," Stone muttered, already bored with this werewolf's idle threats.

Anger flared around Mickey. He looked like he might blow a gasket the way his face turned red.

"I have enough respect for our pack's tavern, which is more than I can say for you. But if you want to fight for her, that's fine with me."

Stone stared at the werewolf for a moment. Mickey Reginald had just challenged him for Ali.

Damn it to fucking hell.

There had been more than one time in the past when he'd been challenged over some bitch he'd been fucking. Every time he'd laughed it off, wished the werewolf much happiness, and moved on to the next willing bitch.

Something inside him wouldn't let him do that now. Ali wouldn't be happy with this werewolf. He was making a public spectacle of himself. Stone had seen him out working with the other werewolves, he didn't have the intelligence to do much more than play gofer. The werewolf would get lost on a run if he didn't follow the rest of the pack. And that might be asking too much of him.

Standing slowly, he took a slow breath. His head needed to be clear with this. Accepting the challenge would have irreversible ramifications. Not that any of them scared him. He could take this werewolf out easily enough. Stone didn't fear losing his life.

It was losing his freedom that had him hesitating.

"Name the place and time," he said slowly.

The instant chatter that started in the tavern rushed through his brain like a disease. He'd just accepted fighting for the right to mate with Ali.

Chapter Nine

ନ୍ତ

Ali wished the slow throbbing in her head would go away. She paced the length of the living room, and then stopped to face her mother.

"I want him, Mom."

"I know, sweetheart." Her mother smiled at her, as if she understood.

Her youngest littermate Joseph darted through the living room toward the kitchen with several other cubs in tow. Ali turned toward her sire, who sat in his chair watching the news.

"I'm not one of the cubs anymore, Dad." Arguing with her sire wouldn't get her anywhere. But damn it, this mattered more than anything. "You embarrassed me when you ordered me home like I wasn't an adult."

Her sire shifted in his chair. He heard her. It didn't surprise her a bit that he remained quiet. He was so damned bullheaded. There were days when she wondered what her mother had ever seen in him.

"Don't you see, Mom?" She tried another approach, appealing to her mother. "I'm twenty-two years old. You know the werewolves have been sniffing around our den for years. If one of them had appealed to me, I would have run with them."

"Like hell you would," her sire growled, not taking his eyes off the TV.

"Stone is different." She continued talking to her mother. "He's dedicated to his den. Look how he traveled all the way out here just to help his twin."

She wouldn't mention how dedicated he was to his twin. Without prompting, Stone's final words before they'd been interrupted popped into her mind.

Then what will you do when I strip you down and give you to Gabe?

She shoved the thought from her mind, fighting off a shiver of desire that rushed through her.

"And remember how he returned to the pack, bringing you all of those supplies and saving you all that money?" She turned on her sire. "And in less than a day he had work here."

"He doesn't even have his own den." Her sire jumped out of his chair, yelling as he pointed at her. "He's wild—out of control. Damn it. He killed a werewolf today. He's drifting through this pack."

"Sounds like someone else twenty years ago," her mother said, and then covered her mouth to hide a smile.

"Whose side are you on?" her sire howled. "You didn't see him today. Stone McAllister went after that werewolf the second we saw him in the clearing."

"Because he was beating his mate," Ali added. "If he were any other *Cariboo* you'd be boasting his morals and fighting skills."

"And the only reason he's working is because I gave him a job." Her sire put his hands on his hips.

"And that was very kind of you." Her mother walked up to her sire, putting her hand on his chest. "We all know you can see when a *Cariboo* is a hard worker. Does Stone work hard?"

Ali's heart skipped a beat when her sire looked down at her mother, his gaze softening briefly. That was the look he gave her when her mother was winning an argument. Ali sucked in a breath, saying prayer upon prayer that he would agree for her to see Stone.

"He's not good for Ali." Her sire focused completely on his mate now, as if Ali no longer were in the room. "Don't you agree? The second things get a bit much for him, he'll be tearing out of here in his fur."

"I don't know if I agree or not, Jonathan. I would have to know him better," her mother said quietly.

The phone rang and every one of Ali's littermates raced from different corners of the house, sounding like a wild pack descending on them.

Jason walked into the living room with an all-important look on his face, looking like a miniature version of his sire.

"Dad. The phone is for you."

Ali walked away from them. This was making her nuts. It shouldn't matter to her so much that her parents approved of Stone, but it did. She knew some of the bitches ran off with *Cariboos* that they'd howled after as soon as they'd graduated. None of them had cared what their den thought.

"What?" her sire screamed into the phone behind her.

Ali jumped, her heart exploding in her chest, and turned around quickly. Her sire's face had turned beet-red and he looked ready to crush the phone in his hand.

"Yes. Thanks for telling me." He threw the phone onto the couch so hard that it bounced to the floor. He turned on her, looking like he was ready to charge.

The spicy smell of anger filled the room, while he slowly raised a fist, his muscles growing while his short gray hair on his head became bushier.

"Jonathan. What is it?" Audry approached him slowly, her hand extended.

Gently she touched his chest, but he didn't seem to notice.

"That *Cariboo* of yours was starting fights down at the tavern. Cook risked taking him on just to prevent his place, your place of employment, from being destroyed." He turned to his mate, looking at her as if she could explain all of this to him. "And you approve of this werewolf for our daughter?"

"Why was he fighting?" Suddenly Ali's den seemed like a cave closing in on her. "Who else was involved?"

And where was he now? Too many questions flooded through her while the urge to bolt out the door, go find him, seemed suddenly more important than making her parents see the qualities in Stone.

Her *Cariboo* was wild. But Ali knew he had convictions. His heart was good. And if he fought, it would be because someone pissed him off for doing something wrong. She frowned, shaking her head.

"I need to find out what is going on," she murmured, more to herself than anyone else.

"I'll be damned if you're going to go sniffing out that *Cariboo*."

There was a knock on the door and Ali hurried to it, aching for Stone to be on the other side of the door when she pulled it open. She could smell that it wasn't him though before she had the door open.

"Sorry to bother your den at this hour." Tip Rochester filled the doorway with his massive frame.

"Is Stone all right?" Ali blurted out before she remembered her manners.

"Ali," Jonathan barked behind her.

Ali stepped to the side, allowing the pack leader to enter.

"Obviously you've heard what happened down at the tavern?" Tip nodded to Audry, and then turned his attention to Jonathan. "I'm here for a couple of reasons. Stone McAllister is the main reason. I'd like to ask you a few questions."

Ali's littermates had gathered in the living room, curiosity filling the air around them.

"Scat. All of you," Ali snapped.

Audry turned to her cubs as well. "All of you to your rooms," she ordered.

Multiple groans followed but Ali ignored them. She needed answers. And she needed them now.

"Tell me if Stone is okay. What happened? Where is he now?"

Tip smiled at her. A fairly large *Cariboo*, he was several years older than she was. They hadn't gone to school together and she'd never known him that well, but the pack consensus was that he was a fair werewolf. He'd always been friendly to her. And although she didn't know his mate that well, she'd heard he had a happy den. She smiled in return, praying her sire wouldn't make a scene and keep her from learning what had happened.

"I'm pretty sure he's just fine." He turned to her sire then, straightening as he cleared his voice. "I smell your anger, Jonathan. But we need to talk."

"What is it?" Her sire looked like he was ready to explode.

"There has been a challenge."

"A what?" Again her sire roared loud enough to rattle the pictures on the wall.

"A challenge?" Ali couldn't breathe.

She looked at her pack leader, and then at her parents.

"Mickey Reginald confronted Stone McAllister in the tavern. Apparently he told Stone to stay away from Ali here. A few words were exchanged and from what I hear, they almost broke into their fur right there."

"Who said they would fight for me?" Ali was almost afraid to ask the question.

"Stone did." Tip looked at her and then to her parents.

"I've got to go." There was no way she could stay here any longer. She had to find Stone.

"You aren't leaving this den." Jonathan pointed to the hallway. "I want you in your room now."

"Father. No." She had to fight to stay calm. But it was high time her sire saw that she was no longer a cub.

Blood rushed through her veins too fast. Stone was willing to fight for her. He wanted her. More than she needed to breathe she needed to be with him. There was no way she could wait. And the last thing she would allow was to be sent to her room like a cub. So many emotions rushed through her that her hair prickled down her neck and spine. Her muscles tightened, the sweet pain of the change quickening in her gut.

"When is the challenge?" she asked Tip.

"They set it for midnight tonight, up the mountain in the first clearing with the waterfall."

"There will be no challenge." Jonathan ran his thick hand through his hair.

Audry went to him, smelling his outrage, and wrapped her arms around him. This was tearing her parents up. Ali didn't want that. She wished she could make them see how she couldn't live without Stone.

"Tip, you've got to find a pack law that backs me on this. Neither one of those werewolves has proven themselves to me. My daughter here is the catch of this pack. Anyone will back me on that. I won't have two hotheaded mutts killing each other over her. Because whoever wins, I'll take down myself." Jonathan sliced the air with his hand.

"Dad. I want Stone. You might see him as hotheaded, but you aren't the one who would mate with him." Ali sighed, fighting to control her emotions and try one last time to reason with her sire. "I know I've always obeyed you. And I don't want to do anything without your blessing now. But you've got to see, I love him. I can't sit here and just wait to see what happens. I've got to go to him."

"He's not even a member of this pack." Her sire stared at her, his anger blinding him from seeing how strongly she felt about this. "He's way too wild for you."

"I've told him before all of this that he had a week to join the pack or leave." Tip's comment hit her hard.

Ali hurried to the door. "Don't stop me, Dad. I'm going after him. You've raised me well, given me a good den, but now you've got to let me go. I need to be with Stone."

"Jonathan," Audry said quietly. "Let her go."

Jonathan didn't say anything, and nor did anyone else. Ali stared at all of them for just another moment, and then hurried out the door, shutting it quickly and running down the walk before any of them tried to stop her.

It was a really cold night, and she hadn't thought to grab a jacket, but Ali welcomed the chill in the air. Her body burned with emotions that clung to her no matter how fast she walked down the street.

There was only one issue that she and her sire saw eye to eye on. The challenge was ridiculous. Mickey was an idiot if he thought he could take on Stone. And she didn't want Mickey anyway. She never had and she couldn't believe he didn't have enough sense to see that.

Lost in thought on how best to deal with the matter, and more than anxious to be with Stone, the walk to the tavern didn't take as long as it usually did. A fair amount of cars were in the gravel lot, most of which she recognized, but none of them were a pale blue truck. Stone wasn't here.

Her heart sank. There wasn't a damn soul she wanted to see other than Stone. Her body tingled every time she thought about how he'd announced a challenge for her. Every beat of her heart pulsed through her, straight to her pussy. Damn. She needed to find him.

She pushed open the tavern door, noticing immediately that the conversation in the place was louder than usual.

"Well, if you aren't the talk of the hour," Maggie, one of the other waitresses, said with a wink as she paused with a round platter loaded with dirty dishes. "You've got that new fighter of a *Cariboo* howling for you, you lucky bitch."

Ali smiled, trying to make light of it. "Have you seen him?"

Maggie shook her head, turning toward the counter. Ali moved among tables, noticing Cook watching her from the kitchen.

"Nope. Cook chased him off when he about took out Mickey right here in the tavern."

Ali slipped behind the counter, her ears buzzing from the chatter that all seemed to be about the fight that had almost taken place here earlier.

"Tell me what happened," she demanded of Cook as she entered the kitchen.

Steaks frying on the large grill filled her nose with their rich smells. But Cook's concern crept toward her when he looked her over. Grabbing a damp towel, he wiped his hands on it.

"Mickey told Stone to keep his paws off you. I reckon that *Cariboo* of yours has a bit too much fight in him. You sure you can settle down a werewolf like that, Ali?"

Cook had known her since she was a cub. And she knew he had a good heart. She smiled at him and gave his arm a squeeze.

"I can definitely handle him. Help me find the number for his den. Cook, I've got to see him."

Cook didn't say anything, but turned to his desk, a pile of papers and remnants of a meal covering its surface. With surprising ease he found the pack directory and handed it to her. Ali grinned at him and hurried to the phone.

"Hello." Pamela answered after a couple rings.

"This is Ali." Suddenly she wasn't sure what to say. "I need to speak to Stone."

"Hi, girl. I'd let you, but he isn't here. He took off on a run, and I'm not sure he's in a mood to go after him."

Oh God. He wouldn't take off, would he? She wouldn't be able to bear it if her sire was right, and Stone truly was no good.

Hairs prickled down her back, raw emotions too intense for her human body to handle, surfacing.

"Do you know where he went?"

"Ali. Sometimes you just have to let them go. Stone is experiencing something I don't think he's ever felt before."

"What's that?" She was scared to ask.

"He's in love."

A lump swelled in her throat so quickly she couldn't breathe. "Pamela. You know I love him," she managed to whisper.

Pamela chuckled. "Yeah. I've guessed that."

Glancing around her, she was grateful that Cook had given her privacy. No one else was in the back part of the kitchen.

"Letting him go just isn't something I can do. If he didn't want me, he'd tell me so." She had to believe that. Her heart wouldn't allow any other truth to surface.

"Knowing Stone, he probably would."

Ali ached to run, her bones popping while she stood there on the phone. "Please. Pamela. Do you have any idea where he went?"

"Tip forbade him to go up into the region where Stone killed that werewolf today. But they could have headed up one of the other trails."

"They?"

"Gabe and Stone."

Ali's mouth went dry. If Stone was serious about sharing her with his twin, she might be running into more than she bargained for. Nervous excitement rushed through her and she was grateful for the smell of cooking meat for covering up the smell of her mixed emotions.

More than anything she wanted Stone. Life would never be dull with him by her side. He offered adventure to her rather tame life. And she knew she would make a good mate for him. No other *Cariboo* had ever made her feel inside the way Stone did.

But if he was serious, and she believed that he was, then taking Stone meant having Gabe too. He would truly unite them as a den.

"Pamela," she said, hesitating. There was no way she could organize her thoughts into words. Her heart raced too hard to focus.

"Go. Find them." Pamela sounded firm about it. "And Ali?"

"Yeah?"

"Welcome to our den."

Pamela had understood. There was so much Ali wanted to talk to her about. But the line went dead. Slowly Ali hung it up, knowing what she had to do. Her legs were like jelly though. And there was no way she could walk back through the tavern, enduring the pack staring at her, whispering about what might happen.

Quietly she slipped out the back door, the intense smell of garbage hitting her hard. She ran across the back parking lot, remembering how Stone had touched her there. He was such a master, his knowing hands touching her in just the right places.

Ali took off in a quick sprint, allowing just enough muscle to put speed to her run. Keeping to back streets, she hurried to the edge of town and toward the mountains. All she could do was head to the McAllister den, and go from there, doing her best to sniff out their trail.

Cold night air slapped against her cheeks, making her ache to be in her fur. It wasn't safe to change yet though. She felt the strain in her human muscles as she started hiking up the narrow trails that she knew so well. Running in her fur would be so much easier, but she wouldn't allow the change to consume her until she was far away from all humans.

Moisture clung to her flesh, clashing with the chill that surrounded her. She wasn't cold though. Her body burned with a need that surpassed anything she'd ever experienced before. She was going after Stone, making him her werewolf.

Goose bumps crept over her flesh when she thought of how she might find him—what mood he would be in. Hell. There was no guarantee that he would be happy to see her. No matter the scenario her overworked imagination managed to create, she couldn't picture him sending her away. Too much hard evidence pointed to him wanting her. He'd come back to Banff. He'd sought her out. He'd come to her when she asked him to. Stone wanted her. Every inch of her body demanded that be the truth.

She began panting as she hiked over rocky ground, the incline becoming steeper the further into the mountain she climbed. A good hour passed before she reached the McAllister den. She couldn't guess the time, but all lights were out. Either Pamela had left, or gone to bed.

Stripping out of her clothes, the night air wrapped around her cruelly. She shook as if a fever consumed her, stretching her body, looking up at the glimpses of stars that peeked through the tall firs that did little to block a cold breeze. Her blood boiled through her. She arched her back, her senses growing more acute with every second as the change grasped her. It took over, allowing her to see through the darkness, smell the variety of scents around her better than any human could.

Her bones popped, stretching while her muscles grew around them. No longer did the cold torture her flesh. Her beautiful fur covered her body, warming her, clearing her head so that everything around her seemed crisper.

Dropping to all fours, she sniffed the air around her. Her heart soared. There were werewolves, and they were nearby. Leaping through the air, she hurried through the trees, the rocks and boulders that blocked her path no longer a trial to climb over or work her way around.

Branches snapped, the small wildlife that inhabited the area darting out of her way. She was at the top of the food line, the predator of all predators. Invincible and in charge of her destiny. Energy rushed through her, giving her new life. Tonight Stone would be hers. One way or another, with or without her den's blessing, she would have the *Cariboo* of her dreams—her soul mate.

A sudden change of the smells in the air brought her pause. Caution consumed her, quickly followed by fear. There were more than two werewolves ahead of her. They were galloping toward her, indifferent to anything around them as they tore at the earth, the smell of them as rich as the scent of the fir trees around her.

Ali slowed her pace, moving cautiously around a large boulder instead of leaping on top of it. She lowered her head to the ground, her hackles rising down her spine, as she sniffed for emotions.

Are you part of my pack?

She didn't recognize their smells. More so, the way they galloped toward her, with purpose and drive, didn't resemble the frisky run of a pack of werewolves enjoying the clean mountain air.

Several of them barked at each other—a warning.

Something wasn't right.

Ali looked down the mountain she'd just climbed. It wouldn't be more than a five-minute run back to the cabin. Her clothes were there. It was her only safe haven.

She jumped when a large *Cariboo* barked from the other side of her. They were ambushing her and her own fears had prevented her from smelling them out.

It was run with all her speed, or risk the unknown. And their aggressive barking and snarling was indication enough that the unknown would probably not be pleasant.

Pushing herself with all the muscle power she possessed, Ali leapt through the air, tearing down the hill with enough speed to send her toppling. Falling paws over head, she rolled halfway down the hill, feeling the sharp rocks tear at her hide.

Their barks were mean, nasty, cutting with angry tones as they cussed each other out. Suddenly the air filled with anger.

Ali was in serious trouble.

Regaining her footing, she managed to dart down the rest of the mountain, with one of them right on her tail. His mean slicing growls chilled her blood.

What the hell did I do?

She roared into the darkness, screaming at them while hurrying to the safety of the cabin. Ali almost slammed into the door of the cabin.

One of the *Cariboo* leapt through the air. She barely had time to register that he would land on top of her when she dared to look over her shoulder. He crushed into her, forcing all air out of her lungs. Large teeth pressed dangerously into the thick flesh at the back of her neck. She felt herself being dragged backwards before she could make sense out of what was happening.

Stop it! Let me go! I haven't done anything! Her cries were more like pathetic yelps as she felt her throat crushing closed, while the *Cariboo* dragging her held on tightly to the back of her neck with his deadly teeth.

Ali barely had time to acknowledge a loud crashing sound when two large and fierce-looking *Cariboo* tore down the mountain and flew through the air, landing on several of the *Cariboo* and sending them flying.

The *Cariboo* who had her pinned by the back of her neck let her go when one of the *Cariboo* who'd just appeared tackled him to the ground.

Ali scrambled out of the way, reaching the door to the cabin where she'd left her clothes.

"Get in here. Change! Get in here now!" Pamela hissed through a barely open door.

Ali looked wide-eyed at the fight going on right in front of the cabin. She immediately smelled Gabe and Stone, and they were taking on four mean-looking *Cariboo* she didn't recognize. Stone tore at one of the werewolves' necks like a rabid werewolf, sending the poor sap flying. The werewolf stumbled over himself, blood smearing his white coat, until he fell sideways, landing and resuming his human form — dead.

Stone took only a minute to turn his attention on her, lunging at her with all teeth bared. His fierce growl was a very simple order. *Get your ass inside now!*

"Come on. Now!" Pamela pleaded through the small crack of an opening. "I've called for help. Get in here."

Ali took one last look at Stone, and then reached down and grabbed her clothes in her mouth. Pamela opened the door far enough for her to enter, and Ali leapt inside, allowing the change to consume her immediately.

"What the hell just happened?" she cried out, as soon as her mouth could form words.

Chapter Ten

❧

Stone had no doubts that he and Gabe could take down the back-mountain den of *Cariboo* who fought like untrained pups. With one of them dead, the others hesitated, backing off quickly. Their conquest was safe inside the cabin. And now the three remaining cowards made quick decisions on whether they wanted to lose their lives tonight or not. They opted to live.

Stone rushed after them when they turned tail and ran back up the mountain.

Fucking cowards! he roared with enough fierceness that it echoed up the mountain while the three *Cariboo* ran off, disappearing into the darkness.

Stone was angry enough to rip a tree from the ground, send it flying across the yard. One look at the dead werewolf lying on the ground, and then at headlights coming up the mountain, and he curbed his temper.

Something told him that his probation in this pack was about to get revoked.

Ignoring the Bronco that screeched over the gravel and skid to a stop, Stone allowed the change to take over. The cold night air did nothing to soothe his fury. Somehow he managed to keep it in check and not tear his clothes.

After a quick sprint up the mountain, and then taking a look at some land that was for sale that bordered the land Pamela's den owned, his spirits had been high on their return. There was no doubt in his mind that the pack grapevine had successfully spread word about the challenge. Ali would have heard of it. One way or another she'd come looking for him. And he was damned ready to see her.

But when the smells had changed, cold defiance adding to the chill in the night air, Stone's senses had gone on full alert. Gabe had noticed it too. Mere seconds had passed before they'd heard the scuffle and howling down toward the cabin.

When he'd seen Ali being dragged backwards, smelled her panic, heard her pathetic yelps, severe protector instincts had kicked in.

No one would hurt her—let alone touch her!

Carnal instincts that would never be tamed took over. Stone hadn't given a thought to how many werewolves would die. All he knew was that he had to protect Ali.

Even now, as he pulled his jeans up and glared at the Bronco that pulled in next to the cabin, his instincts were still too raw for his human form.

Another car pulled up behind the Bronco. He didn't give a rat's ass about any of them. He'd defended Ali. And he'd do it again without thought.

Ali fought to pull her sweater over her head when he barged into the cabin. Taking his anger out on the door and slamming it wasn't an option. Gabe was right behind him. And Tip Rochester behind him.

"What the hell just happened?" Ali cried out, shaking so hard she couldn't get dressed.

Stone didn't bother snapping his jeans. "That was the rest of that mangy den," he barked, hitting the wall hard enough that one of Pamela's pictures fell to the ground.

"Stone!" Gabe yelled at him.

At the same time, Ali yelped. He looked down at her, seeing the terror in her pretty blue eyes and the way her hands shook as she tried to pull her jeans up over her long slender legs.

His anger ebbed just at the sight of her, terrified and helpless.

"God. My little bitch." He reached down to where she sat on the floor, struggling with her jeans, and lifted her into his arms. "Tell me they didn't hurt you."

"Sounds like they were after a little revenge." Tip walked over to Ali, watching while Stone helped her finish dressing. "You okay, Ali?"

Ali nodded, but Stone could feel how hard her heart pounded when he pulled her close. She wrapped her arms around him, burying her head in his chest. Her scent made him drunk with need. His cock hardened, while an ache for her tightened every muscle in his body.

"Everyone is okay, Dad." Pamela hurried over to the *Cariboo* who'd entered behind Tip. "Thank you for hurrying over here."

Stone looked at the pack leader, who watched him and Ali carefully. Glancing past him, he nodded to the older *Cariboo* that Pamela had just called sire.

"Does my den know about this?" Ali asked, looking up at Tip but making no effort to move from Stone's arms.

"They will," Tip told her, his tone serious enough to bar no arguments.

Ali sighed, and then looked at Stone. "I thought they were you. I was coming to find you. I was too close to get away but close enough to the cabin to get back here."

"And I heard the lot of them," Pamela added quickly. "That's when I called you, Dad. And you, Tip. I didn't know how far away you two were," she said to Gabe, and then glanced at Stone. "We're damn lucky you were so close."

"I'd have to agree." Tip crossed his arms, turning his back on all of them as if trying to come to some decision. "You've killed two werewolves today, but you did save Ali's life from what it sounds like."

Stone knew he was talking to him. Straightening, he kept Ali at his side, running one hand down her slender arm. She straightened as well, sensing like he did that the pack leader was about to make a decision.

Stone had no problem helping him along. "It'll be three werewolves dead once midnight strikes."

Tip turned around, giving him a hard look.

"Tip. You can't allow this challenge to happen. I don't want Mickey and I never have," Ali spoke up.

His little bitch had a bad habit of not being able to keep quiet when werewolves were talking. Something he had a feeling he would have to get accustomed to.

"I'll talk to him." Tip nodded to the group and reached for the door. He turned and gave Stone his attention. "I assume you'll see to getting her to her den."

Stone nodded, realizing he'd just gained some respect in the pack leader's eyes. About time the werewolf realized Stone was a good *Cariboo* to have covering his back.

Pamela's sire hung around for another minute or two, and then Pamela and Gabe walked him to his car.

"Why did you run off into the mountains?" Ali asked the second they were alone.

She'd moved over to the couch and he narrowed the distance between them with a single long stride. "I don't go for being pressured into something," he told her.

Ali stood up quickly. "They told me you announced the challenge," she said, worry suddenly clouding her pretty blue eyes.

She nibbled her lip, her scent growing richer while she searched his expression.

"I did." His emotions were still too raw, too much on edge from fighting. He grabbed her hair, pulling her head back while bringing her closer to him at the same time. "No one else is going to have you."

The way her face lit up, her smile spreading, giving her dimples in her cheeks, worked him over harder than he'd anticipated. Something warm melted through him.

"I love you," she whispered, her cheeks instantly turning an adorable shade of pink while her embarrassment tickled his nose.

He shook his head, unable to stop the smile that threatened his own lips. "I know you do," he told her. Although for the life of him, he wasn't sure why.

Her thin eyebrows narrowed, and she instantly started pouting. He tugged harder on her head, watching her lashes flutter over her eyes as she relaxed against his grasp.

"That's not what you're supposed to say," she said quietly.

"I told you I don't like being pressured."

"It's more like you won't admit it to yourself." Again her voice was quiet, her body relaxed.

He had her head pulled back, her neck exposed to him. He could see the red streaks where that *Cariboo* had grabbed her neck. Something stronger than protective instincts surged through him. Never had he wanted to possess, to claim and mark as his own, the way he did right now.

The door opened and Gabe and Pamela entered the small cabin.

"Is she okay?" Gabe asked, walking over so that he stood next to Stone.

Pamela joined him, wrapping her arm around his waist while the two of them studied Ali.

He let go of her hair and she straightened, glancing at each of them. "I'm fine, I promise."

"And now we all know why bitches don't run without an escort," Stone said, intentionally scowling at her.

"Oh good grief." Pamela rolled her eyes, and then reached out and punched him in the chest. "He really is a pompous ass, isn't he?"

Ali smiled. "He'll need some training."

"Like hell," he growled at both of them, and then walked away from them, glancing at the clock.

It was after eleven. "Let's go, Ali. I need to get you to your den and then head out to the clearing. Can't miss my midnight date."

"I'm going with you, wolf-man. Don't think I'm not," she snapped at him.

"You should probably call your den," Pamela suggested.

"Yeah." Ali wouldn't look at him, but turned to the phone, quickly dialing the number. "My sire and mother aren't home," she announced, after hanging up.

Stone didn't really care where her parents were. He wouldn't let her see that he was more than pleased that she'd be staying with him. One way or the other, before the night was over, he'd have her in his bed. Thoughts of her stretched over him, her naked body pressed against his, had him simply standing there staring at her.

"I'm going with you," she emphasized again, not able to smell his true emotions.

They couldn't all fit in the truck. He pulled Ali to him, leading her over to the driver's side, and had her slide over while Gabe and Pamela took the car Pamela's den had given her.

Stone jumped into the truck, and grabbed Ali, keeping her by his side so she wouldn't slide all the way to her door. He needed to feel her, experience the heat of her touch soaking through his clothes. Thoughts of the land he'd looked at with Gabe earlier, of how they could easily put a cabin up in one of the clearings, and of keeping Ali naked in his bed as often as possible kept him busy while they maneuvered their way down the narrow mountain road.

He shook his head to clear his thoughts. No bitch had ever made him think of setting up a den, staying in nights with her. Never had being with just one lady appealed to him. Stone liked the variety, enjoyed experiencing different bitches in the meadow.

So what the hell was this?

He ran his hand down her thigh and she wrapped her arm around his, letting out a soft moan that hardened every muscle in his body.

She pressed her body against his side, her soft breasts torturing his thoughts, making his blood boil. Adrenaline had too recently pumped through him, and still lingered. It would be a hell of a lot more fun to tear her clothes from her body, and make her scream while he pounded his cock inside her heat again and again. He'd much rather do that right now than head out to some meadow and kill some lame excuse for a werewolf. It seemed pointless to fight for something that was already his.

Pack law could be damned annoying at times.

No car could make it up to the clearing designated for the challenge. But half the pack at least had parked at the base of the mountain. Just like werewolves to come out of their dens for a challenge. At the top of the line of predators, werewolves thrived on the kill. Even when it was one of their own, they wouldn't miss the glory of a good fight.

Stone parked the truck, getting out and then holding the door while Ali slid out on his side. It hit him at that moment how quickly he trained her to do such a simple act. An odd memory that hadn't surfaced in years hit him.

"Passenger doors are for cubs," his sire would say as he held his mate's hand and waited for her to slide out the driver's side door.

Damn it. Already he was training Ali to be a mate just like his mother had been to his sire. What the fuck was going on here?

"Stone." Ali ran her fingers up his chest, and then leaned into him while wrapping her hands behind his neck. "Don't fight for me if you don't love me."

He looked down into those sultry blue eyes. Her large breasts pressed against his muscles, fueling the energy that already pumped through him. He put his hands on her ass, and shoved his hard cock against her.

"You know that I do," he whispered, and then nipped at her lip.

"Then say it." She pulled her head back, staring into his eyes.

"I love you." He couldn't remember the last time he'd ever uttered those words.

Something broke inside him, like a dam releasing emotions that had been kept secure and out of the way for years. The raw energy that went along with those emotions coursed through him, making him feel lightheaded. It wasn't a sensation he was accustomed to. But try as he would to shove those feelings back into their safe haven, they wouldn't budge.

"God. Stone. I love you too, so much." Her embrace tightened around his neck and she stretched against him to kiss him.

Her mouth was so hot, so sweet. He wrapped his arms around her, impaling her with his tongue, indifferent to the growing activity around them. Well-developed habits wouldn't allow him to tune the world out though. Always on the watch, the predator in him made love to her mouth while noting the cars and trucks parking around them, the sounds of werewolves arriving.

Heavy footsteps behind him had him breaking off the kiss.

"What the fuck is this?" Mickey Reginald demanded.

Stone took only a moment to stare down at Ali's open mouth, her lips glossy with moisture. Her eyes fluttered open. She'd surrendered completely to him, letting go of her own natural instincts to protect herself. In his arms, she'd relaxed, and for a brief moment looked dazed, while the smell of lust floated heavily in the air between them.

Stone turned around, instinctively putting himself between Mickey and Ali. She stood blocked, with the still open truck door protecting her and his body concealing her behind him.

"Would you rape her right here in the meadow with half the pack to witness it?" Mickey lunged at him, the smell of beer drifting around him.

Stone sneered at the ugly *Cariboo*. "You can't rape the willing," he snarled.

Thick clouds overhead dimmed his vision, but Stone had years of fighting under his belt. Mickey reached for him, ready to send him sprawling across the meadow.

Stone was ready for him though, and sent a quick punch to the side of the *Cariboo*'s head.

Mickey stumbled backwards, letting out a howl. Ali dug her hands into Stone's back, lunging against him, her natural instinct to fight kicking in. With one hand he kept her behind him, and braced himself for the *Cariboo* to gather his wits — what he had of them.

"Our sires discussed our mating when we were cubs," Mickey yelled, pointing at Ali.

"That's a damn shame." Stone knew some of the dens still prearranged matings.

Gabe had gotten around it with Pamela. And he'd have no problem fighting to ensure his right to Ali.

"You're going down, *Cariboo*." Mickey scowled, and came at him again.

"A challenge is only valid in your fur." Tip Rochester appeared out of nowhere, jumping in between the two werewolves.

"He can't fuck her right here in front of the pack before a challenge," Mickey complained, his anger making the air so spicy that Stone about sneezed.

"I don't want you, Mickey Reginald." Ali fought to get around Stone so she could be seen. "I belong to Stone."

"There will be no mating without my approval," Tip reminded her.

"Or mine," Jonathan Bastien barked, pushing his way through the growing amount of pack members who'd formed a circle around the truck.

Gabe and Pamela stood to the side, and Stone noticed Gabe already had the change coursing through him, his shirt undone and too much hair on his body for a human.

Their closeness as twins would have the same energy for the kill coursing through his littermate that coursed through Stone.

He returned his attention to the pack leader.

"I'll fight him according to the tradition of the pack." He peeled off his shirt, and felt Ali take it from him without looking down at her.

Her gentle touch stroked his flesh, igniting nerve endings.

"I don't approve of this challenge." Jonathan Bastien scowled at all of them, crossing his thick arms over his barrel chest. "Mickey, you turned out to be little better than a bum. And Stone here is out of control. My Ali can't control a *Cariboo* this wild."

"I can too!" Ali jumped around Stone.

He grabbed her but at the same time Mickey leaped at her. Ali screamed, suddenly realizing two giant *Cariboo* were about to land on top of her, and darted out of the way. Stone pounded into Mickey, blood pumping through his veins, igniting the change in him.

Mickey toppled backwards, and Stone reached to unsnap his jeans, the group of excited werewolves around him quickly undressing as well.

"No one changes here in the parking lot." Tip turned around, yelling at the pack. "We head up to the clearing for the challenge."

"Ali," Jonathan barked at his daughter. "I will not approve your mating with him."

"Actually, Jonathan, my mate scoured over the written law for me. Ali is of age. The challenge will stand." Tip's words silenced the group.

Everyone turned their attention to Jonathan, who glared at the pack leader. "He's not a member of this pack," Jonathan finally countered.

Tip stared at him a moment, and then turned to look at Stone.

"Make me a member of this pack." Stone didn't hesitate.

The surrounding pack members immediately broke out in quick chatter. He ignored the lot of them. Tip looked at him hard, and then nodded after a moment.

"It's done," the pack leader announced.

Everyone moved quickly after that, turning to hurry up the mountain toward the first clearing. Sounds of running water guided them to the spot.

Mickey broke out in his fur, excitement overtaking him, and split his pants right off him. The *Cariboo* was a damned fool.

Stone turned to Ali, grabbing her in spite of the frustration he smelled from her nearby sire. He ignored the older werewolf. There would be time enough later to get in good with her den.

"Gabe." He turned to his twin. "Keep her with you. Protect her until this is over."

He met his brother's gaze, the seriousness of his request understood in his twin. Stone would fight to the kill. And he knew that in such a case, anything could happen. He had no doubts about his abilities, had taken down plenty of werewolves in his time, but wouldn't be fool enough to get too cocky.

Gabe nodded, pulling Ali to him and putting his arm around her while Pamela held on to the other side of him. "She'll be safe," he told Stone solemnly.

Pamela reached out and squeezed his arm, her hand cold and her nervousness obvious. He winked at her, and then leaned forward and kissed Ali quickly.

"Be good," he told her, not putting anything past the little spitfire.

And they accused him of being out of control.

Stone left them and sprinted up the rocky ground toward the clearing where many of the pack had already dropped to their fur. Stripping out of his pants, he tossed them to the side.

There was no need to even beckon the change. Fire rushed through his veins, roaring through him with an aggressiveness he didn't even try to control. Muscles bulged throughout him while bones popped, distorting and growing, hardening and reshaping until he dropped to all fours.

The night air took on different smells, while his vision changed, everything coming into better focus in the night. *Cariboo lunewulves* danced around him, their energy fueling the adrenaline that coursed through him.

Only one of them had his attention though. Through the crowd, one *Cariboo* began running toward him, maneuvering his way around the pack members, building speed until he flew into the air, deadly teeth and claws extended as he landed on Stone.

Stone had too many pack members around him to move out of the way. He roared into the darkness, hauling up on his back legs, and swiping at Mickey with his front claws extended.

It was a good blow, but Mickey had the advantage of being on top, and took Stone down.

Stone rolled to the side, feeling the sharp ground underneath him poke at his hide. Roaring to release his anger, he lunged at Mickey, ready to take the werewolf to his death.

He would be quick, merciful. Never had he believed in torturing someone until they died. Opening his mouth wide, he clamped down on Mickey's neck, knowing if he punctured the jugular, he could twist his neck easily and end the *Cariboo*'s life.

Mickey howled, and blood filled Stone's mouth. The *Cariboo* scrambled several feet away, managing to prevent Stone from digging into his flesh.

Turning, he laughed, his large white teeth flashing in the night. *Is that the best you got?* The fool of a werewolf mocked him.

Rage soared through Stone. Picturing Ali with this beast, imagining her having to endure a mating to a werewolf she didn't love, was enough to have him jumping through the air, knocking the wind out of Mickey.

Ali had too much life, too much energy, too much happiness surrounding her to have it stifled by a *Cariboo* who would never be able to keep up with her, never be able to keep her in line.

This time when he landed on Mickey, the *Cariboo* collapsed underneath him. Stone didn't hesitate. He went for the neck, burying his teeth deep into the werewolf's flesh.

Blood filled his mouth. He'd done it. Took out the jugular. A skin-tingling gurgle came out of Mickey's mouth. The *Cariboo* jerked underneath him, but Stone held firm.

Lifting Mickey off the ground by his neck, he shook his head hard, shaking Mickey like a rag doll, until the *Cariboo* went still.

Stone let go and jumped back. Slowly Mickey changed back to his human form, naked and dead, surrounded by the pack, in the clearing in the mountains.

Chapter Eleven

∞

Ali was mated. She was a mated bitch. Stone was her mate.

She repeated this in her mind as she sat next to him in the truck well over an hour later. Every time she told herself that, her stomach did flip-flops. No longer would she answer to her sire, but to Stone. And Stone would answer to her.

The smell of dirt and blood, charge energy from fighting, and that all male scent that was Stone, rushed through her system.

He was her werewolf.

"Where are we going?" Ali looked around, confused.

She'd been so focused on Stone it just now dawned on her that they had driven into Banff instead of heading up the mountain.

"To your parent's den."

She noticed he didn't say her den.

"Why? Why are we going there?"

He couldn't possibly be taking her home. Her den was with him now.

Stone didn't answer. His expression was hard, his jaw set, and his emotions still so wired that she didn't dare draw any conclusions from what she smelled on him.

He parked in front of her house, and pulled her out the driver's side. She loved the way he always wanted him close to her.

Her parents were already home, and most every light was on in her den. They would have quite the audience when they entered, and for a moment—well, for a hell of a lot longer than that—she just wanted to be alone with Stone.

Wrapping her arms around him, she stretched against hard muscle, loving the trim solid feel of his body.

"I need you," she whispered and nipped at his lower lip.

Stone gripped her ass, squeezing hard, and then gave it a solid slap. The sting sent fire rushing through her. Her pussy quaked and grew damp against her jeans.

"You'll have me, my bitch. Believe me. You're going to be fucked like you've never had it before." His eyes darkened, the wicked promise sending chills through her. He gave her that crooked smile then pulled her off him. "But first, we talk to your den."

All of her littermates greeted her the moment she opened the door, all talking at once, the boys shaking Stone's hand.

Her sire entered from the kitchen with her mother grinning at his side. "All of you, leave us alone right now." She clapped her hands, and slowly her littermates strayed out of the room, mumbling as they took their time doing it.

"So you have my daughter," her sire said, his expression brooding.

"What he means to say is welcome to our den." Her mother walked up and gave Stone a hug.

Ali's heart soared.

"Where will you take her?" Something, or someone, had convinced her sire that the mating was solid.

Ali had a feeling her mother had something to do with that.

"We go to the pack leader first, get his approval," Stone stated the obvious. "After that we'll stay with my littermate for a couple of weeks. There is some land up Cascade Mountain that I think I might buy. It runs along the Bastien land."

Jonathan raised an eyebrow and Ali looked up at Stone. He'd been planning. She couldn't believe her ears. They would have their own corner of the world, on the mountain.

Her sire started talking to Stone about work. Ali turned when her mother gestured for her to follow her. Entering the kitchen, the first thing she did was hug the bitch who'd given her such a wonderful upbringing.

"How did you convince him?" she asked, knowing her mother had a hand in the civil way her sire talked to Stone.

"I reminded him of how it was when he demanded a challenge for me."

Ali was surprised. "You never told me this."

Her mother grinned. "Once upon a time I had several *Cariboo* howling for me. Of course the only one I wanted, my sire would have nothing to do with. He loudly announced that your sire was too wild, too bullheaded, for his daughter."

"Oh, Mother!" Ali hugged her again, and then worried she'd start crying if she didn't hurry back to Stone.

She couldn't wait to get out of there and on to more pleasurable things—time alone with Stone.

Less than ten minutes later, they left her parents' den and headed to the truck. She walked around to the driver's side with Stone, and then climbed in first when he opened the door.

It didn't take long at the pack leader's house. Tip blessed their mating, and wished them good hunting. Ali was on top of the world when they left.

She would mourn Mickey's death, as they all would. But such was the way of werewolves. It was survival of the fittest. Mickey had wanted something he couldn't have. And she'd tried to tell him. They would attend the burning of his human body, and participate in the traditional werewolf funeral ceremony, as would the entire pack. Such was part of a challenge.

Ali didn't dwell on that though. She slipped her hand into Stone's as they left their pack leader's den, and felt like skipping to the truck.

"Now it's time to initiate you into the McAllister den," Stone whispered to her.

Ali looked up at him, her stomach suddenly twisting in a knot. "How will you do that?"

Her mouth was almost too dry to speak.

"I think you know."

Her heart pattered in her chest when they pulled up to the small cabin. The little car that Pamela drove wasn't there, and there weren't any lights on inside. Stone parked and then took her hand, guiding her inside.

Lust filled the air inside the small living room the moment Stone closed the door behind them. He reached behind her, grabbing her sweater, and sliding it over her head. Next his hands snaked around her waist.

"Kick off your shoes," he ordered and undid her jeans.

She managed to get them off her feet before he slid her jeans down her legs. She lifted first one foot, then the other while he knelt behind her, and pulled them off her.

His mouth was hot against her ass and he ran his tongue over her flesh and then nipped at her.

"Oh God." She had nothing to hold on to, nothing to brace herself.

Stone spread her open with his hands and began licking her from behind. More than anything she wanted to fall forward, but if she did she would fall to the floor.

The sweet smell of her cum filled the room as he made her come.

"God. Stone. I can't stand." Her knees buckled as his tongue pierced through her sensitive skin, stroking and caressing her most sensitive areas.

He ignored her pleas, making a feast out of her pussy and ass as he stroked both holes, lapping at her juices and devouring everything she offered.

Pressure built inside her like she'd never experienced before when his tongue darted over her puckered tight hole. He stabbed at it, making her pussy convulse. And then his teeth scraped her flesh while he pressed his face hard against her, sucking and nibbling until she couldn't take it anymore.

Ali fell forward, reaching out to stop herself from crashing. Landing on her hands and knees, she turned around quickly, reaching for Stone.

"Not yet, little bitch," he told her when she tried to undo his pants.

Instead he took her wrist, lifting her to her feet. "To the bedroom."

She didn't understand. The cabin only had one bedroom, and it belonged to Gabe and Pamela. They must have agreed at some point this evening to give her and Stone time alone. But using their bed?

He smiled at her confused expression and swatted her ass to get her moving. Ali hurried down the short hallway, feeling awfully exposed, completely naked while Stone remained completely dressed.

When they entered the room he pulled her to the bed, and then almost threw her on it. Ali turned over quickly and that was when she noticed Gabe standing in the darkness.

The twins stared down at her, so similar yet so different. Her mouth grew dry, and then too wet as she simply watched them watching her.

Without speaking, both of them began undressing.

Ali had no idea what to do. She slid up the bed, trying to move to a sitting position, but Stone grabbed her.

"That's not where I want you." He grabbed her head, pulling her to him.

His cock throbbed in front of him, hard and eager and smelling of his lust. Adrenaline filled the room, an energy so raw it was intoxicating. Ali closed her eyes, running her tongue over his cock and then sucking him into her mouth.

Her lips stretched over his thick shaft and he groaned. Ali had no idea where Gabe was but she guessed that he watched her give his littermate head. The thought made her wild. Never would she have guessed that having a third party in the room would be so exciting. Knowing that Gabe stood there, that he would probably touch her at some point, made cream flow from her cunt while she took Stone's cock deep into her mouth.

Stone gripped her head, holding her hair while he helped move her mouth over his cock. When she was sure she would gag, he glided slowly out, allowing her a breath before plummeting deep into her heat.

She couldn't help it. She jumped when powerful hands gripped her ass. Large fingers probed her soaked holes, first circling them and then dipping into her soaked heat.

"She's damned tight," Gabe said over her.

"Yeah. It's incredible," Stone almost growled instead of speaking. "Fuck her, Gabe. Experience the gift I've been given."

Gabe didn't answer, but instead pressed his hard cock at the entrance of her cunt. Ali adjusted herself on the bed, focusing on Stone's cock.

Gabe thrust inside her. She howled with Stone's cock in her mouth. Both men growled above her. Never in a million years would Ali have guessed it could feel like this to have two cocks inside her.

Both of them stroking her, adding to the fire that coursed out of control throughout her. So large and thick and hard, nothing in her wildest dreams had ever felt like this before. It was more than she could bear.

Her muscles tightened around Gabe's cock. She couldn't breathe. Letting go of Stone's cock, allowing it to slip from her mouth, she cried out in spite of herself.

"Damn it," she howled, as a wave of passion rippled through her.

"Oh, fuck yeah," Stone groaned, and ran his hands over her back. "Turn around baby. I want some of that."

She could hardly move. Both men grabbed her, adjusting her, until she lay on her back. Stone grabbed her legs, spreading her, lifting her pussy to his cock and then diving in with more vengeance than she'd experienced before.

"Holy fucking shit!" She grabbed the bedspread with her fists, coming so hard she thought for sure she'd black out.

Stone didn't stop. His cock seemed to grow, harden, and fill her so that she knew she would split in two. He thrust again, using more force than before, creating a heat between them that would take her out.

There was no way she'd ever survive this.

And then Gabe took her head, adjusting himself so that his cock pressed against her mouth. The smell of her own cum made her mouth water.

Ali ran her tongue over his swollen cock head, trying him out. She tasted herself on him, learned quickly his own unique shape, and then sucked him into her mouth.

Once again she had two cocks buried deep inside her. And both of them seemed larger than when she'd been on her hands and knees.

She knew she would never live through this. Pamela seemed happy and fine, but Ali doubted she would ever be the same after both of them fucking her.

Her body tingled, her world spinning around her as the two werewolves stroked her with giant cocks.

"Her mouth is as good as her pussy," Gabe groaned.

"I'm one lucky son of a bitch," Stone agreed.

"We both are," Gabe said.

The way they talked over her, while fucking her silly, made her crazy. She loved it. Groaning with Gabe's cock in her mouth, she stretched her legs further, lifting her hands and reaching blindly for Stone.

The two men chuckled.

"I think she's a pretty happy bitch too," Stone said, and then slammed into her so hard that she screamed.

Quickly trying to maintain her senses, she lapped furiously at Gabe's cock, willing him to come. He held her head, and began a slow, concentrated movement in and out of her mouth. He'd adjusted her head, holding it in place while his cock swelled so that her lips were numb from being stretched around it.

Stone had slowed too, and she could tell his body hardened between her legs.

"She's going to drain me," Gabe announced, and at the same time his cock pulsed, filling her mouth with his salty cum.

It dripped past her lips, soaking her face and neck. Gabe howled, pulling her hair while he stiffened.

Then pulling out, he collapsed toward the headboard, allowing Ali to catch her breath. She didn't have more than a moment though. Stone drove into her so hard he pierced her clear up to her belly button.

"Oh shit!" she screamed, reaching for him, her vision blurred as she tried to focus on the wild expression on his face.

He drove into her one more time and then locked deep inside her as he spilled his hot cream into her pussy.

Collapsing over her, his body glistening with sweat, he pulled her into his arms, moving to the side quickly so that she was nestled between the two of them.

Gabe chuckled, and then moved off the bed, knowing it would take Stone a minute or two before he could release himself from inside her. Ali didn't care if it took the rest of their lives. She was more sated than she'd been in her entire life.

"Come here, wolf-man. You need a shower." Pamela stood in the doorway, her hand extended to Gabe.

He walked to his mate, kissing her soundly and then wrapping his arm around her.

"Welcome to our den," Pamela told Ali.

Ali had no clue how long she'd been standing there. Heat flushed over her cheeks but she couldn't think of anything to say.

"Thank you," she managed, and then allowed Stone to cuddle her closer to him.

The other two disappeared and a moment later Ali heard the shower start.

"She didn't get mad." Ali looked up at Stone, loving the peaceful expression on his face.

He barely opened his eyes, but she noticed the glow of contentment. The room was saturated with the sweet smell of sex and of happiness.

"Nope." He ran his finger down her face, touching her where her cheeks still burned from embarrassment at realizing Pamela had watched. "She loves Gabe," he told her. "And accepts how the two of us are. We share what means the most to us."

"And I mean the most to you." It wasn't a question, more like accepting the reality that her mate cared so much for her that he would kill for her, and offer her to the littermate who meant so much to him.

"Yes." He didn't hesitate. "I really do love you."

Her heart swelled and she couldn't stop the tear that freed itself and ran down her cheek. Smiling up at him, she ran her fingers through his messed-up hair.

"It's a damn good thing. Because you and I are together for life."

"I'm looking forward to it," he told her, and then rolled over onto his back, adjusting her so that she lay on top of him.

Ali didn't know what their future would hold. What she did know was that she would always run by Stone's side, kill by his side, and laugh by his side. Life couldn't get any better.

Available from

Enjoy An Excerpt From:

NUWORLD: THE SAGA BEGINS

The village was lively, with people going in and out of different shops. Children and dogs ran up and down the sidewalk, and the women and older girls gathered here and there catching up on the latest gossip. Tara parked the car in front of the grocery and smiled politely at four women standing outside the store. They smiled back and then returned to their conversation with more excitement than ever. She heard them say her name but didn't bother trying to overhear what they said. She could only imagine what gossip was being spread about her now that she was living in Lord Darius' house.

"Ah, good morning to you, girl." Thelga smiled broadly as Tara entered the store.

"And a good morning to you." Tara smiled in return and picked up a basket from the door.

"It's quite an honor you have done your old aunt, being claimed by his lordship, and all." Thelga clucked. "And you only being in our town for such a short time."

Tara grabbed her basket with her other hand to keep from dropping it. She looked at the old lady, quite stunned. "What are you saying?" Tara couldn't do more than whisper. "I have not been claimed by anyone."

"Oh, do you say, maybe you haven't been told. I'm sure I'm right, to be certain. It was my claim told me. He heard from the lord's guards, he did." Thelga leaned on the counter and her eyes twinkled, knowing she got to be the first to share the news. "It happened this way to my granddaughter, it did. She was claimed, and the menfolk had such a merry party over it they forgot to tell her." Thelga laughed at the thought. "I know for a fact there isn't a prettier girl in town than you. I'm sure the lord wouldn't have anyone else to take the likes of you." Thelga saw the look of shock on Tara's face and was trying to be reassuring. She reached over the counter and squeezed Tara's arm with her rough fingers. "There isn't a life a girl could ask for as nice as the one you'll have. Your sons'll be lords."

Tara was so surprised by what she'd just heard that she turned to walk back out of the store.

"Ah, my Lady, your list?"

"Oh, yes…here it is." Tara handed the list to Thelga and then just stood about. She wanted to give Thelga the third degree and find out every bit of information she knew about this claiming. A guard had told her claim? When had Thelga heard this? How long had she known? Tara kept her mouth closed however and stood awkwardly in the middle of the store while a young errand boy took the list and ran through the store gathering the items.

Two young women not much older than Tara entered the store and smiled politely at her. They moved over to the produce, and Tara could hear their conversation easily.

"My mama took a pie to her aunt the other day. The old lady said it was what they'd planned all along."

"I daresay she wasn't in town but a day when his Lordship claimed her. Imagine the likes, all of us having our hopes so high for so long. She comes along so merrily like, and he claims her right off, he does."

"Yeah, and I heard she can't cook, you know. It's her pleasures that sold her, that's for sure." The two girls laughed at this comment, and then realizing Tara could hear them, they started whispering.

Tara's blood started to boil. All of this was simply too much. Hearing that Reena had planned her claiming all along put Tara into a rage. Was it true Darius had claimed her before she'd even gone to live in the house? The only time he'd seen her prior to that was in the alley when she'd kept Torgo out of that fight. Did Reena know at that point and Hilda, too? The entire town seemed to know this casual bit of information and somehow had overlooked sharing it with her.

The young errand boy brought the basket to the counter with the items from the list. Thelga arranged the items in a brown paper sack and then smiled at Tara.

"Don't you worry yourself none about the comments of girls such as those." Thelga didn't move her lips much, trying to speak quietly. "They've all tried for his Lordship and failed. They're jealous, they are. You hold your head high. You should be proud, you should."

Tara thanked her and quickly walked out of the store and to the car. Her eyes burned with tears of anger, and her hands shook as she drove back to Lord Darius' house. Hilda's vehicle died so many times that Tara wanted to pull the circular handlebar from the inside of the car and hurl it out the window.

Darius had asked her about being claimed when they'd driven into the hills together. Had he already claimed her publicly by then? Could that be why she'd been brought to the house?

Tara remembered watching him ride toward his house from her bedroom window, remembered how quickly he'd driven through the hills. That had to be the reason why he had hurried home that morning almost a cycle ago. She had been made to believe she was hired help, yet the whole thing was a facade.

She drove the car up the hill to the house with such a vengeance that the tires skidded on the gravel road. Grabbing the groceries, Tara nearly ran into the house. Darius was in the living room with his guards, and she stormed past them into the kitchen.

"I don't see why you don't listen to reason, my Lord," the large guard who'd attacked her growled loud enough for her to hear.

"Judo, the reasoning isn't sound, it isn't. I'll not hear of it." Darius' growl chilled her blood.

"What's wrong with you? You won't even listen to reason when it comes to that girl there." Mikel, Lord Darius' younger brother, shouted.

"We won't be talking of that today." Darius had a tone in his voice Tara hadn't heard before. There was complete control mixed with anger. His baritone sounded very dangerous.

"Your brain isn't doing your thinking for you, my lord, it isn't. We found the bike, and you yourself have commented on her abilities. Her thighs are wrapped around you so tightly you can't see the truth. She's your Runner! You've let her into this house, and now she'll bring down your kingdom, she will."

Mikel, Tara had noticed, was a smaller build than his older brother, but that didn't appear to intimidate him in the slightest. "Our Papa would be disgraced if he knew what you were doing."

"That's enough!" Darius yelled so loudly that Tara actually jumped.

She quickly started to put away the groceries although her hands were trembling from her anger. She wasn't trying to bring down any kingdom and she sure wasn't going to be anyone's claim.

Why an electronic book?

We live in the Information Age — an exciting time in the history of human civilization, in which technology rules supreme and continues to progress in leaps and bounds every minute of every day. For a multitude of reasons, more and more avid literary fans are opting to purchase e-books instead of paper books. The question from those not yet initiated into the world of electronic reading is simply: *Why?*

1. ***Price.*** An electronic title at Ellora's Cave Publishing and Cerridwen Press runs anywhere from 40% to 75% less than the cover price of the exact same title in paperback format. Why? Basic mathematics and cost. It is less expensive to publish an e-book (no paper and printing, no warehousing and shipping) than it is to publish a paperback, so the savings are passed along to the consumer.

2. ***Space.*** Running out of room in your house for your books? That is one worry you will never have with electronic books. For a low one-time cost, you can purchase a handheld device specifically designed for e-reading. Many e-readers have large, convenient screens for viewing. Better yet, hundreds of titles can be stored within your new library — on a single microchip. There are a variety of e-readers from different manufacturers. You can also read e-books on your PC or laptop computer. (Please note that Ellora's

Cave does not endorse any specific brands. You can check our websites at www.ellorascave.com or www.cerridwenpress.com for information we make available to new consumers.)

3. *Mobility*. Because your new e-library consists of only a microchip within a small, easily transportable e-reader, your entire cache of books can be taken with you wherever you go.

4. ***Personal Viewing Preferences.*** Are the words you are currently reading too small? Too large? Too... ANNOYING? Paperback books cannot be modified according to personal preferences, but e-books can.

5. ***Instant Gratification.*** Is it the middle of the night and all the bookstores near you are closed? Are you tired of waiting days, sometimes weeks, for bookstores to ship the novels you bought? Ellora's Cave Publishing sells instantaneous downloads twenty-four hours a day, seven days a week, every day of the year. Our webstore is never closed. Our e-book delivery system is 100% automated, meaning your order is filled as soon as you pay for it.

Those are a few of the top reasons why electronic books are replacing paperbacks for many avid readers.

As always, Ellora's Cave and Cerridwen Press welcome your questions and comments. We invite you to email us at Comments@ellorascave.com or write to us directly at Ellora's Cave Publishing Inc., 1056 Home Avenue, Akron, OH 44310-3502.

The
☥ ELLORA'S CAVE ☥
LIBRARY

Stay up to date with Ellora's Cave Titles in
Print with our Quarterly Catalog.

To recieve a catalog,
send an email with your name
and mailing address to:

CATALOG@ELLORASCAVE.COM

or send a letter or postcard
with your mailing address to:

Catalog Request
c/o Ellora's Cave Publishing, Inc.
1056 Home Avenue
Akron, Ohio 44310-3502

erridwen, the Celtic Goddess of wisdom, was the muse who brought inspiration to story-tellers and those in the creative arts. Cerridwen Press encompasses the best and most innovative stories in all genres of today's fiction. Visit our site and discover the newest titles by talented authors who still get inspired - much like the ancient storytellers did, once upon a time.

Cerridwen Press

www.cerridwenpress.com